Echoes of Aspirations

JNU to IAS

Love, Dream & the Mussoorie Odyssey

ASIF JALAL

PRABHAT
PRAKASHAN

Published by
PRABHAT PRAKASHAN PVT. LTD.
4/19 Asaf Ali Road,
New Delhi-110002 (INDIA)
e-mail: prabhatbooks@gmail.com

ISBN 978-93-5521-832-2

ECHOES OF ASPIRATIONS – JNU TO IAS: LOVE, DREAM & THE MUSSOORIE ODYSSEY
by Asif Jalal

Edition
2024

Price
₹ 400 (Rupees Four Hundred Only)

Printed at
SS Japan Art, Delhi

Dedication

With gratitude to Amra Praween, my mother

&

Jalaluddin, my father

Who opened the world of books to me.

Prologue

It was July and I returned to the university from home after enjoying accolades. I again got busy with work. I had to work on an academic paper and take the coming Civil Services Exam (CSE) Main in the next two months. I had qualified for the CSE with 400 rank and planned to take this exam once more.

If I cracked CSE Prelim again, I would be at the top in the list of successful CSE candidates. I was fresh from home and worked from morning to evening. I had tasted the fruit of labour, I thought the harder I worked, the better my life would be.

Running and continence gave me wings to fly. I had energy to work on my ambition. Mahatma Gandhi's book said continence gave man a tremendous amount of energy. I kept working on this piece of advice and felt I could drink the ocean. But then everything went into a meltdown.

One after-noon a few days before the CSE Main, I checked my letter box at the hostel gate to see if I received any post. That was a routine act. I had a letter in my box from the Union Public Service Commission (UPSC). I thought it was a letter informing me about the service allocation and an invitation to join the job.

I picked the letter and stepped out of the mess building to take a walk on the open lane with gulmohar trees standing along. I opened the sealed letter and read it. The letter informed me that though I had qualified for the exam and ranked 400 in the total 430 candidates, but I was not allotted any service.

As the implication of what I read entered my mind, the world around me tumbled. I thought how could this be true? I had never heard that one could not get a job after qualifying the competitive exam. The letter was written by a Desk Officer of UPSC. I did not understand anything in the letter except that I was not going to get a job. I felt like vomiting. I returned to the room when I realised I could not walk any more.

With the letter in my hand, I walked into the room of Pradeep Mishra at the hostel and told him about the content. He snatched the letter from my hand, read it and looked at me with disbelief. He said, "If there is one person in the world who could be told unlucky it is you. I have not heard anything like that before." Within a few minutes others on the floor also came to know about the letter and looked at me with sympathy.

***

For a few days, everything looked dark to me. I did not know what to do and where to go. Everything seemed to have slipped out of my hands. Energy and enthusiasm had gone from my body. I asked God what I did to meet such a fate.

A hostel-mate Rangarajan came to me and proposed to go to High Court against UPSC. He talked to a lawyer who asked for Rs 50,000 as fee. I told Rangarajan I had neither money nor energy to fight this battle.

Then, slowly, I reconciled with reality. I realised that a few months of time at the University, which was available to me, was an opportunity to reverse fate. If I did let the time go, feeling depressed all the time, I would go to dogs.

Faiz Mustafa left a piece of paper on my table with the words, "I am not concerned that you have fallen; I am concerned that you arise," in his beautiful writing. I pasted the paper on the wall in front of my reading table.

I started preparation for the CSE Main. I had about two months to go for the exam; it would start in the last week of August. I shuttled between the library and the room for study. I stoped being my normal self, and cut myself from the outside world. I studied and studied. The world outside the campus was terrible, it would crush me if I went out without a job.

I went to the library to beat the monotony. I remembered the fourth floor where Jasmine sat with me. The lift, magazine section, the table, the water cooler, everything reminded me of her. I felt I had become mad. Her images, her voice, the smell of her body did not stop running in my imagination. When I closed my eyes, the picture of her face became more vivid. I wondered what she would have been doing now. How she would have been looking in maroon dupatta. Had she been with me I would have been scaling Mount Everest.

Revision of the notes was the primary task, but as the syllabus of Psychology optional was changed, I had to prepare notes for Psychology. JNU had no department of Psychology, and therefore the library had no book on the subject. I went to the Delhi University library in the North Campus about 20 km away for two weeks. The exercise was not useful as the material on the topics given in the books were not available; research studies to use and quote for writing in answers were outdated; and the books were old. I was tired after making it to and fro North Campus in the evening; smoke on the roads caused headache and summer heat drained all my energy.

❑

Contents

Chapter 1

Leap for the Blue Sky

At 11 a.m. I went looking for my friend Tanweer who lived in a railway government quarter opposite Maulana Azad College in the posh area of the town. He was doing a job in Delhi and had come to celebrate Eid at home. I thought if he allowed I would hang on with him and reach Delhi for studies.

Tanweer was not at home. The staff at his home did not give me a proper reply about Tanweer's whereabouts. As I came out of his residence, I saw Tanweer coming to his home in a tight fitting T-shirt and trousers. I told Tanweer, "Bhai, I want to go to Delhi with you."

He said, "I am returning to Delhi this afternoon at 1.00 p.m. by Purushottam Express. If you want to come with me you are welcome."

I was stressed. I had less than two hours to get ready and board the train with him. I said, "Okay. I will meet you at the railway station."

I walked one km to home along the town's best school Sacred Hearts Academy to my mohalla. I told my mother that Tanweer was going to Delhi that afternoon. If I had to go with him, I would have to be ready immediately.

My mother talked to my father and arranged ₹ 750 and told me, " Hameed Beta, my all blessings are with you. You are God's gift to me and I leave you in his protection." Then I did not understand the import of these words from my mother. Till then, I had never been away from my parents, and had not travelled more than 100 km away from home at Jashanpur. I collected a few clothes, some books, and eatable items in one greenish plastic-suitcase and hired a rickshaw to the railway station. I was full of dreams and confidence. I thought I was going to fly in the sky. Soon, I will be rich and famous.

***

Last evening at 8.00, my father came home from his friend's house after meeting people on Eid celebration. The summer temperature in Jashanpur, a town in central Bihar, was unbearable even in the evening. The walls of the house where we lived released heat like the wall of a furnace. All the family members were assembled on the roof to avoid the heat in the rooms. My father as usual shouted at me and said, "Kam-bakht, mardood, you are good for nothing. My words have no effect on you." Mardood means 'reject', it is a word exclusively used for Satan, as God rejected and discarded him from Eden as per the Abrahamic religious traditions. This was a normal way of my father addressing me, and even on a day of festival.

A lapse on my part could also trigger him to assault me. That night my mother came between us and prevented him from attacking me at the roof of the three storeyed rickety building in Gulab Ganj mohalla.

My father was pissed at me for several reasons. The main one was not that I did not study or roamed around with loafers in the colony. Rather, I studied a lot, and wanted to make a career. I knew only studies could take me out of the sea of poverty and backwardness which was in abundance all around. Recently, my father had brought books by sociologists like K M Kapadia, Harry M Johnson, Abraham & Morgan, and others for me to study. I came across these names and their books in a magazine which a civil service aspirant had read for cracking the Civil Services Exam (CSE). The books were costly, and my father bought them for me after borrowing money .

My father thought that I was irreligious, not fulfilling the basic tenets of religion, not offering prayers on time, and my failing on this front was the cause of all poverty and difficulty in our lives. Because God was unhappy, we were denied His blessings. That was a simple deduction.

My father's anger at me was regular, and unabated. He monitored my activities most of the time of the day, and I failed in his expectations daily, several times. I had no much interest in religious rites and prayer. So I had no respite.

I lived in terror, like a thief at my home. I could be rebuked any time. I tried my best avoiding his harsh words, and when he upbraided me, I kept on thinking his words all the time. I felt my heart was sinking. I was not able to come out of that. The world's beauty and its sparkle was shut to me.

That night I resolved that I would leave home next day and go to a distant world where my father would not be able to shout at me morning and evening. I will just walk away and take a train without informing anybody. The thought of going to Delhi or Mumbai fascinated me, as I was going to complete my graduation from the local college. I did not like to be abused and assaulted for no reason.

***

Jashanpur railway station was a big railway junction and several trains passed through this place. I was going towards Delhi, west of Jashanpur town to realise my dream. I never rode a train in this direction. My colony was located along the railway track. I always wondered where this route took the passengers. When I saw apple-red trains with passengers running on this track, I asked God when he would give me an opportunity to travel on this route.

I took a general category coach's ticket for ₹ 240 from the crowded booking counter and boarded Purushottam Express, which started from Puri and reached Jashanpur at about 1:10 p.m. It would transport me to New Delhi Railway Station the next day at 5:0 a.m. Four coaches were general category coaches, and anybody could buy a ticket and board them, while the rest were open to those who had booked a berth in advance.

The coach was imploding with men, women and children. Entry into the coach was like seeking an entry between the rollers of the sugar cane juice machine. Luggage in hands made the entry all the more difficult. The passengers inside did not want anyone to enter into the crowded coach and pushed the newcomers out. Tanweer and Shamim were also with me in the same compartment. At that time, I did not know how to reserve a berth in a train.

We three entered the compartment with the help of friends and relatives. Dozens of boys of the mohalla had come to see off Tanweer and Shamim. My mother came to see me off at the railway station. We stood near the gate while the train started. Soon the train picked up speed, and in one flash the mohalla Gulab Ganj located along the railway line disappeared. I did not know I was going to miss this mohalla so much in Delhi, and the step which I had taken will distance me from this place for ever.

***

We got down at 5:0 a.m. at New Delhi Railway Station and walked towards Ajmeri Gate from the platform. We boarded blue line bus number 400 and reached Okhla Village, a locality in south-east Delhi, 15-km from the railway station.

Tanweer and Shamim had rented a room in a two storey building with 22 rooms on a floor – total 66 rooms in that building. Tenants of each room paid ₹ 1000 to the landlady whose husband worked in the middle-east. The room without a window for cross ventilation was hot like a furnace in June. One more young man named Babban lived there and, adding me, the room had four residents. All slept on the floor and used a heater kept in a corner to cook breakfast and dinner. My partners mostly baked bread and boiled milk and brought vegetables or meat from the local restaurant.

The lodge had mainly the students or the aspiring students of Jamia Millia Islamia University from western Uttar Pradesh, with a few exceptions to the employed men, as residents. Some of them were intelligent, smart, and highly qualified.

For two days in the room, I was treated like a guest, and then I was told to prepare my meal and live on my own. The warmth of Tanweer changed to bitterness, and Shamim had no good or encouraging words for me. Babban liked himself to be called Babban Yadav and attacked me all the time with harsh words without meaning them.

I told the residents of the lodge that I came to Delhi to work part-time and study. Two-three men were kind and talked to me. They suggested that I look for the job offers and vacancies in 'The Times of India' and 'Hindustan Times', especially on Wednesday. I saw the newspaper and found several vacancies for helpers and attendants. I was not interested in working as a helper. I asked them about an offer for a tutor for students. "You should get registered at a tuition bureau. It will provide you students for tuition," said one of the boys.

Outside the building was a market place—crowded, noisy, hot, and dusty with rickshaw, four wheelers, auto caught in traffic jams and no space to walk for a pedestrian. My room partners who left the room in the morning and came by 7:30 p.m. told me that I should go out and try my luck. Sitting in the room will get me nowhere.

I had to contribute ₹ 250 for the room rent. I came from home with ₹ 500 and after spending ₹ 250, I was left with ₹ 250 for spending on travel and food for one month. If I did not get a job and find a source of livelihood I might be forced to return, which I did not want.

Eighteen years old Tanweer worked as an STD booth operator in the area for three-hours in the morning and got ₹ 500 per month as salary. At 10.00 a.m. he would move to west Delhi to study radiology at an institute. His mission was to go to a gulf country after taking a degree in radiology.

The other guy, 17-year old Shamim, son of a kiryana shop owner at Jashanpur, was a gifted artist, and prepared banners for the politicians and the businessmen. He ran a painting outlet at the roadside in the area. His target was to take admission in the Fine Arts course at Delhi's Jamia Millia. Both Tanweer and Shamim Akhtar worked hard and were hungry for success and money.

I had a great fascination for historical places. Delhi for me apart from a place for realising my ambition was a place with Red Fort, Jama Masjid, India Gate, Rashtrapati Bhawan, Supreme Court, Jamia Millia University, etc. Bus no. 400, which came to the locality, had the names of many of these places written over it and travelled up to them. I rode to those monuments and satiated my hunger for the tour of great places.

One advantage with the bus number 400 and other buses that came in the Okhla area was that Jamia Millia students did not require to buy tickets for travelling. The student had to say 'Jamia Staff', a term which appeared funny to me, to the conductor. The conductor either moved to the next passenger or asked the 'Jamia Staff' to show his or her identity card. I also claimed the status of 'Jamia Staff' some time and availed free rides.

The area witnessed regular violence by the students of the university and fights erupted anytime even when things looked normal. One group of fair-skinned, smart boys with long hair and high-boots coming from elite Muslim families attacked the other group. Within minutes, one could see the students bleeding from head and mouth.

What I saw exemplified the degradation of the community which sent its boys to study in the national capital but the boys on whose shoulders the dream of the parents and the community rested loved brawl and fist-fights more than pen and books. When I returned tired after searching for a job to my room at night I saw the boys and girls crowding the road pavements with tea cups from dhabas, indulging in idle gossip, romance or canvassing for the student union election.

At one time, as I entered the gate of the university, I walked into a green lawn with a statue of Mirza Ghalib amidst pink coloured buildings. Well dressed young boys and girls sat and loitered around. I sat there to absorb the ambience asking God how kind he would have been had he helped me get enrolled there. After spending about an hour at the campus I felt the place was not a university lawn, but a stage for mushaira, an exploding ghazal session. I felt odd that the youths of the community which ranked so low at the socio-economic indicators were fascinated so much by love poetry. They needed to slog and make a career than be drowned in the verses of romantic love.

At the University, I met Ejaz Rehman, a student of my father at Jashanpur. Fair and tall Ejaz was enrolled at the mathematics department of the University. Son of a faculty at Maulana Azad College at Jashanpur, 19-year old Ejaz came to my house at Jashanpur several times, but in Delhi he did not give me importance.

Tanweer knew him and told me that Ejaz was busy in the student union's election and running after girls. He was wasting his father's money. He had fallen in love with an 18 year old girl Ghazala Khan from a royal Rampur family enrolled in MBA.

One morning after taking an appointment to meet him, I came to see him at the university campus. Ejaz came to the university and parked his Yamaha RX 100 in front of the pink library building. Ghazala with a book in her hand saw him from the gallery of the academic building after her classes. When Ejaz looked up, he saw Ghazala in bright red dupatta smiling at him. He left a box of plain muffin for her on his Yamaha's seat and went to the library. Ghazala came down to the bike, picked the muffin box and left a rose bud for Ejaz.

***

I did not know how to cook food but had seen and assisted my mother in food preparation. At the room at Okhla Village, I baked thick bread and cooked daal in a cooker. I had brought jaggery from home to eat with chapati. This was a normal breakfast for me for several days. I calculated that if I ate chapati and daal three times a day, I would manage with expenditure of ₹ 250 on food and ₹ 250 on room rent. I bought a milk pouch some days, but it was wasted after I consumed half of it.

I looked for job opportunities in the newspaper and went to the offices which offered a job. The newspaper printed several job openings at Narayana locality at Mahatma Gandhi Road. I took a crowded bus at 11:0 a.m. and got down at Lajpat Nagar. I asked a gentleman, who also got down from that bus, the way to Narayana. He said, "It was 20 km away."

I said, "But it is on Mahatma Gandhi Road."

He got angry and said, "Mahatma Gandhi Road is upto 20 km from here."

I was shocked. I thought Narayana would not be a suitable place to work because of the distance. I crossed the road to return. I felt like if some vehicle hit and killed me that would be fine. There was no energy in my body. The brain appeared to be foggy. I thought so many vehicles running on the road, but none was mine.

I returned to Okhla. In the room, I spent time thinking about what to do. The closed, windowless room was hotter than the outside atmosphere that June day. Delhi, where I was living, was nothing like the place of my imagination: a place I wanted to go and make a career. The travel in the bus, crowd, smoke and dust-filled road, furnace-like room, were nowhere like what I thought my life would be in a metro. Then I did not know sleeping less and eating daal-roti three times a day, thirty days a month, will ruin my health and intelligence.

Tanweer's idea of life was that sincerity, honesty, and being a gentleman were attributes which could carry the day in Jashanpur, but not in Delhi. Delhi was a different place with a different type of people; it required aggression, speed, and deceit to advance one's career and earn money. He told me to change my attitude, otherwise I will perish, and will have to go back to Bihar as a failure.

I joined an 8-hour job at Maidan Garhi at a dye office-cum-factory after reading a vacancy in a newspaper. It took me about an hour to reach the office at 10:0 a.m. after riding two buses. It was a job performed while standing the whole day. Things were okay for me here except the smell and dust of dye, and the length of my time it claimed, leaving me nothing to spend on study. Besides, the job exhausted me completely. I learned the work here for 15 days and wanted to discontinue as the dust could have caused me health problems. I ate my food sitting outside at the office step in the dust floating on the road. Tears rolled down my eyes as I chewed the food. It was difficult swallowing the food in my dry mouth. Everybody there seemed to be okay and busy with work except me, whose innocent conception of the world was shattered. When I told the manager that I wanted to leave, my expectation was to get a salary for the 15 day work, but he said I will have to work 30 days to get the salary.

I wanted to do a job which could give me at least four-to-five hours for study. At Jashanpur, I had heard the concept of a part time job. Delhi being a metro, I thought it would give me such a job, and I will be able to take competitive exams for jobs like bank clerk, bank manager, assistant grade in government departments, railways station master, railway guard, etc. When I passed such an exam, I would join the job, and would be back to Jashanpur, I thought. That was the sum and substance of my dream. As the environment at home was not good, my father looked for faults in my conduct all the time and as my home's financial condition was hopeless, I had no choice but to leave the walls of my home and look for ways to support myself.

At the lodge, one day, the ill-fitted wash basin slipped from its case when I brushed my teeth in the morning. It broke into pieces. I was scared and did not know the consequences. When the landlady came to collect rent, she asked how it was broken. The residents told her that I was the culprit. I did not expect this from them. The lady in light pink salwar kameez looked at me and told me to pay for the damage. She charged me ₹ 100 which I thought was quite heavy on me.

I tried to sleep on the rooftop, but a swarm of mosquitos buzzed around and humidity laden wind carrying foul smell from dirty Yamuna made sleeping impossible. The windowless room was heated like a furnace on a summer day, cooking meals on a heater made it hotter. Babban kept his stinking socks inside the room. We told him to keep it outside, but his feet smelled equally awful.

I washed clothes in the morning and on Sunday evenings. My body had no energy. I felt I was slowly forgetting what I knew in general studies, social sciences, English language. My English speaking skill became miserable. My roommates chatted constantly or ridiculed me when they returned to the room in the evening. Shamim said Jawaharlal Nehru distinguished himself by studying in a situation far worse than I was living in. I should not complain that they were talking while I held a book in my hands. My approach was not to engage in confrontation with them and keep silent. I knew my three roommates were doing job, and I needed to live with students, who had ambition and a career goal like me.

In all this, my room-mates were comfortable. They were not tortured like me with the heat, dust, crowd and uncertainty. They also cooked in the room and ate five chapati with daal and sabzi. While I counted time spent on cooking, walking to the bus stop and washing clothes, thinking that I would have utilised this time on my studies, they seemed at home with the circumstances and enjoyed cooking spicy vegetables.

Sometimes I would go to the local mosque even when there was no time to offer prayer. I would sit, offer prayer and ask God to help me. The mosque appeared to me serene, spacious, and clean in comparison to the outside world and my room.

I got hold of Norman Peale's book 'The Power of Positive Thinking' in the room. I read its several pages but it did not impress me. When everything was bad in my life there was no point in thinking positive or believing that things were good in my life. But later I realised that that was a wrong way to interpret the book which is immensely useful for everybody—rich or poor, successful or failure.

I again went out looking for a job in pharmacy, factories, STD booths. I spent one whole day in Laxmi Nagar area talking to the factory managers for a job. One guy told me to learn driving and take up taxi driving. This was now going to be one month after my arrival in Delhi.

Some suggested that I go to a tuition bureau. Others told me that my accent was Bihari, parents would not like their wards to be tutored by me. I visited one bureau at Lajpat Nagar, and paid ₹ 200 for registration. The bureau in-charge, a middle aged lady in salwar-kameez, looked at my face, clothes and shoes with slight contempt in her eyes.

She asked, "Which subjects could you teach?"

'Any subject upto 12th standard, Ma'am.'

"You mean Maths, Physics also for 12th?"

"Yes."

"I don't think you are sure about what you are saying."

The lady thought how this boy who could barely speak could teach Maths and Physics. She sent me to one family for class 8th standard in Defence Colony. The family name was 'Bhasin'. I rang the bell at around 5:0 p.m. A gentleman opened the door and asked me about the reason for my visit. After a few questions, he said he was not in need of any tutor. I tried a few more families without success. Then I changed my plan.

One Sunday when Tanweer was at the lodge washing clothes, and cleaning the room, he told me to go to a nearby factory at Gaffar Manzil near Jamia Millia campus and enquire about a job. The secret was that Tanweer had worked there and left the job sometimes back, something which he did not tell me. If the owner of the factory had employed somebody at his place, there would be no vacancy for me. Tanweer told me not to mention his name to the owner as that might prejudice him against me.

Hearing this opportunity I became very excited and waited for Monday to come. In the morning on Monday, I took bus no. 400 running between Okhla Village to Jama Masjid and got down after one stop. I walked to the factory through Jamia University in the direction Tanweer had given to me. It was an embroidery factory with about a hundred tailors, everyone working on a machine. It was located in a two storey building with huge halls and a tall black painted gate.

I entered the building and walked into the cabin of the owner Zaheer, a man in 30s . He required one assistant who could supervise the work, collect the items from the tailors, and maintain stock of the items. I said, "I needed a job. I would be very grateful to you sir if you give me an opportunity to work at your place." I tried to show him my certificates which I carried in a folder. Sitting on a chair under a fan, he thought for a second and said, "Okay, you can start work from today." My happiness knew no bounds. I thanked God and started the work.

The tailors there were all aged between 20 to 30 years and came from Uttar Pradesh and Bihar. Zaheer's younger brother John with a large mane of hair, who loved riding a Bullet, assisted him at the factory.

This was also a whole day standing job, moving from one machine to another. But what surprised me here was that the employees had to work 12 hours from 9:0 a.m. to 9:0 p.m., and only Sunday afternoon was off. It was something atrocious. I was locked inside the hall in the tube light in the noise of hundreds of embroidery machines the whole day. The only break was a half hour break for lunch at 1:30 p.m.

The job brought pain in my life. I would get up at 6:30 a.m. and rush for the morning ritual, and then prepared breakfast and lunch in the room. I would board a bus at 8:30 a.m. for the office. After the whole day's work, I would return to my room at 9:30 p.m., cook chapati and daal, ate and slept like a log of wood. I had no energy, no ambition, only darkness as far as I could see. Within weeks, my muscles shrunk and I looked like a malnourished, emaciated boy of 14.

One afternoon, John, the younger brother of Zaheer, in a medallion yellow shirt, saw me eating chapati and jaggery at the office table. Since I did not know how to roll chapati, it was thick and a part of it remained unbaked. The tailors next to me said they did not know how I survived on this kind of food. John was overwhelmed seeing the food and he told me to come out with him. I sat on his motorcycle which stopped at a nearby dhaba. He told the dhaba owner that I would take lunch there daily and he should not charge me a penny for the lunch. Other workers also dined there. That day I saw and tasted rajma for the first time in my life, it looked like swollen capsules to me. The normal, tasty food of the dhaba appeared to fill me with instant energy. Till today, I am trying to meet and thank John for his that day's act of kindness, but I could not succeed.

Tanweer told me not to negotiate for the salary. "First get the job and then you will think about the salary," he said. I knew even if I got ₹ 500 for a month that would give me a lease for one month in Delhi. But at the end of the month, I got ₹ 1200 in an envelope. This was far beyond my expectation, and was sufficient for my two month's expenditure in Delhi. Seeing the value this amount had for me, I forgot the hardship which I endured to earn the money. With this much money, I felt like I would buy a plot at Ashoka Road in New Delhi.

I worked at this office for one more month. The sound track of "Tu Cheez Badi Hai Mast Mast", "Ole Ole" and other similar songs played in the hall the whole day and subdued the noise of the machines. I developed a distaste for these songs and never liked to listen to them as they reminded me of those difficult days. During this period, I had no opportunity to see the sun's brightness, the beauty of the blue sky, the greenery of trees, or feel a whiff of the wind. I stood within a tube-lighted hall for 12 hours a day for almost 30 days in a month. It was a terrible experience which I could not get myself off. After earning ₹ 2400, an amount sufficient to back my stay in Delhi, I stopped going there. I did not tell Zaheer that I would not come next month.

Thus, Tanweer not only brought me to Delhi but also helped me get a job which gave me a financial wherewithal to hold on to the city.

❑

Chapter 2

Books, Flowers and the Moon

With no job, I had no idea what to do now. I had just a sense of relief from the terrible routine of 12-hour a day at a factory with closed gates. After seeing the world for about three months in Delhi, I was a bit wiser and less affected by the deprecating remarks of Tanweer and others.

One morning, I went for a walk in the shanties at the Yamuna river basin. The polluted river with water hyacinth floating over it touched the walls and fronts of many brick-and-tin houses. I stood near a house, and told a middle-aged man that I was a tutor, and if anybody was interested in tuition for their wards for a small fee, I could come and teach there. I offered to teach for ₹ 100 a month per student.

He told me to wait there, went to a few residents around and discussed my proposal with the children. The parents agreed and I started teaching three students.. I sat with three children on a bed sheet in an open place in the foul smell from the river.

Thus, I arranged an income of ₹ 300 per month in an hour walking ten minutes from my room. In 10 days, I got 23 candidates, and thus arranged a tuition income of ₹ 2300. It was like I had hit a jackpot. I would stay in Delhi, I was sure.

I went to the locality and taught the ill-clad, stunted children—boys and girls. After two hours of work, I returned to my room and sat to study. My life was coming closer to my dream. I studied and thought I would conquer the world. I would be bigger and more successful than everybody around.

Then God sent another 'Farishta' in my life. He was Zubair Khan, a smart, tall civil services aspirant from Kolkata, studying at a coaching-cum-study Centre of Jamia Millia. He preferred white shirt on black trousers. I would see him cooling boiled milk in a pan at the lodge before he left for the Study Centre. I did not know anything about him except that he looked like a student and lived at the lodge. He would see me busy with books sitting in the room. One day he asked me a few questions and invited me to study at the Jamia Study Centre where he studied. He said though only members of the centre were allowed to study there, I could sit at the centre with his support.

Next day, I got ready and walked with him to the Centre— which was officially known as Centre for Coaching and Career Planning at Jamia University in Jamia Nagar. It had a big hall, an air cooler, dazzling lights, good chairs, and a noise free environment. Zubair Khan was like *'dada'* of that place and he wielded enormous influence over the Jamia employees working and the students studying there. He was seen as a candidate who will crack the exam for sure. He studied from 9:0 a.m. till 11:0 p.m. with small breaks in between. Full of ambition, his face shone bright.

About 30 young men and women visited the Centre and most of them prepared for civil services exam, and some for the Common Admission Test for admission in top management institutes, and admission in foreign universities.

I saw the study Centre, its facilities, warm white lights, woven wood-chairs, and felt I was now closer to my dreams. With this place to study, I will crack nothing less than the civil services exam, I thought. I started going to the Centre. I thought a shelf of books and a Reynolds pen in my hand with a place like this to study were sufficient to raise my status and empower me to change the world. To rise above the crowd, I required nothing more. I will work hard and realise my dream. With this much facility, I was at par with the most privileged and powerful in the city. I would crib for nothing, ask no more facility from God.

One of the visitors to the Hall was Sophie, a 20 year old lady from Delhi, preparing for admission to Faculty of Management Studies, Delhi. Another was Ranjith Martin, a 21 year old clean shaven, English-speaking, slim Keralite, preparing for the civil services exam. Martin came to the Centre in white shorts, and sports shoes.

Zubair told us he was studying to enter into civil services to fulfil his mother's dream. Otherwise, he did not require a job. He was not a wretch, jobless like us. He had a well settled business of sports shoes manufacturing at Patna's Boring

Canal Road. He said his full time occupation was street-fights, gun-firing and drilling holes in the head of rowdies before he came to Delhi for civil services examination. He spoke about his background and plots of his battles with a sombre face at the running ground in the evening while the sun was to set.

He said when he did not pick a fight, he was not able to concentrate on his studies. One fight kept him charged for studies upto a week. After that he required another fight to sustain his interest in studies. For months, he kept his head tonsured and tied a black scarf over his head to look like a black-cat commando. He smiled a little, spoke good, fluent English, and ran in a navy-blue tracksuit for about one hour in a jumbo-sized green lawn of the university. Except for his propensity to pick a fight, I thought he was an ideal candidate for the IAS.

The approach of the people in my surrounding was that if my father and grandfather had not done something big then I should not aspire for civil service. Because of this approach I did not dare tell anything about my dream or aspirations to anybody. Very common refrain was 'Apni shakal dekhi hai?' Because my face was not handsome, I did not tell anybody that I was preparing for the services.

Today, a huge amount of material is available on the internet, especially on YouTube. There is a competition among the experts and successful candidates for informing the aspiring candidates on how to prepare for and crack the civil services exam. Then we had only competitive exam magazines to reveal the secrets of success in the CSE.

I would cook breakfast of daal and chapati for the morning and afternoon. A pouch of milk I could afford now but half of it would spoil in an hour when I left it in the room for the Centre after drinking half of it. At the Centre, the students ate together. They got food from a tiffin service which provided food similar to home cooked food. When they saw me eating daal and jaggery, they shared their food with me. Ahmad Aamir, a close friend of Zubair Khan, and also a native of Jashanpur district, told me to stop bringing food and eat from his tiffin with him. His offer overwhelmed me, but I continued bringing my food and receiving vegetables from him and others.

Now, study and visit to the Centre was everything my life revolved around. Civil services aspirants at the Centre, especially Ahmad Aamir and Zubair Khan, were extremely kind to me. They interacted, and shared books with me, and treated me like an equal. The community life around the Centre was interesting, but I do not like to deliberate on it any more.

With the Centre was attached another hall working as library-cum-reading room with rich collection of books. It also housed the office of the grey-bearded librarian of 55 years from Barabanki town of Uttar Pradesh. The librarian spoke all the time in Khariboli Hindi in high volume sitting on his chair. His beard and face reminded me of Mirza Ghalib. He loved using profanities and the f-word in his one-sided talk during his office hours at his table. He discussed rape crimes reported in the newspapers in a great detail with the students of the Centre. His high decibel talk ensured that a reader did not understand what he read at the library.

Centre conducted entrance tests once a year, and only the members could visit the reading hall. Ahmad Aamir once took me to the posh restaurant of the area 'Monish

Kada' and I had a taste of the non-veg food for the first time in Delhi after I left home.

One evening, one of the students at the Centre, Rashid, told me that a family was looking for a tutor in the nearby locality, if I was interested I could go and teach. The family had a son Javed and a daughter Lubna studying in secondary school. I agreed and visited the family after walking about 15 minutes. The family offered me ₹ 800 for the tuition of the two children. Life became even better. I stopped going to the poor students at the bank of Yamuna. This I regret till today, but the ambition which was driving me gave me no option. I could not walk to the two destinations for teaching as they were in different directions.

After 15 days, Javed's father asked me if I was interested in teaching the son of a Member of Parliament. This was something I did not expect even in my dream. I said, "Yes." They gave me an address and I visited the white-painted two storey MP flat at South Avenue near Teen Murti, and joined the new assignment in excitement. I had never been to this area, and did not know in what kind of accommodation our honorable representatives lived. I had to travel through two or three buses to reach there.

This was not a correct decision on my part, as it took me two hours in making to and fro, and it left me no better to take any more work. I accepted the offer with the hope that this would open to me new opportunities which I was not able to foresee then. I had seen some youths hanging around a Member of Legislative Assembly (MLA) or a Member of Parliament (MP), and calling shots. But I had no such intention, I knew my studies would take me far ahead in comparison to working like a hanger on to a politician. Anyway, after tutoring his son for more than a year, I did not benefit from this break and the MP treated me like nobody. The wife of the MP was kind to me and his son was an adorable 11 year old boy. The good thing was that after a negotiation, I was able to reduce the number of days to three in the week for tuition, and tutoring at this place enhanced my respect at the Centre.

The Centre conducted an annual test to induct the aspirants preparing for competitive examinations. Most of those studying there had already taken the test, except me. I took the test and scored 85 marks out of 100. Zubair Khan was disappointed with me and told Ahmad Aamir that he expected me to top the exam and score 100 out of 100 marks.

I studied at the Centre with full devotion. I felt now I was on the track to my destination. I read in the library the lines of Oscar Wild: "With freedom, books, flowers, and the moon, who could not be happy." I felt with the books and the time to study them, I would scale the blue sky. I arrived at the Centre at 9:30 a.m. and studied there till 9:0 p.m. I had low energy because of simple food, but my spirit burnt with ambition. I believed by working hard, one day, I would own a house like the bangalow covered with the lush greenery standing on the way to the Centre. The admission to the Centre gave me an identity card which I could use as "Jamia Staff" to travel on the bus. The identity card was a precious possession for me. When I was alone I took it out of my pocket and gazed at it with pride.

***

During this period, I went to Jashanpur for a few days travelling in a general compartment. I told my parents and friends about my life there. My parents were satisfied with my progress and they hoped I would do good in my life.

A friend, Salman Taj told me that he wanted to come to Delhi with me for studies. I welcomed him and he accompanied me on the train. In Delhi, I thought it was a good time to part company with Tanweer and his group as our wavelength did not match. I found a room in Sarai Jullena area and started living there with Salman Taj. The place was a bit far from the Centre and required taking the bus to reach the Centre. My movement to Julena pained Tanweer, he confronted me saying that I was not worthy of his trust and care. Shamim said they brought me to Delhi and guided me at every step, but when I got a foothold I dumped them. I tried to reason with him and Tanweer but I failed. After leaving Tanweer, I never met him despite my best efforts.

Salman Taj proved to be a good friend to me and we never lost respect for each other. He became a pillar of strength for me. He was in many ways very different from me. I was docile, ready to bend and avoid confrontation, low on confidence, physically weak, ruminating over difficulties and limitations of my life. He was physically strong and smart, never ready to take bullshit from anybody, sure of success, and he believed like legendary boxer Mohammad Ali, 'Humble people did not go far.' His father died when he was a young boy, his mother brought him and his two brothers and a sister as a school teacher. He remained awake at night for long, and slept till late in the day. The room had an LPG connection and a stove. Most of the time our meal was daal and chapati.

Salman Taj prepared for admission at Indian Institute of Management for a Master of Business Administration degree, while my target was civil services and other competitive exam which could get me a job. He read the

Longman English dictionary word by word, page by page. Till then the only English dictionary I knew about was the Oxford Advanced Learner's Dictionary and that too through my father. I told him a dictionary was mainly a book for finding the meaning of a word and not for reading like a novel. He said a dictionary tells you also about the rules of usage of a word, its root, grammar, etc. It was much more than a meaning throwing book. He wanted to read the dictionary completely and then take another book.

I did not protest. I knew he was in one orbit and I was in another. We will soon separate and travel in different directions. But the moment of separation came unexpectedly and too early.

❑

Chapter 3

Two Tests, One Dream

In April, a student at the Centre, Kalaam Ahmad went to Jawaharlal Nehru University (JNU) and brought a dozen forms for admission to the graduation course at the University's School of Languages (SL). They gave a form to me also. Until then I had no idea about the University, its entrance exam and admission schedules, and the type of courses it offered. They told me to apply for graduation in languages like Russian, Persian, and Arabic. Many meritorious students were not takers of these subjects and it was easy to qualify for them. The only catch was that we were all graduates, and the university had reserved most of the seats for those who had done plus two, leaving only a few for those who had done graduation in any subject. Such candidates were called Preference II (P II) candidates. Still we hoped to get into the university. Admission at the university will give one a hostel room, mess facility, access to a rich library and an excellent environment for study and interaction with the best of the minds.

I went to the University with Kalaam Ahmad on bus no. 615 to deposit the form and saw the university campus for the first time. Its brick architecture, greenery, clean roads and the youths on the campus fascinated me. But I thought it was a home to the wards of the rich and privileged people of the country. The boys and girls who lived in those red-brick hostels and studied in dreaming, tall buildings under unbroken blue skies were sons and daughters of Mittals, Tatas, and Birlas. My dream to enter this university will not be realised.

On the day of the entrance test, in May, I started at 6:0 a.m. on a bus to take exam at a Kendriya Vidyalaya in Rohini area. I travelled 40 km changing several buses on the empty morning road. I had not taken breakfast, and traffic smoke caused nausea. All the way, negative, weakening thoughts tore me, I was not confident of qualifying it, and was going just to try my luck. The questions were easy, and I thought I stood some chance. After the exam, I forgot about it and focussed on exams for jobs like Bank Probationary Officer, Railway Guard, Assistant Grade, Assistant Section Officer in Central Secretariat, etc. I worked on English language, arithmetic, reasoning, etc. and solved objective type questions. I thought if I worked on these for one or two-years, I would get some job and my life would be a bed of roses.

While working for these exams, my writing and speaking skills were ruined. I read mainly the passages given in the question paper, and therefore my word power also deteriorated. I felt scared. But the most important factor for my academic decline was lack of a nutritive diet. A meal of daal and chapati two or three times a day was not good enough to nourish my brain and body. But I did not know what was wrong and I had no solution for the problem.

In the first week of July, I went home for a week to meet the family members. I was away from home for almost a year. The images of houses of my mohalla, gullies, roundabouts, incidents, friends, my family members troubled me all the time. But my ambition drove me on the lonely road in Delhi. At home, I told my friends that I studied at a Centre of Jamia University. The name of Jamia aroused fascination like that of Oxford University among my friends who were slightly better than me economically. After the break, I boarded the crowded general compartment of Purushottam Express again, travelled most of the distance standing on the train and reached Delhi. The days in Delhi were rainy, leaves of the tree were fresh and roads completely wet.

JNU entrance test result was declared in the last week of July. Kalaam Ahmad came to see the result at the university's administrative block. He returned to the Centre at 4:0 p.m. and said Zubair Khan, Ahmad Aamir and I were selected for admission in the Bachelor of Arts (BA) in Persian and Russian languages. People sitting in the hall came to me and congratulated me, Kalaam said the admission started on 30th July.

The result was something unexpected, and it was like too good to be true. I thought the days of my difficulty were going to be over. I was a student of JNU. I will live on the beautiful campus and study with the best minds of the country.

***

From Okhla area, I took bus no. 507 and went to the University. I reached the administrative block in a bus crowded with boy and girl students. The academic complex building was made of red-sandstone. I stood with my documents in the queue for admission. Clouds hung in the sky and monsoon rain had made the campus look dreamy. The university officials in the admission hall sat in a row in different halls scrutinising the documents. When I reached the table, the official looked at my documents and said those documents were not relevant. I said they were marks-sheets, admitcard, caste certificate, etc. He mumbled something and threw my documents. My hopes fell apart, I picked up the documents and came out of the admission hall thinking what to do. Had the opportunity which could change everything in my life slipped away? I stood at the gate of the block, saw hundreds of boys and girls flocking to the block for admission. One guy in lounge here saw me and guessed I was in trouble. He was a student of the university. He asked me if I had taken admission. I said they told me to go back home, I had not brought all the required documents for admission.

Two activists came with me to the official and talked to him. I stood one-metre away praying to God to help me. After a minute of discussion with the two student activists, the official called me with the papers. He saw the documents again and gave me an admission receipt of ₹ 220. I knew the importance of this receipt. I was then a student of the university and things promised to get better. I thanked those guys, walked to the bus stop and came back to the

Centre. I shared about the incident with Ahmad Aamir and Zubair Khan. They said all is well that ends well.

***

As I had done graduation and, I took admission again in a graduation course for a language, I was not going to get a room at a hostel till all those enrolled after doing their plus two had got rooms allotted. I will have to wait at least for one year. Then Ahmad Aamir came to my rescue. His friend, Imran Ashraf, was enrolled in M. Phil at a language and literature course at the university. As a senior student he enjoyed a single seated room. He accommodated me in the very first week of my admission.

Now there was pride in me, energy in my body and hope in my eyes. I had good, nourishing food—milk, butter, meat, curd, sweet-dish. I had never tasted food which was served in the hostel till now in my life. All very tasty—many times better, more nutritious than what I was eating at home.

***

Imran Ashraf, my host at Sutlej Hostel, was a religious man and expected me to offer prayer daily and observe fasting for one month. I had no issue with prayer but fasting for a month squeezed life out of me. He got up at 4:0 a.m., took a bath in cold water even during winter, and offered prayer. Sometime, a few of his friends joined him for prayer. Then I could not sleep in the room. And getting up early without completing sleep left me tired and drowsy the whole day.

Imran gave me the impression of an austere monk. His wants were simple. He slept on a thin mat on the bed, sometimes on a bed-sheet on the floor. He indulged in serious discussion and espoused higher values. He was

not a careerist, he believed in destiny and was not scared of uncertainty in life like me. He received a Junior Research Fellowship and focussed on academics. His eyes were drowsy by 10:0 p.m. as he got up at 4:0 a.m. He was kind and generous to me. I indulged in discussion with him on religious issues, our views diverged but I took care that I did not annoy him.

***

My father came to Delhi to see me. He got in touch with my host and his friends and requested them to counsel me, as I was off the track in his estimation. The wish of my father was to make me a monk who fulfilled at least the basic commandments of the religion, of which offering five times prayer a day was the first and the foremost. I had no issue with the prayer for five times except it made me wake up very early and visit the mosque five times, every prayer taking almost half an hour. That I thought and still think is a huge toll on time. But he wanted more than prayer from me.

At Jashanpur, my morning started with my father's cuss words because I kept sleeping during the morning prayer. He said I slept while God offered abundance during the morning prayer; poverty and lack of God's grace was the direct result of lapse on my part. By noon, he kept a vigil to see whether I was readying myself for the afternoon prayer or not. The pattern repeated for the rest of the three prayers. He would not talk to me for weeks for not being prompt for prayer. I had to suffer sometimes for failing to offer prayers and sometimes for not being prompt for prayer.

He sought to make me a perfect Muslim. He thought studying for hours or acquisition of knowledge will not make God happy. It was action and the religious performances which will win God's pleasure. Even Satan was very knowledgeable, but that did not help him in salvation. Knowledge was good to the extent it gave us an understanding of good or bad, and a job. Beyond that, interest in knowledge at the cost of God's worship was an act of arrogance and futility. But I knew if I had to get a job, I would have to study for hours. A casual approach to study will take me nowhere.

The basic philosophy of my father consisted of the idea that this world was like an old hag and the worldly life was temporary. He said, "Real life started after death. All we needed to do here on the earth was to prepare for life after death. Prayer and remembering the Creator should have priority of place in our routine. We should not be studying and seeking a career goal all the time. Getting a clerk's job by studying and observing religious ritual was better than qualifying for the IAS exam without prayer."

This appears very logical. But a full time work of remembering and loving God does nothing to fight debilitating poverty, and deprivation in which I grew. Wealth was to come from rational, responsible, and goal directed action. This I realised and learnt from my studies and observations. Another conclusion which I drew after seeing large-scale poverty all around was that if the family size of a person was small, even a poor person had a fair chance of coming out of poverty. But if one's family size was large, even a wealthy person was going to see ruin in his life.

Now, while I lived in Delhi out of my father's influence, he did not stop tiring himself of the objective of reforming me. He built pressure on me through Imran Ashraf and others. But they saw me beyond redemption.

***

During discussion with them, I argued that if religion stayed upto 10 per cent in man's life, it would be beneficial. But if religion constituted 80 percent of a man's concern, his life would be miserable and a failure. God created man not for full time rites, rituals and prayers. Man's life on the earth would be better if he indulged in photography, studies, river-rafting, romance, service to the fellow being, and so on. This kind of argument jolted the group, so I cut the discussion short. There was no point trying to convince a person who thought I had gone off track.

One of the push factors at Jashanpur was my father, but he was again in my life in Delhi. He did expect me not only to offer prayer but a host of other things which I do not want to discuss here. But the saving grace was that he could not cut my food or assault me here. He could only send messengers to me who would tell me I was not on the right track of life and I would have to grieve at my "misconduct" at a later stage of my life.

***

JNU about 10 km from Okhla village was located in a different corner of Delhi, and my ecosystem which was created at Okhla was dissolved. I had to restart my life here. I could not go to Okhla to tutor my students. But I required money to pursue my studies. My parents sent me money orders in the range of ₹ 1000 whenever they could manage. I was everything for them, and my happiness and safety bothered them all the time.

Then one evening, Akhlaq Waris, a student at the university, during dinner at the mess table at the Sutlej Hostel offered me teaching a student for tuition at a DDA flat in front of the university campus. He got a fee of ₹ 500 from me and told me to go there. The student was a class VI student at Delhi Public School. I went to the flat and talked to the father of the student. Both mother and father of the girl student were examples of refinement and decency, though the student was a bit complex and egoistic. She played mind games with me, and parents had to intervene to control her. This family introduced me to another nearby family originally from Gujarat with three children studying in VI to VII standard. These two tuition with time to time assistance from my parents were to take care of my expenses.

To run across the academic centre, library, hostel and the flats for tuition in no time I bought a cycle in ₹ 2000. The cycle attracted derision from some quarters but I realised I would be able to attend to all the responsibilities if I had a vehicle to move fast.

I felt lonely most of the time. There was nobody to talk to, to share my feelings. Even if I had a friend I could not discuss my personal issues. Life was like a machine. I attended class, visited mess, tutored students, sat with books in the library—I was all the time on the run. I felt like weeping all the time, thoughts were chaotic and depressing. One day I sat on the rocks, and wrote about my problems in the class notebook I carried. That made me feel a bit better.

***

Life at the Persian language centre was nothing which I imagined an admission to JNU would give me. The university students of other Centers and Schools treated the students of the Persian Centre as non-serious students. Two girl students studied in the whole Centre and the boys across the batches tried to stick around them. I saw it was not a Centre for bright and ambitious students. Most of the

students belonged to one community, displayed low level of sophistication. Students at the campus held the view that the School of Languages (SL), the only School offering graduation (Bachelor of Arts) degree in languages, and students enrolled themselves there for graduation course, somehow did not fit in the institution of higher learning. Culture at this School building was different, somewhat akin to a college at University of Delhi.

Telling anybody at the campus that I studied at the Persian Centre did not evoke a positive response. I felt I was not enrolled at JNU despite being at JNU.

Prof Jamshed, a faculty at the Centre, seemed hostile to the students in the classroom. He bore the grudge against the Arabs for extinguishing the flames of Zoroastrianism in Persia (Iran). He made frequent remarks against me in the classroom, and stressed that the Iranians and Indians belonged to one race—Aryan—and the two shared huge commonality. He showed common words in Persian and Sanskrit languages, and a host of similar practices in the two countries during the ancient time. He said the Arabs conquered Persia militarily, but Persian civilization awed the backward Arabs. Persian civilisation possessed so much strength that it later became Muslim civilisation, the rulers all over the Muslim world during the medieval times adopted Persian language and practices at the courts and in their territory. All this was fine for me, I shared his pain but I was not ready to face his anger in the classroom. I, in the 20th century in his class in Delhi, was in no way responsible for the developments of the 7th century in the middle-east, I thought.

Anyhow my objective was not to enter into a quarrel with anybody. I had to stay, study and pass the exam for a job. Everything was fine till I could achieve that objective; what I had got here was a blessing. I could not complain.

***

In Jashanpur, Maurya University declared results for graduation courses of its colleges. I scored distinction in Sociology (Hons) subject with History and English literature. Now, I targeted admission in JNU's prestigious School of Social Sciences (SSS). It had renowned faculties and its students achieved great distinction in their career. One student was then chief editor of the Economic Times. Admission in this School was a license for sure success in life.

But the general standing at the university, particularly among the students of the Persian Centre, was that a student of School of Languages was not admitted in the School of Social Sciences (SSS). I heard this view not from one but dozens of students. They gave the example of several 'brilliant' students who later qualified civil services exam with a social science subject but could not crack admission test for SSS. I doubted this theory, as the University gave admission to students of any School or Centre through a written test. The faculty who marked the entrance test paper could not know whether a candidate was a student of the School of Languages or otherwise. Yet I was given the examples of so many students of the School of Languages who failed to get admission in SSS that this theory almost stood tested and established.

I thought let it be so, I will break this jinx. I will park my ship at the harbour of SSS. I reminded myself of the words of Abraham Lincoln, "I do the very best I know how-the very best I can; and mean to keep doing so until the end."

I stopped listening to this argument or telling the SL boys that I aimed to appear at the entrance test for SSS.

I approached one senior at Sociology, Fahad Ahsan and requested him to guide me. Fahad told me to go through the Indira Gandhi National Open University (IGNOU) booklets on BA Sociology and memorise everything written there. He also told me to solve the previous year's question papers for the MA Sociology entrance test. He introduced me to a student from Manipur who had IGNOU booklets. I kept talking to other MA students of the University, they were helpful and cordial.

One day I was studying Sociology on the fourth floor of the library. I saw a student with the book 'Main Currents in Sociological Thought' by Raymond Aron, a popular book of Sociology, which I had gone through. I said, "Hello Sir."

He became attentive to me and asked in which centre I studied. He said he was a student of Sociology at SSS. I told him "My ambition in life was to join SSS." He smiled. After talking to him for a few minutes, I realised my command over the subject was better than his. I felt confident that I would get through the entrance test.

***

At the Persian Centre, I met Faiz Mustafa, a student of MA, an extraordinary mix of energy and passion. His face shone bright and he spoke English like the famous British Prime Minister Winston Churchill. I wanted to imitate his diction, delivery, pause, and vocabulary. In a tucked maroon shirt, and grey Bata Power shoes, he looked as if he would bend the sky.

Most of the time, he was in high spirits. The ambition, thoughts, and doubt which seemed to have flagellated and propelled men like William the Conqueror and Alexander the Great, disturbed him also to achieve the extraordinary. So many days of life had passed, when he would become successful? This thought seemed to worry him all the time.

Course at Persian Centre was light and two hours of work apart from attending three-to-four classes daily was sufficient to keep me afloat. I spent the rest of the time reading Sociology for admission at the university. I walked from Sutlej Hostel in the morning to attend classes, came to the hostel mess for lunch at 1:30 p.m. and went to the central library and finally returned in the evening at 8:30 p.m.

When I walked to the School of Languages in the morning or when I returned to the hostel in the evening, I gazed longingly at the SSS (which we called triple S) building. I thought one day I would attend classes there and will be a student of SSS.

Many smart and beautiful girls, mostly from Delhi, were enrolled at SL. The red-brick beautiful School building was like a fashion ramp- smart faces with trendy dresses and fashionable haircuts walked around while boys stood or sat along the wall, the desks, and parapets. Boys discussed about the girls—who was going along with whom, what was the size of Anita's dress, how Pooja appeared in goggles and so on. My classmates at Persian Centre, though not equally well dressed, nor fluent in English, participated in the race. But they stood no chance of winning the heart of a girl. The fact that there were no girls in our class made the possibility of interaction and romance with a girl nearly impossible. Yet nothing dampened their spirit.

My approach was realistic. I had come to study here and go out with a job. Romantic entanglement was a distraction.

Moreover, I stood no chance of getting the attention of a girl with my ordinary dress and look. I knew this area was a waste of time for me.

***

It was March and forms for filing for admission in Sociology were being sold at the pink-stone building housing the administrative complex. I bought a prospectus for admission to MA at SSS. Faiz Mustafa suggested that I file forms for admission in the School of International Studies (SIS) also, where the courses were less rigorous and the students had more time to study for the civil services exam. I filled up forms spending ₹ 200.

I took the end-semester exam for Persian paper and had 10 days to go for the entrance test for SSS and SIS. I read IGNOU BA Sociology notes as many times as possible, and solved previous year's question papers. I appeared for the MA Sociology entrance test on May 17. Kendriya Vidyalaya at the old campus of JNU, a walking distance from the Sutlej hostel was the exam centre. I wrote as much as I could--relevant and irrelevant things. Writing tough words I thought would impress the examiner. At 12:0 noon. I was free. I walked to the hostel for lunch in the scorching sun and went to the school again for a test for admission in SIS. At 5:0 p.m., I came out of the exam centre. Sun was still scary. Plants along the way were dead, only thorny babool trees seemed to resist summer's haughtiness.

After dinner, I took a walk with a few friends. Nobody asked me about my test. I thought what I did today was going to determine the rest of my life. If I got admission in SSS, things were going to be good. If I missed it, life was going to be a walk through a scorching sunstorm.

After the exam, I thought to go home at Jashanpur. Most of the students, including my classmates at Persian centres, left the campus after the end-semester exam for two-and-half months long vacation. I stayed at the campus for one month, read Santayana and William James at the library, but did not understand them much. The deserted campus looked lonelier. Most of the students around were busy submitting dissertations and theses. Rajiv, a senior student of Economics, asked me at the library, "Why don't you go home? Break is important. You would come fresh from home and study with new energy."

"Yes, sir. I will go." I felt good that he was concerned for me."

Next day, I picked up my suitcase, and boarded the general class compartment of Purushottam Express with a ₹ 200 ticket. After the night's journey I reached Jashanpur. I had a surprise at home. I had a sister newly born. I took her in my lap and kissed her.

***

My father was still no different to me. After the first day of courtesy, he stopped talking to me. He saw that I was not offering prayers five times, and therefore I was good for nothing. I felt being boycotted. When in a good mood he talked on some issues but he did not want a counter argument. A talk with him was a monologue. I replied on any issue in yes or no, according to his wishes.

Because of my father's attitude towards me, I felt I was a thief or an intruder at home. I regretted coming to my parents. I kept silent at home most of the time. I met friends, told them about my 'great' life in JNU. After some days, I felt Delhi was calling me. There was no life worth living till I did something big. I lifted my teflon suitcase and went to Jashanpur railway station. I bought a ₹ 200 ticket for the general class compartment and stood in the crowded coach.

❑

Chapter 4

Campus of Dreaming Red-bricks

Purushottam Express reached New Delhi railway station at 5:0 a.m. I waited for bus number 615 at the bus stop. The railway station was a scene of dirt, poverty, and smell. I rushed to bus stand towards the Ajmeri Gate with my plastic suitcase. Bus was yet to arrive. I sat in a nearby small green, crowded park. Men, and women walked and jogged. Outside the park along the wall, young and old men slept on the footpath. After 40 minutes the blue line bus arrived.

I felt hungry, but did not want to spend any money on tea or snacks.

Finally, the bus arrived, and it ran through beautiful Lutyens Delhi, Prithvi Raj Road, Bikaji Cama Place, Munirka and then into the university campus. As the bus entered the campus, the air smelled sweet. I felt I was at home. Here my dreams would take wings. The yellow flowers on the amaltas tree hung low. I was again at the place of my dream. Life held promise for me. I got down at the bus stop and reached Sutlej Hostel. It was about 7:0 a.m.

Imran Ashraf, the resident of the room, had finished namaz and read Fazail-eAmaal, the treaties by a hadith scholar Mohd Zakariya Kandhlawi on the merits of good deeds. I entered the room and kept the suitcase in a corner. Imran Bhai looked at me and said, "Congrats, Hameed. Your name is in the Sociology selection list." I was stunned. I had qualified for admission in MA Sociology at the School of Social Sciences (SSS). He said, "You are ranked 4th in the selection list. You will get a hostel-room in the first list." These were the sweetest words I could hear. This was a turning point in my life.

***

While I was at Jashanpur I did not know about the result. All the time I was praying to God for my selection in SSS. At Sutlej Hostel, before I could wash my face or take breakfast, I rushed to the admin building of the university. My heart raced fast. At the admin building, on ply boards, the names of the selected candidates were type-written—names of thousands of students, including poor and underprivileged like me. I saw my name—Hameed Akhtar; I was one of the 60 candidates selected for the Sociology Centre at JNU.

I returned to the hostel. Everybody who knew me congratulated me. For the first time in my life, I won appreciation from so many people. Now I was in the mainstream course at the University. Now being enrolled at the University meant really being at JNU. I felt I got my destiny.

The Sociology Centre at the University was called the Centre for the Study of Social Systems (CSSS). It was one of the reputed Centres at SSS. Finally, I was at the building which I looked at daily morning and evening. The three letters —'SSS" —of brass shone golden and bright.

***

I took admission at CSSS paying ₹ 246. It was a long distance from the day when I had landed at New Delhi Railway Station for the first time in search of opportunities, and now when I had got admission at CSSS. I had no money, no extraordinary talent, no connection with big people, yet I believed I would do extraordinary. I would have everything which was required to live a life of dignity.

The classes started at the Centre. The composition of the class was very different from what I had experienced at the Persian Centre. Students came from different states of India, and from eight other countries like Denmark, South Korea, Japan, etc. and fifty per cent of the class was formed by girls. The classmates were gentle, soft spoken, and friendly.

The faculties were well-known faces. They had books published from reputed publishers and their articles appeared on a regular basis in the national dailies. They were like rock-stars, they excited and inspired us. One girl classmate said one professor was so handsome that she would say yes to a marriage proposal from him. One story did the rounds was that Prof Devender Sinha while studying at the university married a beautiful lady classmate and her father, an army officer, after hearing the news of the marriage of his daughter came to the university with an axe to kill the groom.

The faculty gave a reading list for the course. I tried to read all that was given in the reading list of the course of study. I loved reading and thought if anything could bring change in my life, it was study of books. I thought the study was a way to prosper in life, to achieve all which I could not get in my life till then. I must get out of poverty and deprivation. I must own a car, a house, a beautiful wife. I must be rich and famous. I thought the harder I worked, the more successful I would become. University campus was a battlefield. I had to develop skills, plan and strategy and emerge victorious. If I missed this opportunity, I would die in poverty and failure.

Reading from the lists, which contained the books or chapters of the eminent authors of social sciences including that of economics, philosophy, history, sociology, etc., I realised studying Sociology at JNU was a tough proposal. Themes in books were abstract, thought profound, the sentences lengthy, and words difficult and unfamiliar. Many times faded photocopies with small font size of relevant portions and chapters of many books were given. Original books of Karl Marx, Emile Durkheim, Max Weber, MN Srinivas, Dipankar Gupta, etc. were to be read. But reading and understanding the difficult text was both a challenge and a joy.

***

I tried to be active and participative in the class; I asked questions and made observations. The teachers encouraged intervention, participation and divergent thinking. The classmates respected their fellow classmate's right to hold an opinion. I did not attend classes in a proper way till I got enrolled here, and I enjoyed every moment of it. I thought this was the best India could offer me in social sciences. I was in awe and thrill all the time.

At the class, I met Jasmine, a sweet girl with curly hair from Kerala. One day she sat next to me, and wrote every detail of the lecture. Her handwriting was beautiful. I said, "You write very fast." She smiled and continued. She was not allotted a room at a hostel yet. After the classes, she went to her Legal Guardian (LG) near Hauz Khas in Delhi to stay with them.

***

I was allotted room no. 152 at Periyar Hostel. Red-brick, three-storey hostel building stood amidst big boulders, tumbling vines, and tall gulmohar trees. With more than 200 rooms, it accommodated 300 plus students enrolled in Centres like foreign languages to economics studies. Every room had a balcony where the leaves of neem, and babul trees rubbed the shining brick walls of the building.

Two students lived in a room designed for one student. My roommate was 20 year old Sameer Khan, proud of his smartness and muscular body. Enrolled at SL in French language, he shared with me techniques of getting fair and being presentable. To convey to me that I was a dark-skinned, despicable Bihari fellow, he often told me that he was scared seeing my face at night in the room.

I smiled at his subtle invectives. I felt I was a bushman from Kalahari Desert. I knew there was no point taking a fight with anybody on such an issue. I had to cover miles, and not waste my energy in such petty comments.

When I saw the room, dazzling light, good tables and chairs, I thought with so many facilities in my life, the civil services examination (CSE) would be a cake walk for me. Things looked under control. I thought these things were the best things life could offer me. I felt thankful to life and God.

Sameer came from an upper class, wealthy Muslim family. He said his ancestors came from Turkmenistan and made India their home. He asked me about my caste. I said I used to sweep the municipality road in my town before coming to Delhi. He realised I did not like his question and he did not ask me this question again.

I read somewhere: it does not matter whether you can be proud of your ancestor's. What matters is can they be proud of you. I reminded myself of these lines and kept cool. I also remembered reading the words of the American novelist Ernest Hemingway: In life it doesn't matter where you come from; all that matters is where you go. It is a mantra for all strugglers; they fight against the demons of privilege and prejudice.

After his repeated talk of his ancestors, I wrote these lines on a piece of paper and pasted it on the wall above my study table.

The personality of my father had made me a dabbu, timid, a person who could tolerate a lot of nonsense from others. I lived in fear of my father's anger and physical assault most of the time. Because of that I had no courage to confront Sameer. In childhood, when somebody assaulted me, I did not give him back because of my weakness. I told myself I would become a person worth reckoning and that would be my revenge.

Sameer's girl-friend Farah Mirza from his Centre came to him at the room and passed the time talking nonsense. His relationship with her was complex, and they had fights also. In a short sleeved shirt and cotton skirt, she would sit there even for two hours. During such times, I went outside the room and sat at the Godavari dhaba, waiting for her to leave the room. Sometimes I went to the library, read Schopenhauer under the milky tube light, and returned after hours. But I would find Farah Mirza had yet not finished her meeting. One evening, I did not leave the room when she came. They talked in whispers. I looked at the pages of Emile Durkheim, but I could not understand a word from the book, and had to leave the room, defeated.

***

The faculties kept us busy with work, presentation in the class, seminars, syndicate papers, etc. Jasmine and myself, apart from three other students, were part of one syndicate for writing a paper on "Patterns of Culture", a concept given by the American anthropologist Ruth Benedict, and for making a presentation in the class. I loved the name 'Ruth' and thought she must be beautiful. While reading her, I came across her words, "There are two kinds of opportunities: one which we chance upon, the other which we create." We all divided sections of the paper after preparing an outline and decided to read on the topic and discuss the paper at least once in a day.

The library's reader section dazzled with light. Smart girls and boys sat in rows with books, paper and pen. Relevant library books were badly underlined. Jasmine with her hair on her shoulders sat on a wooden chair and scribbled on her notepad with a pencil. Books of authors Rrajeev Bhargava, S Kaviraj, TK Oommen lay around her. I sat two rows behind her and read a paper on 'Argonauts of the Western Pacific' by a British anthropologist Malinowski. After an hour I went for a 5 minute walk, but Jasmine continued with her books and notes. I went to her and asked her how it was going. She said she had got the relevant material and was making notes on the topic. I said we could go for a tea break to the library canteen. She said, "Okay."

The canteen was located behind the library on a mound with three sides of precipice and dense forest. Nature was at its best and students preferred sitting outside on the granite boulders amidst leaves of thorny plants. We walked looking at the big posters with quotes of Vladimir Lenin, Mao Zedong calling for the red revolution.

I ordered two cups of tea and aaloo-bonda and sat on a bench. Nearby, peacocks jumped on the plants and rocks. Jasmine said, "We would make a good write-up and presentation."

"I can also present it in the class if you want," she added.

Abishek S, a class-mate, joined us and exchanged something with Jasmine in Malayali. They laughed, I could not understand why they laughed. I said, "Abhishek why don't you talk in English so that I can also understand."

"You need not understand everything man," he said.

Abhishek S had passed out from Dayal Singh College in Delhi. His father, an architect, had served in the government of India in the capital. Abhishek S was politically active and interacted mostly with the Keralites.

He kept talking with Jasmine in Malayali. I thought why and wherefrom this idiot had came. I waited for him to go so that I could talk to Jasmine, but he was in no mood to leave.

Twenty-year old Michel, who served as a waiter at the canteen and favourite of all visitors, brought our order on a tray and served us. After the tea, I felt Jasmine and Abhishek would sit there longer. I told Jasmine I would leave and went to the library.

Next day, all the members of the tutorial assembled at the library canteen and discussed the progress. I took the lead and tried to coordinate and give a shape to the paper. Michel brought for us thalis of crispy masala dosa in the humid evening. Jasmine in a cream shirt and trousers said she would start the presentation, introduce the topic and speak on her section and then the rest of the participants would speak.

After three days of work we made a presentation, each member spoke on a unit of the paper in the classroom. The faculty and the classmates appreciated our work.

***

My clothes during this period were ordinary. My highest aspiration was to wear a T-shirt, jeans and a pair of sports shoes. Dress did not appear to be an important factor for one's stature and reputation on the campus. What mattered was what and how one spoke, where one's articles were published, what marks one scored in the tests at the University. Many students from good families wore slippers and went to the classroom. It was fashionable to look ordinary, and espouse high ideals.

The university gave merit-cum-means scholarship at the rate of ₹ 350 per month to every student if he/she produced a low income certificate of his/her family. The scholarship came once in six months or in a year. The mess charged a bill of about ₹ 700-800 per month.

***

My next door neighbour was Surya Prakash. We called him Surya Althusser because he was too much in love with French authors and philosophers and he threw their ideas and names like bullets from a machine-gun.

One evening he told me to go for a walk after dinner. The taste of the delicious custard was yet to settle in my mouth. At 9:0 p.m. it was drizzling, and Delhi's sky held more rain. I was in no mood to drench myself with a man in the monsoon evening. But he forced me to come out of my room when the FM radio was playing Kishore's 'dilbar dil se payare dil ki sunta ja re'.

We walked in jeans and sleepers. As we came on the main road near Godavari bus stand, Dipali Mukherjee with open hair came from the opposite direction. She told Surya, 'Hi. Kahan they tum,' in a husky voice. The two got close, while I waited for Surya to finish talk with her, and move for a walk with me. But something cooked between the two, and after 30 seconds Surya said looking at me, 'Okay, Bhai, see you again.' The two moved under an umbrella in the neon lamp post.

***

The class ended at 1:30 p.m. with a lecture on structuralism theory by Levi Strauss. It was an abstract topic for the students. After the class, most of us walked towards our hostel. I saw Jasmine with her notebook bag near the SSS building gate.

"What are you thinking, Jasmine? Come for lunch at the hostel," I said.

"No. I will take something to the canteen."

"After the class, will you go to the library or to your LG?"

"Bus is crowded at this hour. I will study for some time and then will leave the campus at 3:0 p.m."

I said, "Okay. I will see you off near the library canteen and will go to my hostel."

We walked towards the canteen. Jasmine said classes were boring. She had studied Economics in graduation and everything was new to her at the university in Sociology. She was not able to understand the books prescribed in the reading list. "What you read, please discuss with me. I will also get some ideas."

I said, "Fine, Jasmine. But it is not so difficult."

"No. You have studied Sociology in graduation. You are okay because of that. I never thought Sociology could be so difficult."

"Maybe it will be fine after the first semester."

"My father wanted me to go to Delhi School of Economics (DSE). But I landed here."

"This is also a good place. Equal to DSE or better."

Near the library canteen, she told me to join her for lunch. I agreed. We took masala dosa and returned to the library. I read an essay by sociologist Davis Moore sitting next to her while she read Duncan Mitchell's 'Dictionary of Sociology' familiarising herself with the sociological terms, concepts, theories, and names of the sociologists.

***

Friends, class work, reading, new environment—initially all gave me a high. But I knew I had a very short time at my disposal and my goal was to get a job. I filled up forms for Bank Probationary and Assistant Grade Exams. The exam pattern was objective type questions on general awareness, arithmetic, English language, mental ability, and so on. Proficiency in solving questions on these topics required regular practice. I had left practising and solving such questions long back. My vague goal now was to qualify the gazetted officers' exam conducted by Union Public Service Commission or Bihar Public Service Commission.

I used the SLR cycle for attending library and tuition. Students and friends did not like me cycling. Assembled at the dhaba, taking tea and discussing academic or political issues, they commented when I rode the cycle to go anywhere. Students mostly rode motorcycles and cycling was considered infra dig. Road at the University was undulating, cycling on it was a bit difficult but I continued with it. It gave me speed and I attended more work than was possible without the cycle.

***

Jasmine was now allotted a room at Godavari Hostel, opposite Periyar Hostel, with Neelgiri Dhaba between them, after a month. One evening at 4.0, I went to buy a Reynolds pen at the dhaba. She was standing there to take kachuri which the vendor was frying. It had rained in the after-noon, and the evening was humid. Seeing her there, I said, "Hi Jasmine!"

She said, "Hi! You are here?"

"Yes. I live in Periyar." She looked beautiful in a denim workshirt.

"Eat some kachuri."

"No. It is very spicy."

"Ok." She smiled. "You did not explain Talcott Parsons to me. He is absolutely pedestrian but he has laced his theory with technical terms."

"I will do it when you have time. Please let me know when you want." I bought the pen and walked back to the room.

Neelgiri Dhaba was a rendezvous of memorable characters, ideas, and a stage for happening events. Here a crowd of beautiful and intelligent people sat on the steps and discussed Adam Smith, C. Wright Mills, Noam Chomsky and Francis Fukuyama. It was a parade ground for ambitious, sharp, and beautiful people from all over campus. Vehicles with red beacon light came and stayed parked near the hostel for the daughters of the rich and powerful. The poor and have-notes also strutted around there. There was no social bar in interaction, or mixing. All felt equal. Everyone was courteous, busy in his or her own world. Eyes of men did not leer, glances did not offend anyone.

In the room, I took 'The Pioneer' editorial and read it. I was thinking about Jasmine. How seductive was her smile, how sweet her voice.

Sameer was getting ready to go out. He said, "Bhai, a newspaper story is one day old. Editorial in a newspaper is a commentary on an issue published one day ago. So in effect you read stories which are three days old."

I said, "Anyway, they are worth reading." I was thinking about what Jasmine told me. I did not want to talk to Sameer and ruin my mood.

That evening it rained and the sky thundered. After dinner at the dining hall, I walked to my room. Sameer was busy with Farah Mirza tasting food delivered from a restaurant near Malai Mandir. I came out of the room and went to Godavari Dhaba and looked for Jasmine if she was there. She was gone.

I thought of going to Jasmine's hostel and calling her for a walk. But I restrained myself thinking what if she declined? I walked alone on the road under the yellow light of lamp posts. The smell of soil filled the air, leaves and yellow flowers rolled on the tarmac. Then I saw Abhishek S walking with a classmate. I was stressed thinking whether it was Jasmine. When I moved closer, I saw it was Sanyukta, a senior in our Centre. I heaved a sigh of relief and returned to the common room of the hostel where the boys whistled at the songs of "Hum Aapke Hain Koun..!" My roommate was yet to finish dinner with the beautiful Farah Mirza. So, I stood in front of the television and saw the strain in the love story on the screen.

***

For the first time in my life, I got so many friends and acquaintances. Until now I was shy, hesitant, inward looking. I did not like meeting anyone. Now I had a crowd of boys and girls, all friendly and helpful.

Friendship here was based on the commonality of class room, Centre, School, or State to which one belonged, and hostel, etc. If one started from the hostel to the library building or to the KC shopping centre, one met, greeted and exchanged ideas or incidents with dozens of students on the route. Just meeting and interacting with so many students made me feel wonderful. The students of various backgrounds interacted freely and participated together in various activities. There was no snobbery or if there was, then it was restrained. Elitism of any sort by anybody was denounced. Students from rural background could be found interacting with beautiful girls from elite, urban families. In the outside world, such a girl would not even look at such a boy. The feeling of differences on the basis of caste and creed was minimum. Here I felt that I was more than a person from a community. My identity as a boy of a community was foregone, other identities like being a student of social sciences, a part of a hostel, a boy from Bihar, etc. were recognised above my religious identity. Students generally were not critical of others, they did not look for the negative side of other's conduct and nor passed nasty comments. People avoided making comments about one's look or colour or a girl's character even behind that person. If somebody said that a boy looked like an auto-driver then the one who said this broke some model code of the University.

***

On Sunday evening at 9:0 p.m. I went to Jasmine's hostel and told the security staff to call her. I had not seen her since Thursday and was wondering where she was. While at the library or taking tea at the dhaba in the evening I looked for her but she was nowhere.

The security staff gave her a call and she came down in a denim work-shirt with rolled sleeves. I said, "Hi Jasmine! How is it going?"

"Oh! I was getting bored. I am tired of reading books and papers."

"We can go for a walk."

"Where? I am in no mood to go anywhere."

"I did not see you for the last few days. So I came to say hello to you."

Then she thought for a while and said she would come for a walk.

She came out and we walked along the lonely road. She said her father never discriminated against her. He told her if she did two things, she would have all the freedom. One was that she should stand first in the exam in the class, and secondly, she should not enter into an affair with any boy. He said he would get her married with a boy of her choice at a later stage. He said at that age she was young and was not able to make a correct choice. So she should wait. She complied with these directions of her father, but living with these two conditions did not leave any joy in her life.

"But now you can have a boy of your choice," I said and laughed.

"But the boys around me are boring and duffer."

I did not ask her what kind of boys she wanted. I said, "But this university is full of bright minds."

We kept walking slowly. For the first time in my life I was walking aimlessly at night with a woman. I looked at her face, hair and bare forearms. She looked so seductive that I could do anything to spend a moment with her. I looked at the moment of time and told it to stop so that I could absorb her company.

Jasmine said, "I will go now." We turned and reached our hostels. I did not study a word that evening and slept at around 2:20 a.m. I did not know what had happened to me. For the first time I was not thinking about the books and study and the problems at my home. Jasmine danced in my thoughts, what she said and how she said replayed in my imagination.

***

Friends, class work, reading, new environment--initially all gave me a high. I was happy with progress in my career. The fear and uncertainty stood a little away from me. My target was the civil services exam and entering into All India Services like Indian Administrative Service (IAS) or Indian Police Service (IPS). But it was a vague target, and there was no stepwise plan to execute it. Every other youth like me aspired to crack CSE, and there was nothing special in what I wished for.

But, I knew I had a very short time at my disposal. I intended to start preparation for CSE, but life was very hectic with classes, exams, and term-papers.

The students prepared for the civil services exam surreptitiously, without sharing their ambition with the fellow students and faculties. If a professor came to know that a scholar was preparing for civil services exam, he would oust her out of the centre or make her busy in academic work to ensure that her ambition of a career in bureaucracy was frustrated. A student taking the civil services exam was using the infrastructure of academics for a career in bureaucracy.

Those preparing for civil services were looked down upon among the student community. They were seen as careerists, those who had betrayed the cause of people and jettisoned the higher ideals of life. Preparing for the civil service exam while receiving Junior Research Fellowship (JFR) was a higher treason. The first rate brains pursued the academics. One who was preparing for civil services was a cuckoo chick in a crow's nest.

I met Sunder Kumar, a 22 year-old senior at the hostel, and asked him how I should approach the CSE. Sunder was a native of Patna, and was enrolled in MPhil. He had appeared for an interview in CSE and enjoyed a good reputation among the students. He advised me not to go for the CSE while doing MA. He said, "If you prepare for UPSC at this stage, you would score low grades in the MA course and the faculties would ensure that you are not selected for the MPhil course. MA syllabus is very heavy and MPhil is slightly okay. So MPhil is the best time to study for CSE and make a career."

I was a bit convinced with Sunder's argument, and I walked out of Sunder's room thinking about his advice. But I wanted to work more. The MA course, though heavy, was not enough to tire me completely. I was in a hurry. I wanted to prepare for the exam and qualify it. I did not want to wait for another two years to start taking the exam. What would be the situation in my life after two years, nobody knew. Why should I wait? I walked towards the administrative block thinking what to do.

***

It was 5:30 p.m., the day was cloudy and pleasant. Jasmine was coming from the library towards her hostel with classmates Kavita Thakur and Anju Saini. I looked at her and said, "Hi."

She said, "Hi! Where are you going?"

Students walked to their hostels with their note-books and bags while the evening sun from the western sky sent abundant orange colour on the earth. Henna plants with fresh leaves fenced the residential quarters along the way.

"I am just taking a walk."

"Okay see you." Her dupatta with a silken edge hung down from her shoulder. Her hair was a big bun held together with a hairstick. I thought to engage her, but she seemed to be in no mood to talk to me.

She moved towards the hostel. I forgot about the CSE and felt attracted to her. I strolled ahead and thought about her. I became conscious of what I was wearing and how I looked. I went further towards the administrative block where two students were sitting on dharna against the administration demanding roll back of increase in hostel mess fee. The university had given some hostel mess to a private contractor who charged the students fee for the food preparation apart from the expenditure on food.

That evening I walked with Surya Prakash after dinner. I saw Jasmine marching in a protest procession to Ganga dhaba against desecration of the statue of a political leader in Pune. She walked along with a senior student of the Centre for Economic Studies and Planning (CESP) Ragni Gupta, who held a mashal (torch-light). The processionists, after a short speech on poor and voiceless people and the need to speak for them, spoke against the university administration and then dispersed. I thought to catch up with her somewhere on the way while she returned, but she spent more time with the student leaders and activists. Then I returned to the room and stared at the pages of Thomas Kuhn, philosopher of science, under the table lamp. Kuhn broke my belief in scientific certainty. He wrote, "Far from being magisterial in its objectivity, science was conditioned by history, society, and the prejudices of scientists."

***

Professor Amulya Banerjee, our faculty at CSSS, told the students to read the original texts of the classical authors and not the substandard text or run of the mill writers.

Reading the interpreters of an author or a guide book will not benefit one in the way reading the masters would do. He said reading even 20 pages of the original text of the authors was thousand times better than reading a guide book sold on a stand in a stall.

Reading classical theorists like Emile Durkheim, Max Weber and Karl Marx was many times more beneficial than reading sociologist like Abraham and Morgan. The language, the breath of thought, the way of expression of the masters, the references in their writings, their genius could not be captured and conveyed by the interpreters. This was a great insight and it stayed with me. We now read books published by Allen and Unwin and Routledge.

He said he would make out from our answer sheets whether we answered the questions after reading the original text or 'market notes'.

The reading list was tough and intimidating. A student of Sociology was supposed to read the original text of Karl Marx and Friedrich Engels, Anthony Giddens, Thomas Kuhn, Robert King Merton, Karl Popper and Paul Feyerabend, Levi-Strauss, C Wright Mills, Robert Nisbet, MN Srinivas, Terry Eagleton, Dipanker Gupta, Immanuel Wallerstein, Eric Hobsbawm, Davis & Moore, to mention only a few.

But the mature among us did not fall to the baits of teachers like Prof Amulya Banerjee and read notes and books of graduation level. And they scored respectable B plus grades in the exams. The best students scored A plus and A, the minimum one scored was B, or in rare case C plus. B plus was equivalent to about 55 per cent of the marks.

***

Every professor standing near the green-board with a chalk stick was an inspiration for us. Many times when they lectured, my thoughts wavered to their profile, gossips about them, lady faculty's tall-thick hair, and their dress rather than what they taught.

Prof Shaili Raman, who taught us feminist theories, would tell us, "Never accept the expression which comes easily. Think of the alternative ways of doing things and writing." Professor Harjot Singh had a high opinion about me. He talked to me at length and considered me a serious and good student. He answered my questions in the classroom and the day when I did not raise any point in the class he asked me what was the matter, why I was silent.

Prof Mukul Sharma taught us sociologist Herbert Spencer's theory of social evolution. He elaborated on Spencer's notion of a self-made man who overcomes all his frailties and odds. According to Spencer, after the industrial revolution we will have a class of superman on the earth, and all the unfit will have no place here.

***

I had learnt the English language by building the word power. The first book my father taught me was one IXth class English book of Bihar School Education Board titled 'Stories for Pleasant Reading.' The second book with the same title Part II was prescribed for Xth standard. He told me to note down the difficult words in a chapter, he would write their meanings. I memorised the meanings of the words and then he explained each line.

When I read the chapter again on my own I could understand every line, this was a magic. If I read a chapter myself after memorising the meaning of those words I could not go much ahead. It was only after he taught that I could understand the chapter. But it amazed me and boosted my confidence tremendously. I saw that if one knew the words then one could understand the English text. Reading about 200 pages of both the books raised my confidence and put me on a track which changed the course of my life.

Then I took the third book and the fourth book. I was unstoppable. English newspapers, magazines, English books around me raised my curiosity and fascinated me. I wanted to know what was written in those pages carrying beautiful, expressive photographs.

But newspapers, and magazines were not easy to understand. I got hold of 'India Today', and 'The Sunday', and 'The Times of India'. I realised that while my school text book was a cakewalk, these magazines and newspapers were tall walls to climb. While I read them and failed to understand them, my thoughts wandered and understanding them became difficult. The way my father coached me for the school story textbook, he was not going to do the same for the newspapers and magazines. However, more work and better vocabulary power would make me understand newspapers and magazines also.

And the ability to understand the English language put me on a different track. Otherwise I would have been roaming around in Jashanpur town till today. It opened to me a vast pool of knowledge, and inspirational thoughts which were otherwise not available to me. I became a lifelong collector of English vocabulary, which enhanced my level of understanding.

Friends told me that the ultimate level of command over English language was the ability to understand the editorial of 'The Times of India' newspaper. I took the newspaper and read the editorial without making head or tail of it. But I continued reading it with the thought that it was my way to salvation. Those days, 'The Times of India' editorial exhibited higher literary quality and profound analysis. Currently, it is simplified and truncated.

Anyway, despite my reading habit at home, I found the reading list and material given at the class in JNU insurmountable. I found many books which made a few simple points in several pages written in tough English. Exams questions were to be answered and term-papers were to be written using these books and reading material.

***

The result of the mid term test had come and I was among the top students of the class. The result gave me my ranking vis a vis the classmates. But the end semester exam result was going to show a clearer picture. I needed to work equally hard in the coming days to stand in the top crust of the class.

Jasmine stood somewhere in the middle and was okay with a B-plus grade. She was not very serious; campus life, friends, participation in the various activities like procession, protest, public meeting, etc. interested her more.

Classmate Abbas Nasir would give me treats, or loan me money when I required. His father was an executive engineer in the public works department in Bihar. He was never short of money and lured me to write his term papers. He had graduated in Philosophy from Deshbandhu College in Delhi, and was well versed with Plato, Aristotel, Karl Marx, Immanuel Kant, Witgenstein, and others. I enjoyed listening to him. He told many things about philosophy and philosophers in a story form, which I did not know despite being acquainted with the philosophers. He said philosophy was the mother of all sciences. Aristotle wrote about 10 lakh words, only 20 per cent of his writings were available for us to read. Rousseau read Plutarch's 'Lives' at the age of seven. His most famous quote was: "Man is born free, and everywhere he is in chains. One man thinks himself the master of others, but remains more of a slave than they are." Abbas said there were two sources of knowledge: revelation and reason. Man could go near God not only through religion and revelation but also through reason and science. I loved listening to his snippets though I knew most of the things he said about the philosophers and their theories.

One of his favourite activities was reading Khushwant Singh's column "With Malice Towards One and All' every Saturday in 'The Hindustan Times'. He would tell me the saucy jokes from the column.

***

Different bodies in the university organised regular talks and public meetings on various burning issues. One favourite place for public meetings was the hostel mess which accommodated about 200 students as audience, and speakers ranging from the university professors, policy experts to union government ministers who came to address the students. The talk, always held after dinner at around 9:30 p.m., was entertaining and educative. It also provided one an opportunity to see eminent men of the country, and benefit from their ideas and style of expression. I attended these talks and felt inspired by the speakers. I saw many politicians and intellectuals whom I had seen on television or read about in a newspaper. Jasmine in contact with the student bodies was active in organising such talks, writing pamphlets informing the students about the topic and speakers, or contacting the speakers to invite them for the talks. The talk ended at about 11:30 p.m. after question and answer sessions.

***

Though I rejected my father's recipe for a good person, the spiritual and religious questions, a kind of permanent convulsion, did not spare me. I thought what would happen to me when I die, what God wanted from us human beings— his worship and remembrance all the time, or running of the workshop of the world. Whether man or his spirit survived death? Whether our action determined the course of our lives or everything was fixed, we were puppets with our strings in the hand of God? The environment at the university was not such that one could debate religion and spirituality. Everybody discussed economics and politics. Even psychology, which focussed on an individual, her emotion, motivation, learning, intelligence, attitude, etc. had no place in discussion.

As per the Muslim's belief one was accumulating sin in tons simply by failing to offer prayer. God will incinerate those who did not pray five times. Any active misdeed was not required to earn God's wrath. A crime will earn one additional sin and curse. That was a terrifying situation.

I was not bold enough like Ludwig Wittgenstein who dismissed the question of life after death saying, "The real question of life after death isn't whether or not it exists, but even if it does what problem this really solves."

I read a Nobel laureate from France who said human beings after their death suffer the fate which follows the fate of a crashed computer. Jawaharlal Nehru in the 'Discovery of India' broached these issues and said, "Essentially I am interested in this world, in this life, not in some other world or a future life. Whether there is such a thing as a soul, or whether there is a survival after death or not, I do not know; and, important as these questions are, they do not trouble me in the least...The real problem for me remain problems of individual and social life, or harmonious living, of a proper balancing of inner and outer life, of an adjustment of the relations between individuals and between groups..."

These words had an impact on me and I decided to suspend the questions about soul, sin, God, life after death, etc. which constantly inveighed me.

I reasoned if I had money, a house, a naukri, I would fulfil the basic requirement of a religion better than if I was poor and hungry. Only two-to-four years of focussed work, suspending the demands from other quarters, would give me everything. But if I tried to be everything, I would get neither God nor Mammon.

***

Jasmine came to my room at 8:0 p.m. Electricity was gone and I was studying with a candle lamp. Some boys could be heard singing songs while others walked in the corridor talking with fellow students. Surya Prakash had gone to take bath in the wash-room. I was yet to go for dinner.

She said, "Why are you hitting your head on the wall in the dim light? It will ruin your eyes. The whole world is outside, enjoying the beautiful evening. And you are reading boring pages of mad philosophers."

I looked at her bright dusky face. What a surprise, I thought. If somebody passed near the door of my room, I thought it was her feet. I wished to tellI her she looked gorgeous and I wanted to marry her. That you are the feeling of my first love, you are my first wish, you are my thirst. I folded the book and wondered why she was there at dinner time.

"Jasmine, I was thinking of you."

"Did you have dinner? Let us go outside or to the library canteen. Fish preparation there is excellent."

I thought how much money was in my wallet. I remembered it was ₹ 50. Two people could have dinner with this much money at the library canteen.

I said, "Hostel mess food is also good. Today is Wednesday. They have prepared mutton gravy and custard."

"I do not want to eat mess food."

"Ok. We can go to the library canteen. We would go outside some other time."

I wore shoes and washed my face. Sameer had gone to listen to the lecture of the French embassy to listen the French philosopher Michel Foucault. She stood on the balcony and looked outside the road lit by the yellow light of the lamp-posts. She said she did not like the cold climate. At Malappuram, even on 25th December, the temperature was 30 degree.

We walked out. Boys standing at the hostel gate stared at us. Her eyes shone with idealism. I felt guilty that she lived for the weak and the poor and I was busy with myself. What good did I do in the life of anybody today, I questioned myself.

I said, "Today I read a few pages of 'Wuthering Heights' by Emily Brontë. It is great reading."

She said, "Yes, I read one chapter in my school English book. Something about a boy named Heathcliff. But I do not like novels and fiction. I like serious stuff—writings about economy and society. About change and revolution. Not the fiction which drives you from the real world."

"But this book is lovely. An amazing description of the English countryside, roses and daffodils, snowy mountains and rivulets with a storm of human emotions, moonlight, blue sea and silent nights with characters in difficulty.

"This is what I am saying. It lulls you. Transports you into a world where you feel everything is okay. You become blind to the agony and distress of the people around you," she said.

I did not want to argue with her. I knew argument was the surest way of making an enemy out of a friend. I became silent and heard the noise of insects in the forest in November evening. Sky was clear and the moon looked pale. Numerous kikar trees stood silent. A nilgai roamed on the dry leaves and woods of the trees.

I thought what she wanted from me. Simple friendship and companionship or more than that. Would she live with me till the end? Should I ask what was in her heart? Would she laugh if I said I loved her? We reached the canteen.

We ate fish and rice with spoons sitting on the rocks under the night sky. A bulb lit the area in front of the canteen and the sound of a song by Hemant Kumar on the FM radio reached out mildly from somewhere.

After the dinner, we walked back to the hostel. I left her near the hostel gate and said, "See, you." Udai Pratap, son of an IAS officer and a student of MA Political Science, stood with Neha Gill, a resident of Godavari hostel, at the gate. He held her hand and said, "Neha, your hands are so beautiful." Then he kissed her hand. Neha blushed and walked inside. I walked through the crowd on the steps of Godavari Dhaba and reached my hostel.

***

My urge to prepare for the CSE persisted. Graduation was a qualification for appearing at the CSE. I was enrolled in a masters course. Why should I wait for two years to appear at this exam? After discussion with Sunder Kumar, I went to Amrender Singh, who had qualified for the CSE and got allotted Indian Police Service (IPS). He told me to study sincerely at the Centre for at least two semesters. Those who start preparation for civil services exam right from the beginning lose both in academics and in civil services. One should impress the faculties with sincerity and good grades in the first year. In the second year, one could take liberty as the teachers knew that one was a good student. Most of the students did this. Instances of an MA student joining civil services were a few. Getting admission in MPhil was not difficult, even an average student qualified the entrance test. For qualifying the exam one should read diverse subjects, that would pay one even if one failed to qualify the civil services exam. Amrender Singh had qualified for the civil services exam while doing MPhil course.

***

Between all these came Dipawali. On the initiative of Sasikumar, all classmates assembled near the junior Kendriya Vidyalaya on the campus at 9:30 p.m. We fired crackers. Jasmine had gone to her legal guardian in Delhi. In her absence, I felt sinking but I did not let anybody realise that. Priya Jhingan had brought a box of sweets for the batchmates. Alka Jamwal dressed in a blue tube top looked dashing. Laxmi Naagar sat along with Ankit Srivastav sending feelers that she would date him. The norm at the university was that more than one boy could court a girl. The moment the girl showed interest in a particular boy, other boys interested in the girl would lay their arms and stop wooing her. Laxmi's other aspirants in the group surrendered. While love between the two was being played out, we exploded crackers, screamed, jumped, and ran helter skelter on the empty road. Some moments were scary. I threw a cracker up above, and it came back near the face of the most beautiful girl of the class Puja Bhagra. But she was not injured with God's grace. After this, we sat and played antakshari songs. The night was beautiful and we did not want it to go.

Now, it was 2:30 a.m. and some classmates pressed to call it a day. We packed, and returned. On the way back, Nirupama Menon sang Hindi film songs in a sweet voice under the smoky sky. I was happy that by the end of the session I was not feeling sick without Jasmine. But when I reached the room, she again came into my thoughts.

***

Now the mid-semester exam came over my head. I had 20 days to go. Jasmine asked me for the class notes, and the notes on the syllabus I made reading with books prescribed by the faculties. I said, "Okay".

On Friday evening at 7:30, I went to deliver her notes at her hostel gate. Sunil, the security staff, a native of Rewari district of Haryana, was busy calling the hostel-mates for the visitors. Men and boys came in Ambassador, Opel Astra cars and Mahindra classic Jeeps to meet the resident girls or to go with them somewhere. White tube light dazzled the security post at the hostel gate, which had a table and a telephone set to receive a call. The roots of the banyan tree dangled over it. I thought it was a mela. Beautiful people came to the university, showed their talent, and were replaced every year with another set of beautiful people. But the mela was continuous, only the characters changed. I saw from a group of girls Jasmine emerging. She said, "Sorry, you had to wait."

I said, "No issues."

She took my notes and said, "Thanks so much. I will return them on Monday morning."

Her eyes were expressive, they shone bright. I thought how comfortable the lives of these girls were. No worries for money, a vanity parade all day, excess of everything in life, no uncertain future like mine.

I said, "Bye," and walked back to my room. I thought how she looked at me, how lovely was her smile, what she must be thinking when she smiled.

Rumi's line "Gamble everything for love" crossed my mind.

***

On Sunday, I went to her hostel at 2:0 p.m. after lunch. I thought she would be in the mess and I would meet her. I waited for her; she came out after 15 minutes in capri pants and a white T-shirt. She said, "Hi!"

"Hi, Jasmine."

"What's going on? Busy with books."

I said, "I came to take class notes of sociological methods."

She smiled and said, "Um...You are sure you came for class notes?"

I did not know how to handle this question. I said, "I was getting bored. So I thought to disturb you. I did not see you after Friday afternoon."

"I was at the hostel. Did not go anywhere. I get entertained at the hostel itself. You have all kinds of people here."

"Would you come for a short walk?"

"Abhi? Now? Isn't it hot outside?"

"I think it is pleasant. We can take a round of the Godavari Hostel."

"Okay, chalo. Let us go." We came on the main road near Godavari bus stop and walked towards kendriya vidyalaya. Peacocks ran across the empty road.

I was feeling uncomfortable. I did not know what to say to her. Then she said, "Which book are you reading for social movement?"

"I am going through the book of MSA Rao, though it is an old book and speaks nothing about the contemporary developments."

"Yes, it is difficult to find books and studies on Indian society and developments. Indian researchers and academicians write or publish a few books."

"Because of this, we get to know more about the western societies than about our society."

"If you find something then share it with me. Or explain the topic to me. We can sit somewhere and discuss."

The amaltas trees along the road stood silent. They were witnesses of batches of students coming to the university, absorbing knowledge in its ambience and leaving the campus in India's service. We reached the trijunction near the admin block. I wanted to walk more.

"Have you gone towards the Parthasarthi rock? It is amazing."

"I have heard a lot about it. But it is a lovers' point. We are not lovers yet . So no point going there."

"But we can walk on the main road towards the East Gate."

The pathway to Parthasarthi rock through the kachcha track broke from the mettled road going to the East Gate of the Campus. We walked further on the silent, lonely tarred road. Jasmine had not been to this side of the university yet. A few bikes with university boys and girls passed us. Now a group of nilgai looked at us from the bushes.

"My God! See what is there."

"That is a nilgai."

"This area is thick with trees and thorny bushes."

"Yes, we are walking on the last patch of Aravali."

"I never thought I would be studying in Aravallis, so far away from home," she said.

"Who is at your home?" Jasmine.

"My father, mother and a young brother."

"And what about you?" she asked.

"Father, mother, brother and sisters."

"You are the eldest?"

"Yes."

She suggested that we should now return. She was not used to taking a walk like me. We turned back towards the hostel.

A scorpion walked on the metal top of the road. Jasmine picked it with a stick and put it on the roadside lest it was crushed by a vehicle. We reached near the residential complex Dakshinapuram where our hostels were located.

"I will come to your hostel this evening. If you liked the walk we could go again in the evening," I said.

She said, "Okay." and walked into her hostel.

***

End semester exam drew closer and everybody became busy. My target was to score A grade in all the four papers. Given my performance in the mid-semester tests, it was quite possible.

Prof Devender Sinha awarded low grades, scoring A grade in his paper was a certificate of being brilliant. Prof Devender's mother was of British origin and his father came from Lucknow. He knew the names of most of the students of the class and addressed them by their first names. He looked dashing and wore branded casuals. Other professors awarded average or better scores in the range of A minus and A grade.

***

Jasmine, sitting at the steps in front of the massive red-brick SSS building, turned the pages of Sociologist KL Sharma's book. She wore white jumper and light-green silk salwar and appeared stressed with the exams. She said she was tired of frequent exams. "I am busy all the time memorising and revising things."

I said, "My father did not tell me to study even once in my life. But now I feel I am sick of reading and exams."

"I want freedom from this cycle of exams, term papers, and seminars."

"Life here is not for joy, Jasmine. I was happy and proud when I got enrolled here. But the burden here is always more than I can carry. You feel you are in a grind."

"Let's go to the canteen. We will have coffee. Don't depress me."

We took coffee sitting at the boulders. Peacocks screamed in the nearby bushes. I looked at her neck and glowing arms and thought she wanted just temporary company or something more from me.

***

During the end semester exam, Jasmine told me to guide her and make her revise the whole syllabus. I sat with her in the evening in the soft winter sun on the marble steps of the library building and ran over the whole syllabus of a paper whose exam was scheduled the next day. I was myself stressed and I wanted the whole time for myself. But I could not say no to her. Anju Sani and Abbas also joined us. Abhishek S while entering the library stood there and made faces. He thought I was doing some scam.

At the exam, I gave answers to the questions without beating around the bush. I pushed myself to write fast and more, as a good result was going to open avenues for me. Still, I had no idea where I stood in the class vis-a-vis other students. Exams of four papers came to an end on May 5 when the heat scorched the earth.

***

After the end semester exam, Jasmine went home boarding Trivandrum Rajdhani Express at 10:0 a.m. I went to see her off at the railway station. Most of the other students had also gone home and the campus was deserted. I spent time reading books, sitting on a rock or at the steps of the library in the chilled winter wind. When I had classes and exams, or friends around to talk to or take a walk, I felt okay. But now I felt lonely and depressed most of the time. I wore a shirt and a sweater but cold wind tore and shrunk my existence. I thought how I had spent my last six months and how I should spend my days in the coming semester. The thorny kikar trees had shed their leaves on the pathway connecting the academic complex with the hostel area. I walked to the library in jeans and slippers and poured over the pages of books on religion and philosophy.

I thought my father was responsible for difficulties in my life. He did not prepare me for the battle of life. If one did not study in a good school, did not speak English at the age of five, one did not receive nutritive diet when one was in one's mother's womb, then nothing could change one's life for the better. That is, one could not catch up because one was handicapped. I thought all those around me were rich and privileged. I was the only one suffering that kind of challenge.

On December 12 night at 9:30, after dinner, alone in the room, I felt I should talk to Jasmine. The whole day I did not speak to anybody, and I felt like a prisoner living in solitary confinement. I thought Jasmine must be happy at her home with her parents. Her town Malappuram must not be this cold. I collected her home's phone number from my notebook and walked outside in slippers. At the PCO at Godavari dhaba girl students stood in the line. I thought my turn to make a call would come after 30 minutes. Still I waited and dialled her number. A gentle man who must be her father picked the number. I disconnected the number. After a minute, I dialled again but the same person picked the phone. I had no courage to say on the phone that I wanted to talk to Jasmine. I did not know how the person on other side of the line was going to react. I returned to the room. Will Durant's book 'The Story of Philosophy' was waiting for me at my table. Abbas Nasir had come to my room and was flipping the pages of KL Sharma's book 'Indian Society'. FM Radio played the songs "Mera Jiwan Kora kagaz, kora hi rah gaya."

"Where had you gone Bhai?" he said.

"I had to go to meet somebody."

"Jasmine Madam is not here. Whom had you gone to meet?" Abbas wore a Nike cap and held a pen in his hand to underline the book.

"I had gone to call her at PCO."

"Now you are in love," he said while keeping his eyes on the books.

I did not reply. I switched off the radio, took a sip of water and sat on the bed under a razai with Durant's book. I planned when Jasmine returned from home after the break, I would maintain distance from her. I was studying less because of interaction with her, and when I held books I was thinking about her. If I want to succeed, get a job, I would have to break from her. The fault was not hers but she being around me I could not put my concentration on the pages of the books.

The university opened after one month of winter break. Students got registered again for the course, as every student was supposed to get registered after every six months—once in January and then in July. Students came charged after one month's break from their homes in different states. Some students like me chose to stay and study. For me going home was not a better alternative. At home criminal gangs operated with impunity and shot dead young men from the opposite gangs or even an innocent man on suspicion. And I had nothing at home in Bihar like a room, table and chair, light, green campus, where I could study and write the story of my destiny. So, it was better to stay here and cover the distance of my goal. Of course, some seniors like Shrikant Verma wondered what kind of an idiot I was who did not like going home.

***

Jasmine came to the university on January 7. The security staff at my hostel called me. I was reading 'History of Sikhs' by Khushwant Singh. The violence described in the book was abominable. I left the book and walked down to the gate thinking about Banda Bahadur, a 17th century Sikh warrior. Jasmine was standing in blue jeans and a maroon jacket.

"Hi! How about registration? Are you done?"

I said, "Yes."

"Come with me. Tell me how to proceed."

I walked with her towards the administrative complex and helped her register for the second semester at the counter in administrative block. I asked her about her family members. She said everybody was fine at home. She said her younger brother had plus-two board exam after a short interval but he had a break-up with his girlfriend. Because of that he wept most of the time instead of preparing for the exam. She said the weather at her home was pleasant but here in Delhi it was freezing cold.

After a three hour walk with her from one building to another for her registration, we returned. It was lunch time. Cold wind caused shivering, but the campus was full of young and bright faces. When we reached the Nilgiri Dhaba, she said, "Okay bye. We will meet in the evening or tomorrow."

In the room, I changed the dress and went to the mess. The cook had prepared rice, rajma, raita, pumpkin, etc. The food smelled good.

After lunch I went for a walk with Abbas Nasir. I kept thinking how I spent the first half of the day. I thought I should not have gone with her. A person was useful when one had some value. That value to a person came from hard work. If I stopped working, studying, being knowledgeable, she would go from me.

I thought I should act to become a model for the future generation and leave a legacy. Why should my life revolve around a girl? My family was in a desperate situation. If I made a love story here with her, that would not change their situation. I should use my time, rise like a sun, and glow in the sky.

Abbas said, "What are you thinking? Lost somewhere?"

I said, "No. I am very much in front of you."

"Has Madam come back?"

"Yes, she is at the campus."

"You did not meet her?"

"I met her. She got registered today."

"She would make you busy now."

"She has already made me busy."

I returned to the room after a 20 minutes of walk. Curd in the food made me feel drowsy. I took up a page and started writing a note on cultural relativism. Writing activated my brain and repelled sleep. Anthropologist Franz Boas arguing on cultural relativism said cultures of different groups could not be ranked in a hierarchy with the western culture at the top. All cultures had merits and demerits. He said, "I often ask myself what advantages our 'good society' possesses over that of the 'savages' and find that we have no right to look down upon them ... We 'highly educated people' are much worse, relatively speaking ..." Boas had earned PhD in Physics and had interest in Geography.

***

I continued benefitting from Faiz Mustafa even when I joined CSSS. He introduced many authors to me. But his favourite was Bertrand Russell and his classic book was "Why I am not a Christian." He said when he had to go for a talk or participate in a debate, he read a few pages of this book. He would often quote Russell: "The fundamental cause of the trouble is that in the modern world the stupids are cocksure while the intelligent are full of doubt."

Compelling expression and opulent prose of the book electrified his tongue. When he spoke standing with the teekwood lectern at the SSS Audi or the hostel mess, thick accolades and prizes came flying to this master of wordsmith.

He said "Rhetoric is the art of ruling the minds of men." Debating and speech-making should not frighten us. Fear during public speaking was a normal thing which afflicted even a conqueror like Napoleon Bonaparte. If you do not work on this skill, you will not go very far in your life. He told me to read Aristotle's 'The Art of Rhetoric' for mastering the skill of oratory.

He shot dozens of inspirational sentences at his audience with ease from the monumental works of Friedrich Nietzsche, Mohammad Iqbal and Sri Aurobindo.

I did not like Urdu poetry. I thought it was a sign of fall and decadence. But on Faiz Bhai's recommendation I started reading Mohammad Iqbal. Each line of Iqbal told one that man was not born to live an ordinary life. One was a luminous ball, a divine essence, an intense whirlwind. The soul of man was shaped with the essence torn out of God. Man was created for ceaseless action, for being restless, for flying to the unknown. The sky and stars were for his conquest. The law of Physics was a myth, it could not impose a limit on his will. Man could not afford to remain low and down.

Listening to Faiz Mustafa fired me with optimism, hope and self worth. One evening, with thick hair parted like that of Amitabh Bachchan, he sang the song 'Ruk jana nahi tu kahin haar ke, kaanto pe chal ke milenge saaye bahar ke' near the student union office. A flicker of light fell on we four-to-five friends, sitting on the rocks with the wild bushes, while babool and kikar trees stood behind us. Jasmine said Faiz Mustafa Bhai sang with passion, he poured his soul into the song. That was true. When Faiz sang, passion lit his eyes. His voice and the song made us all serious. Abbas said, "Sir, give me bahar (spring) without the condition to walk on the thorns." We all smiled.

***

Mid-sem exam had arrived. Jasmine was also down with the burden of exams and term-paper. She had difficulty in writing the term paper on abstract topics. Her engagement in political activities at the campus did not leave her much time for studies. She had to write 5000 words on Scottish anthropologist James Frazer's thesis that mankind progressed from magic through religion to science. She sat at the steps of the Centre's brown-brick building and discussed with me the format of the term paper. Her dupatta appeared to be blowing out from her shoulder after every gust of wind and I lost concentration from the topic.

She said, "I am not getting the head or tail of it. What does the Professor want? What should I write?"

I sat next to her, and I told her how to approach the topic. She noted my points on her notepad. Prof Mukul Sharma walked past seeing us.

"Would you suggest some books?" she said.

"I have photostat material on magic and science. Some articles are published in Seminar Magazine and Economic and Political Weekly. Use them all. It would make a good term paper."

"Oh! You are so good."

The class time had begun. We walked into the classroom and took seats. Prof Sharma lectured on Frankfurt school sociologist Theodor Adorno. He wrote a famous line of Adorno with chalk on the green board: "Talent is perhaps nothing other than successfully sublimated rage." He smoked cigarettes and spoke in between. Now the awe with which I used to look at him when I first attended his class was gone.

***

After the class break, Jasmine had gone to protest with other students at a site of jhuggis against the university administration which had ordered labourers to vacate their jhuggis. The labourers were employed in construction of an academic building, and after the completion of the building, they were told to leave the university. The students shouted slogans saying the unjust system should go.

Jamine's note-book and other material were lying on the desk in the classroom. I picked them and gave them to her at the protest site. She said, "Stay with us. Where are you going?" She looked to be in a bad mood.

I said, "The administration would throw them out. We cannot do anything."

"So, we should be mute spectators?"

I said, "I am going. After 1:45 p.m. I would get no lunch at the mess."

"These poor are losing their hearth and home and you are worried about your lunch."

"The administration may call the police. It would be difficult. I am going."

Her eyes burnt and veins on her forehead bulged. She saw that she could not make me stand there. I walked in the winter sun. The images of the half-naked dress of jhuggi children and fear in their eyes kept staring at me. I had no solution for their displacement.

***

That day in the evening she was coming out of the library with some photostat material holding near her chest. I saw her, turned my gaze away and stepped in the library. At the seat, I picked up the book 'Homo Hierarchicus' by Oxford University Professor Louis Dumont. I was thinking about Jasmine and could not understand any word of the book, which dealt with the caste system in India. Then I saw somebody come and stand near me. I looked up at the face. It was Jasmine.

She bowed down to me and said, "Why are you so weird? At least you could have given me a smile." She banged at the table and walked away before I could reply. I got up and rushed behind her. Her red cotton dupatta waved as she walked towards the library gate. I wished to put my face in her dupatta, and say sorry.

I reached to her and said, "Jasmine."

"Go to your books. You are a careerist with no human feelings."

Careerist was an abuse at the university. A careerist was not committed to the larger human cause, he was a self-seeking creature, a parasite who took from society, used tax payer's money but thought nothing to give back to the world, to the poor and helpless Indians.

She walked towards the hostel. I walked behind her. I said, "Jasmine, I am sorry." But she did not look at me. I felt forsaken, I did not commit such a mistake that she should behave like that to me. She walked to her hostel gate and I stood there. Abbas sat there at the Nilgiri Dhaba gossiping with a guy about a persian mystic Al-Hallaj who was executed for saying "I am the Truth". He looked at me and said, "What happened? Is Madam angry with you."

"I don't know. But she is not happy with me."

"Did you tell her something?"

"No. I was not with her at the protest site today. So, she was offended."

"That is a small issue. She will be fine by evening. Just tell her you are sorry."

"I have already told her sorry."

"No issue, tell her sorry again when you see her."

I walked back to the library. I asked God, "Why are you doing this to me? Why was I in such a bind? I had come here to study but a girl was ruining my plan."

God did not give me any answer. I went to the water cooler and gulped two glasses of water. In the magazine section, Bijoy and Sasikumar were sitting at the stairs. I joined them in gossiping and returned to the hostel at 8:30 p.m. for dinner.

***

Jasmine did not speak to me for two days. I sat next to her in the classroom. I said something to lighten her mood but she kept her face stern. I looked at her thick, black hair, bracelet in her hands, her jacket and shoes, and forgot she was angry with me. I thought if she became my friend I did not need anything more in my life. But what was in her heart I did not know.

Then in the evening, after the classes, I sat alone on a rock near the library and asked myself, "Why are you so upset? Why do so many negative thoughts badger you? Lose yourself in work, hard work. They will give you success, recognition, and freedom from insecurity. Work on your weaknesses, prepare yourself for the battle; you are here to make a career, not to write a love story. Time will go, and you will have nothing in your hand. People around will use you, waste your time, and go away."

I got up and walked towards the hostel when the sun setting in the west painted the earth red. I was feeling hungry, and wanted to eat something. Dinner was to be served after an hour. At the hostel gate Saurabh Ranjan,

Surya Prakash and Vikas discussed American academic Samuel Huntington's thesis of 'clash of civilizations'.

In the room, I sat on a chair and kept thinking. I told myself my study was like the prayer of a Hindu monk. A saint prays single mindedly with love and dedication without doubt about the existence of God. I will study without doubt that my studies would take me to the top. I should fight the odds—odds for me were poverty, boredom, distractions by friends, lack of confidence. People said JNU was a factory for producing IAS officers. I should go out as a proud product of this factory. The university could be privatised any day, and that would make higher studies costly. Instead of indulging in student politics, gossip, romance, I should focus my energy on studies. Study like a yogi whose passion to see and meet God overrides even his basic needs and desires. I should visualize that I am also doing 'tap' for achieving the goal of my life. And if Jasmine is a goal, then she could be achieved if I had a job and status; not by roaming around with her. I remember Christoper Marlowe's time. "Money can't buy love, but it improves your bargaining position."

***

One afternoon, while I was waiting for a bus, one Norwegian classmate, Nora, stopped her white Fiat car and called me. I told I was waiting for a bus to go to Saket locality for some work. She offered me a lift. I protested and said I will travel by bus.

She said, "No worries, I am going that side."

I sat next to her and moved on to Aruna Asaf Ali Marg. I had to collect ₹ 2000 from a person to whom my father had given at Jashanpur to deliver that to me. I told Nora I heard the name of Norwegian playwright Henrik Ibsen from my father.

"Yes, he is a big name. Father of modern theatre in Norway. Second only to Shakespeare," she said, accelerating the vehicle.

She looked white like milk, and did not understand English much, but always smiled. She had got a scholarship from the Government of India to study here. Apart from Henrik Ibsen, the other thing I knew about Norway was that milk, cheese, and yogurt were produced in that country on a large scale. She said one famous line of Ibsen was that the strongest man in the world is the one who can stand alone.

Sitting in the car I saw outside, the world looked better from the light green tinted window glass. I remembered nights in Okhla when I slept without food.

At Saket, I again told Nora that I would return on a bus. But she brought me back to the hostel. I thanked her profusely and went to my hostel.

In the room, I was thinking about Nora's kind gesture. I felt everybody around me was rich and privileged. Being able to sit and interact with them was a matter of pride for me, an achievement in itself. Life had brought me from a small mufassil where boys around me were poor and loved guns and gang-war. From those dark-lanes, I was at the best university of social sciences in India. I did not hope for such a jump in my life, though I worked for this world. Still I felt the larger share of credit for this change in my life was to God. The best thing at the university was to be treated as an equal, as a friend by everyone here.

***

The seniors of the Centre threw a party for freshers' welcome at Teflas, an uber canteen of the university.

Everybody wore one's best dress and reached the venue walking in the twilight. The seniors welcomed and talked about the university's high tradition. The freshers had to introduce themselves and say or perform something for entertainment. Shrikant Verma in jeans and shirt and Maithili Jha in cotton sari stood in the centre of the hall and said everybody will share the story of his or her crush. The order caused a sensation in the hall.

Priya Jhingan came near the dias and said she had no such experience. Then a senior, Sunder Kumar, told her to sing a song. She stared at the ceiling and started singing the Hindi song "gairon pe sitam apno pe karam" from the 1968 movie 'Ankhein' in a seductive voice. The song made the mood of the occasion sombre. All eyes were on her face and her dusky shoulder-top, covered by curly hair. Everybody clapped at her performance. Others came and introduced themselves. Most of them said they had no experience in love.

Shrikant Verma and Maithili Jha felt nobody will speak on a topic like 'first crush'. So they made an amendment and told us to share some interesting stories about themselves.

Abbas came forward on the dias and said, "Raahein kaisi bhi hon, ham shauk se guzarte hain."

Everybody clapped. Then he said, "I did not have a crush but I will tell you about the crush of my class-mate Ranbir." Abbas had graduated from a college in Delhi. He said, "My class-mate Ranbir fell in love with Prof Rashmi madam at my college. He wrote a letter to her and gave it to her in the assignment he submitted. Madam was an adhoc faculty at the college, who had just finished MPhil and had qualified for the Junior Research Fellowship (JRF). She did not respond to the 17-year-old Ranbir's overture and thought he would cool down after some time. She thought if she made an issue out of Ranbir's gesture, that may affect her continuity as a faculty at the college . But Ranbir was emboldened. He took Madam's silence as her consent. One day she called him on the lawn at the side of the classroom and told him that what he was doing was a mistake and she would initiate a disciplinary proceeding against him.

"Ranbir told her he would die if she did not respond to his love request. Ranbir attended his class and classes of other students and batches wherever Madam lectured. Madam lost concentration in the class, and felt insecure. Ranbir came from Palwal district and was son of a lawyer in Delhi."

Abbas was going to continue but seniors shouted at him, "Bas, bas. Okay. Enough." Abbas did not know that madam Rashmi was a student of this university and was known to the seniors. The story told here would have travelled far and wide, so Abbas was told to cut. But the cut disappointed us.

Then came Sasikumar in a black suit. He was a graduate in Philosophy from Madras Christian College, Chennai. We had too many philosophers in the class of sociology. He said, "Seniors and friends, this evening we are talking about love. I will add something here about love. It is sad if a heart does not know how to love, if it is not drunk with the red wine of love. If one is not in love, one cannot enjoy the red sun, dancing tulips near the stream, silvery glow of the moon. Every place whether a temple or a mosque is a shrine of love. The day you do not love is a day wasted. A sound wakes our heart when we fall in love with someone. The lips of those who love are in a state of perpetual pleasure. Lovers are patient and know that the moon takes time to become full." Sasikumar then closed, saying "Thank You." Everybody clapped.

Jasmine sang an English song, "Rebel girl, rebel girl/ Rebel girl you are the queen of my world…When she talks, I hear the revolution…" Singson, a classmate from Nagaland, played guitar for the singers.

Abhishek S came forward and sang the song, "O lal dupatte wali, tera naam to bata…O kaam to bata…"

After the introduction and songs, we had dinner and dance. I did not know how to dance or sing, I stood in one corner seeing others mingle and shake legs.

We also had a group photo and then we dispersed. I left Jasmine at her hostel gate.

***

The next day, I met Jasmine while she returned to the Godavari Dhaba at 10 p.m. after a protest against a university authority at his residence against the "anti-student" policies of the university administration. I was on the way to my hostel after a short post-dinner walk.

She said, "Tomorrow evening, we will go for 'Mission Impossible' at the PVR Cinema near Vasant Continental."

I said, "What? I am busy with some work."

"You are always busy. If you do not come along, I will request Abhishek S."

I was shocked at her proposal and the alternative. I did not want her to go around with anybody. Her indulgence in political activities and interaction with boys caused me much stress. If she went to the cinema with Abhishek, that would be atrocious.

I said, "But I have to study. I have very little time."

"It will take three-to-four hours in total. That is like skipping one-third of your study. I mean evening studies." I realised there was no use arguing with her. I will have to go.

I agreed. Next day in the evening, we went to the movie hall. Before that I requested a mess staff to keep my food. I borrowed ₹ 500 from Abbas Nasir. I told him that I would write all the four term papers for him each paper in 5000 words for this much money. At the movie hall at Vasant Vihar, I bought two tickets from the counter for ₹ 198 and went inside. I felt I was doing something against my core belief and objective. Jasmine had no intention to ruin me. But the way things were developing I was digressing from my goal.

I visited a movie hall for the first time after coming to Delhi. I felt that visiting a cinema hall was like going to a brothel. At the mohalla in my home town it was only the bad characters who loitered around a cinema hall. If my father saw me, he would have killed me, I had no doubt.

I could have said no to Jasmine, but when she insisted on something, I had no courage to defy her.

The movie ended at about 10:30 p.m. We took ice cream from a Mother Dairy vendor and walked to the hostel. I did not offer her dinner at the restaurant around, nor did she ask for that. The restaurants there would have charged more than the whole month's mess bill for food for two persons. In a brown sweatshirt with the JNU logo she walked along with me silently. Some patch of the path was unlit. She felt scared and held my right arm tightly. In the lit portion, she released me. She asked me, "What are you thinking?"

The scene of Prague shown in the cinema revolved in my mind. I said "I am thinking how to go to Prague."

"It is a beautiful city. When you get a job, you can go there." she said.

"If I get a job I would go all over the world. I will first tour the globe and then fulfil my other obligations."

We took a short cut to the university through the staff quarters amidst a thick grove of trees. I took her soft hand and felt I touched red charcoal. She kept walking with her hand in my hand. This was for the first time I held her.

The road was deserted, all the doors and windows of all the houses were closed. Dogs barked at some distance. I pulled her hand to my mouth and kissed it.

She said, "What are you doing?" and pulled her hand down.

I kept quiet and walked further. Our hostels were about 600 metre away.

I took her hand again and put her palm on my mouth. Her palm was warm while my face chilled. I had a sensation of stars coming round close to me. I put my one hand on her right shoulder. She removed it by her right hand.

"You are teasing a girl who is lonely."

"Oh! This lonely girl is so powerful that she can finish me in a second."

I took her hand again and kissed it.

"Will we reach the hostel? Or do you want wildlife to kill me?" she asked.

"We are already near the hostel."

I asked her about dinner. She said she would eat something on dhaba. I said "I have told the mess staff to keep a dinner thali for me. You can come for dinner."

"It is now late. I do not want to go to the boys' hostel at 11 p.m."

"Okay." I kissed her hand again and left her near the hostel. I rushed to the dinning hall, picked the plate and went to my room. Sameer was sitting with Farah Mirza in the room. I ate the food sitting on my study table and flipped through the pages of India Today magazine. I was thinking I was no different from Sameer tonight. I did today what Sameer did every day. I was on the way to fall. I hated myself for what I did that night.

***

All this time, religious questions kept tormenting me. The talks of religious scholars created a feeling of guilt in my consciousness. Simply by not observing religious practices, one was enhancing one's detention in Hell by thousands of years. Many times I discussed religious issues with friends at the cost of my studies because they agitated my mind.

Over the period of time I made a few conclusions about God and religion. The trick was that because I had reached conclusions about an issue after lots of thinking, I should not think on those issues again and torture myself unnecessarily.

One conclusion was that a human being was incapable of finding God. As a pigeon couldn't understand the symphony of Beethoven because nature had not given it capability to do so, a human being was incapable of seeing or touching God. Humans could not know God with the given five senses. The claims to do so were bogus. One should not waste time on that.

Secondly, the religious rites, rituals, books, etc. which we had got to observe and believe were actually human creations. Thirdly, science had demolished the conception of the cosmos which had God sitting above the earth on the Throne of Universe in the sky looking at our activity and dispensing justice.

Nobody, who died, had returned. And nobody returned after death to tell us what happened after death. All talks of life after death by a person while living on the earth were at best a guess work.

Nevertheless, the creation, symmetry, beauty and complexity on the earth and heavens pointed to the existence of a power and creator, but he was not like the one the religious teachers described about. God was not like a Father or a King observing our every action and rewarding us according to our performance. Had it been so, there would have been no injustice or poverty on the earth. Rather, God was aloof from us, was not much bothered about the violence and oppression we wrecked on the weak and the powerless. He had created a law where the best and fittest won the day, and the honest and the weak suffered.

God stood with the powerful; with those who had tanks and swords; those who had legion and missiles. Not with the men who were weak or poor. Human life did not count much for him. He was not striving with us to fulfill our dreams. We were alone in our struggle.

God was not coming to help the weak. He did not hear our cries. He did not lose his sleep when a croc ate a fish, or humans slaughtered another human.

The prayer which we offered to win his favour were our inventions, and perhaps he was not bothered by what we offered to him or not.

These conclusions were based on my thoughts, studies and observations. I had seen poor girls offering prayers but living in hunger and being ravished by the greed of the villain. I had seen a family of a wife and daughter wailing but the young and sole breadwinner of a family sinking to death. I had seen earnest prayer defeated against the blow of a tyrant. If prayer as provided by the religion worked, there would have been no bloodshed on the earth, the weak would not have been defenceless, millions would not have died in hunger. I had seen "bodies being sold in lanes and market places caked with dirt and bathed in blood."

There were more conclusions about religion and the nature of God, and I kept most of these conclusions as final reality for myself. Yet I was open to revise them in the face of new evidence.

These conclusions helped me keep sane. When the nature of life, injustice on the earth, ascendance of evil, the question of life after death, uncertainty all around, battered me, I reminded myself of these conclusions and told myself there was no use wasting time on thinking about them. I was not going to get any answer.

***

While going to the class, I saw Vivek Yadav hurrying to the class. He told me to explain WW Rostow's stages of economic growth. He had missed the lecture of Prof Raj Kishore while he explained Rostow's theory. I did not want to ruin my joyous walk through smelling yellow flowers to the SSS building. I said Priya Jhingan yesterday said Prof Raj Kishore was so handsome that if he proposed to her she would immediately marry him.

"This is a shame for us," said Vivek.

I succeeded in diverting his attention. I said Priya is a graduate from Gargi College. She was asking about you. Vivek, "What do you mean man?" he said. Vivek had done Hons in Political Science from BN College, Patna.

We reached the class. Fifty year old Dhruv Narayan was writing on the board the name of English political scientist Benedict Anderson and his book 'Imagine Communities' in the class. He discussed Anderson's definition of 'nation'. 'Nation is an imagined political community - and imagined as both inherently limited and sovereign. It is imagined because the members of even the smallest nation will never know most of their fellow-members, meet them, or even hear of them, yet in the minds of each lives the image of their communion...' I took a round view of the class and found Jasmine was not there. I sat next to Neelu Khanna. She jotted down everything the professor said. I was feeling sick as I had hardly slept three hours last night.

During the class, Dhruv Narayan asked questions and our reaction to Andersons' views on 'nation', 'language', and asked whether he should clarify further.

I kept silent while others said something. The professor looked at me expecting I would say something but I kept silent. He said, "What is troubling you?"

I was a bit surprised by his question but I said, "Sir, I am not feeling well. I could not sleep last night."

"Why? What happened?"

"Sir, I went to the bed but sleep did not come."

"Don't worry. Such things happen during this period of life. You must be thinking about somebody."

I said, "Sir..."

The whole class giggled. I sunk my head down in embarrassment. When I looked up, I saw he was smiling and looking at me. This was an unexpected attack.

***

In the evening before sleep, I picked up Vikram Seth's book 'A Suitable Boy' which I got issued from the library. The book, the story line, location of the story at the bank of Ganga, sentence structure, even its paper, fascinated me. I thought about Seth's elite schooling at Doon School and his Oxford University education and compared that with my less than ordinary life. I continued reading the book even when the end-semester exam approached and finished two-third of the book. Somehow I was bored with the Sociology books as most of the books were regurgitation of the ideas, concepts and names. There was nothing new in them.

I knew reading books of Sociology would give me scholarship, better grades and recognition in academics. And reading novels or books of Spinoza, Plato, Montesquieu and Russell will satiate my intellectual curiosity and entertain me, but would not reward me. Yet I read books which fascinated me, not what the MA course demanded from me.

Apart from focusing on the contents of the book, I looked at the words and sentence structure of the writings. I observed how the authors composed sentences, wove magic with words, shot ideas which changed the world. My father used to quote Rudyard Kipling's line, "Words are, of course, the most powerful drug used by mankind." Kipling said these words addressing the Royal College of Surgeons in London. I tried to absorb the words and expressions in the books.

I came across several authors like Karen Armstrong, John Grisham, and of course Batrand Russel who wrote one book a year, over 30-40 years in their career. Their career and distinction fascinated me and I thought a career as a full time author was a great choice.

***

In the mid-term exam, I was attempting a question. I had no wrist watch and wanted to know the time. Abhishek had left the room after submitting his paper, so I thought one hour must have passed. An invigilator, who was an administrative staff at the School, in a light pink shirt, sat with his big stomach on a chair to oversee us.

Jasmine sat on my left side and scribbled on the note-sheet rapidly. I asked the invigilator what time it was sir; but he was drowsy and did not look towards me. I asked him again, "Sir, what is the time now?" He stared at me and signalled me to write answer without creating a disturbance. But I did not lose courage and asked him for the third time. Now, he was angry and was at the verge of kicking me out of the room.

Jasmine saw him infuriated. She told me to wait. Then she said, "What time is it, Gupta Ji?"

In response to her query, the invigilator got up from the chair, and rushed to Jasmine, brought his head down to her face and said "How can I help you, Madam?"

"I want to know time, Gupta Ji."

"Oh! It is 11:25 a.m., Madam."

Okay Gupta Ji. Thanks. The 56- year old Gupta Ji returned and took his seat. Jasmine looked at me and said, "This is how time is asked." I thought at my college in Jashanpur, Gupta Ji would have faced a difficult time today while returning home.

***

Many of my friends observed fasting during the Ramazan. But I did not fast because fasting left no energy in my body. I could not study or attend the normal duty as a student. Sun scorched the earth, and it appeared as if a cataclysm was to envelop the existence. I thought I would have all the time for fasting and prayer after I passed out from the university and got a job. One month of fasting meant one month of no work. That is, I will be able to work one less month on my task in comparison to others, while I should be working more. In 'Glimpses of World History', Jawaharlal Nehru mentioned about Napoleon's life which was full of intense activities and a hunger for more. Nehru said Napoleon had amazing energy and vitality; his coworkers were exhausted but he worked tirelessly for 18 hours in a day. He went into detail and had a wonderful memory. His ambition was to match Alexander's achievements. So I thought why should I make my day invalidate with hunger and lack of energy.

For me, God wanted men to work to the extreme, beautify this earth, realise our potential as humans, ride on a horse from one end to the other. Man was to live in the state of perpetual restlessness or what Mohammad Iqbal said 'talatum', not an inactive corpse, sleeping during the day on his stomach. Thus, I had chosen to eat food and work hard.

I guarded myself from social pressure and criticism. Many students hated me for not fasting. But I came across Dale Carnegie's idea: 'Any fool can criticise, condemn and complain—and most of the fools do.' When people stared at me, I ran this quote in my mind, and found courage to move on. I told myself I should strive, seek and find and not yield. This world was mine, I could change it, I could transform it.

I saw many students who observed fast did not offer prayer or follow other basic religious duties. Some only kept themselves hungry. They watched movies on TV and flirted with girls. I thought if I did not fast but gave all my time to studies I was more pious than them.

***

Then came the Eid festival. I longed to celebrate festivals with my family members. At home, lots of preparations were made for a festival. But now I was in a world where I was busy with work all the time and the festival came suddenly. Around me were many friends and acquaintances to share joy, but they were no substitute for my blood relatives.

In my mohalla, life seemed to be a cycle for celebration of festivals. A festival was followed by preparation for another festival. A festival demanded preparation of special dishes, meetings, visits by relatives to each other's place, stitching of new clothes, prayer to the Almighty, and so on. But the world in which I lived, a festival arrived, stared and passed. One was busy at work till the evening before the festival and the festival arrived like an unannounced guest. One had no idea what to do with the D-day. Dozens of friends did not compensate for the absence of parents.

In the morning, I offered prayer. I bought sweets and other material and offered them to my friends and classmates. Besides, students celebrated Eid Milan at the hostel mess in which the Vice-Chancellor and faculties also participated.

Abbas said, "You are not meeting Jasmine these days. Go and talk to her today."

"I do not want to go to her. She is a storm. She would uproot me from my tentpost. I stop studying after meeting her."

"That is your problem. She does not tell you to stop studying."

'Yes, that is right. But this is how I feel after meeting her. Nietzsche said: "A trueman wanted two different things--danger and diversion. That was why he was so drawn to a woman, nature's most dangerous plaything. She is an absolute risk."

That evening, Jasmine came to my room, ate sweat and said hello to Farah Mirza and Sameer Khan. Farah Mirza wore a white fancy cotton shalwar kameez. Her chubby wheatish body, curled strawberry long hair, her height made me think she was a fairy from some other world. We just exchanged the words--Hi and Hello. She responded with a half smile. I switched off radio when she came to the room looking for Sameer in his absence. Jasmine did not show an awe for Farah Mirza but that day even she was impressed by her and said, "You look sweet."

***

I had liberated myself from many shibboleths. But one thing which still bothered me was the concept of destiny and predetermination. The common sense among friends around me was that what one was to achieve, what was to come in our lives—success or failure, happiness or worry, wealth or poverty—everything was determined by God. Our action or inaction was not going to have an impact on that. In support of this thesis were given instances of people who did nothing but achieved everything and people who strived a lot but got a naught.

Success or failure was something which will fall our way at the given time. All our effort will make no difference.

This was a terrible philosophy for a man of action. If God had preordained everything then what was my role in this world. This belief system made me feel imprisoned. I saw it was poison to the mind. It did not goad one to strive and struggle. It told me to wait and watch. It killed our genius and creative freedom.

I realised that if I wanted to do a thing I would have to demolish the authority of this Book of Fate. My reading kept throwing me ideas and quotes about destiny and its role in our lives. Shakepeare gave a contrarian view about destiny when he said, "The fault, dear Brutus, is not in our stars, but in ourselves."

One person who helped me break the prevalent concept of destiny and inactivity was the poet Mohammad Iqbal. His view carried weightage because he studied religion and was seen as a scholar with authority.

He said one's destiny was to achieve what one desired. Destiny was not a framework written for human beings which casts limits to what one could achieve and what not. Rather, destiny is a set of possibilities which one could realise with one's work and effort. Destiny of an individual does not mean that a full-fledged event lies for him in the womb of the future. Rather, every moment in the life of an individual and society was new, original, undetermined.

Iqbal said to exist as a human in this world did not mean that one was bound by fetters. Rather, it meant one could create reality from moment to moment and one was absolutely free from casual consequences. The existing belief of people about destiny left no scope for human or God's freedom. World with such an idea of destiny was not a world of free people. It was a stage on which puppets moved by a string controlled by a master. It disinherited man from any responsibility for his action.

These were powerful words. Because these words came from a person well versed with the scripture, I accepted him. I convinced myself that my destiny was not written. I was giving shape to my future with the work I was doing there, the books I was reading, the way I used or wasted my time. I realised that I would have to work to reach my destination. I should not wait for good results to come. It was my action which created my prize. If I sat idly and waited for the prize to fall, it would never come.

I saw many people around, who believed firmly in the theory of destiny, and did not work hard. They could have done better and achieved more if they believed that it was not destiny but their action that determined their life.

This change in the belief was a revolution in my thought.

***

End semester exam had arrived and the university was to close for summer vacation after 20 days on May 5. I had submitted my and Abbas's term papers. Jasmine did not have complete class notes and lacked confidence to take exam. She was busy with elections and political activities and had less time for her studies. She had to bring out pamphlets, speak in the public meetings, and invite speakers for speeches on national issues at the campus.

She told me to help her revise all the points on a topic, and on the likely question to be asked. She came to my room or sat with me on the pavement under a lamp post in the evening and discussed the points. I told her I would not be able to sit with her the evening before the exam. And on other days, I could sit with her for one and a half hours. She said, "You had no choice and would have to sit as long as I wanted."

It was a tough call for me as I wanted time to read and revise my notes. I thought her insistence and demand would ruin my exam and grade. I could not say no to her. She was ill-prepared for the exam. Had I told her no, that would amount to ditching somebody in distress. When she was busy in political activity, it was at the back of her mind that she would extract assistance from me and I would stand by her. If I did not help her now, she would break up with me permanently.

I sat and sang to her tunes at the risk of my studies and grades. I remembered reading, "Man for woman is a means." Abbas also joined the two of us. I revised the points which I had studied with the books, photostat material and notes. Because I had to explain things, I could revise half of what I would have revised for myself, and I could not study anything more.

In the exam hall, she sat next to me and asked some points. Most of the time I could not listen to what she asked and hence could not rescue her. Once she asked me the spelling of German sociologist Max Horkheimer. Because of my failure to help her, she stared at me and sometimes smiled. She wrote in beautiful handwriting at a rapid pace.

In the evening after the last exam, she told me to accompany her to a restaurant. At 8:00 p.m. in the blue line bus we went to the Mughlai Darbar at Malai Mandir. The FM Radio on the bus played the song 'Kya khoob lagti ho… Badi sundar dikhti ho' by Mukesh and Kanchan. I thought I was studying to succeed and marry a woman like her. If she said she would marry me, I would stop striving. At the restaurant, she said I helped her in the exam after a lot of pressure from her. It did not come voluntarily from me. I thought this girl bound me with a duty to rescue her and lowered my grade.

***

After two days, all my friends left the university to enjoy summer vacation. Alone, I sat in the library with Balkh born mystic Rumi's Masnavi by Oxford publication. The book was available in six volumes. I had come across the quotes like "Do not feel lonely, the entire universe is inside you" by Rumi, but had not read his work and did not know there was so much depth and resplendent beauty in his writings.

Shrikant Verma, a senior enrolled in PhD at CSSS, saw me in the library and told me to go home. He said there should be balance in one's life. I should give time to my parents and to relatives also. We were not machines tiring all the time for a rational goal, but humans with feelings, needs and emotions. He offered me cash if I had no money for a train ticket to my home at Jashanpur. His classmate Anjali Verma had joined IAS and was doing field training in Delhi. She came to meet him at the hostel in the evening in a vehicle with red beacon light.

After a few days, Shrikant Verma told me again to go home, but I stuck with the red-brick library building. I did not go home despite his repeated advice and devoured the pages of the works of Baruch Spinoza, a 17th century enlightenment philosopher, sitting near a window of the library. I read the yellow broken pages of Spinoza's book. God had whispered to him:

"Stop praying and giving yourselves blows on your chests, what I want you to do is to go out into the world to enjoy your life.

"I want you to enjoy, you sing, have fun and enjoy everything I've done for you.

"Stop going to those gloomy, dark, and cold temples that you built yourself and that you call my home.

"My house is in the mountains, in the forests, the rivers, the lakes, the beaches. That's where I live and express all my love for you.

"Stop blaming me for your miserable life; I never told you that you were a sinner.

"Stop being so scared. I do not judge you, nor criticize you, nor ever is angry with you, nothing bothers me, nor do I devise punishment. I am pure love.

"Stop asking me for forgiveness, there's nothing to forgive.

"If I made you...I filled you with passions, limitations, pleasures, feelings, needs, inconsistencies...of free will.

How can I blame you if you do or say something out of that which I put in you? How can I punish you for being as you are if I am the one who made you?"

While returning to the hostels through the fallen fern-like leaves of kikar trees on a hot day, I thought over the words of Spinoza.

❑

Chapter 5

Hearts in its Tears

Now it was the end of July and the university was to open after summer vacation. Rain had made the university beautiful. I thought of some points as guidelines to navigate the coming semester. It was like a new year's resolution. The first was to avoid Jasmine. I should not meet and interact with her when she returns from home. Secondly, I should cut down on time-wasting discussions with friends at the campus. And lastly, I should not care about what people had to say about me or what I was doing.

I continued visiting the library and reading books. The prime motive of reading was the belief and expectation that it would make my life better and would give me money, fame, reputation and recognition.

For me, every moment was a fight of thoughts in my mind. One moment I felt I would survive, swim across, do great, and the other moment I thought nothing good would come in my life. The cacophony of thoughts never stopped, doubts ran uncontrolled. The train of negative thoughts were compulsive, uncontrollable and continuous. I did not know that negative thoughts could be replaced in mind with positive thoughts. Some friction with somebody, someone's negative comment or irascible behaviour further depressed me. Because I was aiming big, I rubbed people around. Many times I felt I would not be able to make it. I should rather return home and do some work at Jashanpur.

What further dampened me was frequent spells of fever, at least once in a month or more than that. Fever did not leave me fit to contest the challenges. Then I thought the feverish condition was an addition to my existing challenges, and I should fight it like other challenges. I should not surrender.

***

Jasmine had returned from her home in the last week of July after summer break. She came to my room looking for me on Friday at 4:0 p.m. I was busy with psychoanalyst Sudhir Kakar's book, "Inner World: A Psycho-Analytic Study of Childhood and Society in India." Sameer Khan, my room-mate, told Jasmine that I was away and must be in the library. She took a piece of paper and wrote, "Hi, dear Hameed, I came to see you. Meet me when you return to the hostel. Jasmine." She left the piece on the table and walked out.

I returned to the hostel at 8:0 p.m. I had worked enough to my satisfaction that day. I thought the time was like water flowing in a river. I was satisfied if I had picked some water from this river and made use of it. If I did not use water, that water would go and would never be available for me for use. I saw her note on the table and thought about what to do first-- whether to eat meal at the mess or go to her hostel. I took dinner as I was hungry and thought I would go for a walk with her after dinner.

After gulping the food, I rushed straight to her hostel from the mess. I wanted to see her, and share things with her. There was nothing better than walking with her on the campus road under the neon lamp posts. I did not do that because I first wanted to achieve a status, a car, a house in life. I told the security staff at the gate to call Jasmine from room number 107.

The guard came and said the room was locked. I told him to go to the mess if she was there having dinner. He came back and said she had gone to her LG.

"How do you know?" I asked the security guard. He said, "Jasmine Madam's roommate Kavita ji told that."

I returned to the room and sat on the study table. The next two days were holidays. She went to her legal guardian in Delhi and was to return on Monday. I did not know how to spend two days. How could she go without meeting me? If she had to go to her legal guardian, why did she come to my room? I was fine without her anyway. Then, I remembered sufi poet Rumi's lines: "Lovers don't finally meet somewhere. They're in each other all along."

***

I filled up a form for the Bank Probationary Exam. The exam was scheduled after three months. I practised arithmetic and reasoning for one-two hours daily and aimed to crack this exam. Life would at least become stable if I got a job. After joining a bank as an officer, I could have prepared for other exams like Civil Services Exam (CSE). This exam tested a different set of aptitude and skill, and had no similarity with the CSE pattern, or the course I was doing at the university. In fact this exam ruined one's reading and writing ability, as it tested one with objective type questions. I thought this exam would be a plan B, and if I had to leave the hostel and the university, job at a bank would be something to fall back upon.

On Monday, Jasmine came to the university and went to the admin block for registration. I saw her in the library standing in a queue to collect library tickets. I went to her and said, "Hello Jasmine! When did you come?"

It was raining heavily outside and the rain droplets entered with strong wind at the library main gate. She smiled and said in a soft voice, "I had visited your room in the hostel. You were absent. I came this morning from my LG."

"I did not know you were to come on Friday."

"I called you on your hostel landline phone. But I could not talk to you. The runner did not call you."

"Okay, I will pull him." I was thinking it was good I was not informed. Otherwise she would have made me come to the railway station.

She told me to stand with her in the queue and not to go anywhere. She asked me how I spent the summer at the hostel, why I did not go home, how were my friends and what were the grades of other batchmates. She collected library tickets from the counter, and went to the magazine section and flipped through the newspapers. I followed and sat next to her. Priya Jhingan read there old issues of 'The Illustrated Weekly of India'. At about 2:0 p.m. when the rain became slow we walked to our hostels for lunch.

***

The 4th floor of the library housed literature and the 5th floor philosophy books. Silence hung over the floors, except occasional murmuring of boys and girls sitting here and there with books and notepads.

I picked up books and sat with a chair and table near the window. The floors had no air conditioning but the temperature was bearable even during summers. All the forest and buildings within the university campus were visible from here. After a lunch of rice and curd, I felt sleepy while reading. I washed my face and fought the sleep. A cup of tea would have been the solution but I had no money to afford it.

But when Jasmine came to the floor or I saw her sitting somewhere in the library with Sociology books, I lost my sleep without an antidote. After seeing her, I could not read or understand a word. If she sat next to me with a book, the rate of my breath increased and I lost concentration. One day I tried reading from 3:0 p.m. to 6:30 p.m. in the library, but I failed. I did not dare ask her whether she could concentrate on books when she sat next to me. But she appeared normal, underlining the book and making notes from them.

When I read a book at the library, the stories and episodes in the book unfolded in my imagination in Bihar. The characters in the books moved and acted in the locality

I lived in. For me, Zarathustra of Nietsche walked and sermoned on Gautam Budh road at Jashanpur. Michelangelo carved the ivory structure of the beautiful woman at Patna Gandhi Maidan. Baruch Spinoza meditated and wrote on God and ethics on the roof of my neighbour Bilqis Jahan in Gulab Ganj. Prophet's Ta'if journey was near the area of my playground and Abu Jahl lived a stone throw distance from a primary school in the locality where I played with Asma. I did not know how my brain processed the information.

During such a reverie, Jasmine would walk, hush something in my ear and bring me back to reality.

I always felt that after studying I would go and settle in Bihar. Delhi for me was a place for study, getting a job, and making a career. The place for living and enjoying life in my imagination was Bihar, and Jashanpur. It was a land which I could worship and die for; it was the most sacred piece of land for me on the earth where my friends and relatives lived, where the girls whom I liked breathed and walked with their hair down.

***

As the classes for the third semester started, my health begun to fail. My stomach became upset and nothing worked to normalise it. I could not digest food and my energy level plummeted. I visited Dr Bansal at the university's health centre but medicine did not help me. I visited him several times; he told me in the end that I had a syndrome which could not be cured. I did not know what to do. I walked a lot thinking that walking will make my stomach fine. But it did not help me. I became weaker. Friends told me that I was losing fast muscle and weight. I could not work even at the half of my capacity. I was burning with ambition but my health grounded me.

Jasmine told me to go to AIIMS but getting treatment there was not an ordinary task. I went there early in the morning, got registered at OPD and consulted a doctor. He prescribed lots of tests. After seeing the test reports, the doctor could not detect any problem. He said I was normal, but under trouble because I was stressed and suspicious about my health. Then I decided to consult some other medical expert.

When allopathic medicine did not work, Fahad Ahsan suggested that I visit Majeedia Hospital at Hamdard Nagar in Delhi, where a hakeem prescribed unani medicine. I went there on an auto rickshaw at 4:0 a.m. and stood in the queue in the dark. I consulted the 90-year old hakim who wore a crisp, white kurta-pyjama and white beard. He gave me thick tasty paste-like medicine boxes. I asked him what was my problem. He said, "Your liver is a bit lethargic." His medicine worked and my condition improved slightly. But my performance in the class and the exam deteriorated.

***

I realised if I wanted to succeed, I would have to keep in check the movement of Jasmine in my life and thoughts. I thought about this many times but I did not succeed. She met me and talked to me and all my resolutions were swept like dry autumn leaves. Now I had to take concrete steps to bar her in my life if I wanted victories . I started with avoiding sitting close to her in the classroom. Next, I left the class-room before she walked out from there so that I had no opportunity to encounter her. I also did not go to the hall or floor in the library where she was studying. I avoided the places like dhaba, canteen, routes, etc. where she could be present. She kept herself busy in political activities but when she had time, some personal work, studies, exams, writing term-paper, or other such work, she looked for a pound of flesh from my body.

***

Ankit and Laxmi Naagar's came closer and could be seen together most of the time in the campus. Ankit's parents died when he was six-year old and he was brought up by mother's sister at Jaunpur in eastern Uttar Pradesh. Laxmi Naagar came from Himachal Pradesh and had converted to Christianity under the influence of a bishop. She told Ankit also to embrace Christianity. He accompanied her to a methodist church at R K Puram locality on some occasions. She loved wearing blue jeans and khaki leather boots. She had got some assignment with the United Nations Population Fund and visited Lodhi Colony in Delhi. Ankit's aunty came to know about Laxmi Naagar and told him that she would sever her relationship with him if he continued meeting the girl. Ankit loved Laxmi deeply and did not know whether he should side with his aunty who had brought him up or with the lady of his love. However, his relationship with Laxmi was strained.

***

Prof Raj Kishore lived in a villa adjoining the hostel. He was a political activist-cum-teacher. He was eloquent, handsome, and charismatic. Students kept him surrounded all the time. Sometimes students walked to his office or his residence to hear his views on political developments. He had a cult following. A proponent of Rammanohar Lohia and Jayaprakash Narayan, one could listen to him for long and get enriched. In the class-room, he familiarised us with Immanuel Wallenstein's world-systems theory, Swedish economist Gunnar Myrdal, Walt Rostow's stages of economic growth, American political scientist Lloyd and Susanne Rudolph, and hundred other names and theories.

***

Whenever I read any material, including the abstract academic writings, I came across facts and information which inspired me to work harder and focus on my target. For example, Sigmund Freud said civilisation was possible because we sublimated our sexual urges. That is, one should hold the sexual energy which is building and rising in the body and which wants a release. And then one should spend this energy for writing or painting and other such creative work. This motivated me to conserve and channelise my sexual drive on the task at hand. In Sociology, the concept of 'culture of poverty' convinced me that the rich and the poor have different values, and the economic reality of their life was a reflection of their values, attitude and practices, and vice-versa. I concluded that I should change my values and attitude if I wanted to rise in life. In Karl Marx's writings, I loved the idea that it was "possible for me to do one thing today and another tomorrow, to hunt in the morning, fish in the afternoon, rear cattle in the evening, criticize after dinner, just as I had a mind, without ever becoming hunter, fisherman, shepherd or critic." I knew this was practically not possible, but it appeared sweet. I came across such inspiring message anywhere and everywhere, even from a song of a Hindi movie.

Professor Hari Lal a faculty in the Hindi department at the university said during a public lecture that two books influenced him the most in his life. One was Jean Jaque Rousseau's 'The Confession' and the other was Jean Paul Sartre's "Being and Nothingness". I went to the library and flipped through both the books.

I believed Jean Jaque Rousseau to be a university professor at a place like Oxford, writing books. Rousseau was a first rate philosopher and intellectual for me. I had come across his name with John Lock and Hobbes hundreds of times in the context of 'The theory of social contract'. But when I read "Confession", my impressionable mind was in for a shock. He was nothing like the learned intellectual I had imagined.

When I knew about his constant poor health, debilitating poverty, complex affairs with women, I felt what I knew about him was wrong, and my health was better than him. At one place he wrote, "I remembered that after the defeat of Nicias at Syracuse, the Athenian prisoners supported themselves by reciting the poems of Homer. The lesson which I drew from this specimen of erudition, in order to prepare myself against poverty was to exercise my admirable memory in learning all the poets by heart."

At another place, he wrote, "I certainly cannot have been born for study. For continuous application tires me to such an extent, that I am utterly unable to devote more than an hour together to close study of the same subject... When I have read a few pages of an author who must be read carefully, my mind wanders from him and is lost in the clouds."

He says about his care-giver, a 12 year older woman, Madame de Warens: "Remember that, in this condition, thirsting after women, I had never yet touched one; that imagination, need, vanity, and curiosity all combined to devour me with the burning desire of being a man and showing myself one. Add to this, above all, that my tender and lively attachment to her, far from diminishing, had only become warmer everyday, that I was never happy except with her; that I never left her except to think of her; that my heart was full, not only offer goodness and amiability, but of her ..., her form, her person..."

So much was my misconception about my intellectual hero that reading these words, I looked at the cover page to check whether I read Jean-Jaques Rousseau or some other person.

The other book, which was Sartre's "Being and Nothingness", made no sense to me and I left it after reading about 100 pages. I heard a lot about Sartre, his novels, his marriage with Simone de Beauvoir at the campus from the students-- all these fascinated me. The book "Being and Nothingness" was based on the lecture Sartre delivered on existentialism. It argued that it was our action which determined our life. We as human beings were free to choose an action from a range of actions at a moment. That action and choice shaped our future. It was a scary proposal; God was not doing the things for us. We were responsible for our destiny. One wrong choice of action and everything could change.

I read several pages of this book, but it was a challenge to me. My belief was that if I failed to read a book, that meant I was defeated by it.

"The Critique of Pure Reason" by the German philosopher Immanuel Kant was another book which found mention in every forum on the campus. From class teachers to seniors talked about this 600 page thick book. Abbas Nasir said a person who couldn't understand the Critique was mentally still a child and was not grown up. I wasted several hours trying to read and understand this book. It was full of difficult terms and concepts. Unless one knew about those concepts, one could not understand it. Abbas said Kant was the greatest of the modern philosophers, and he was to philosophy what Nicolaus Copernicus was to astronomy. He bridged the discord between the empiricists and rationalists.

***

I read wherever anything was available on the art of writing. But such books were few and far between at the university. I came across Bertrand Russell's book, "My Philosophical Development' where he said he wished to write in the style of the 19th century English philosopher J S Mill. I got Mill's book and went through his "Three Essays on Religion." The sentences were long, and difficult to understand.

Russell, however, said all imitation was dangerous. He said nothing could be better in style than a Prayer Book and the Authorized Version of the Bible, but they expressed a way of thinking and feeling which was different from that of our time...A style was not good unless it was an intimate and almost involuntary expression of the personality of the writer...But although direct imitation was always to be deprecated, there was much to be gained by familiarity with good prose, especially in cultivating a sense for prose rhythm. He said there were some simple maxims which a writer should follow: 1) never use a long word if a short word will do; 2) if you want to make a statement with a great many qualifications, put some of the qualifications in separate sentences, 3) do not let the beginning of your sentence lead the reader to an expectation which is contradicted by the end.

Sadly, there were no books on writing style and techniques on the racks in the library. One was to learn how to write oneself or one was supposed to know correct English writing when one came to the university. Aftab, a senior, told me when he wrote an article he kept five books open on the table and used terms and expressions from them in his articles. He had a few articles published in 'The Times of India' on political issues.

The academic writing did not impress me much, as it was deliberately made tough, verbose and abstruse, as if the author did not want more people to read and understand her work. A journalist on the other hand wrote in an easy and lucid style; she tried to invite and hold the attention of the reader; her interest was to make more and more people read her.

Reading at the Magazine Section of the library I came across an article in 'University News' magazine published by the University Grants Commission. The author of the article observed that in the Indian universities the level of the students was so poor that they passed out as graduates and masters but they had no capacity to write one correct, coherent paragraph. Even PhD degree holders struggled to write one page in English. Their power of expression and writing capability was miserable. It was like the report by an employability assessment company which found that 80 per cent of the graduates in India unemployable.

This article impacted me hugely. I thought if I did not learn correct English and writing skills in the university, then I would not be able to learn it ever in my life. It was like one came to the city of gods and returned after shopping and trekking.

***

Papa visited me again. He stayed with a friend and came to see me for a few hours at the campus. He gave me ₹

5000 for expenditure. It was a huge amount of money but it was borrowed money and we had to return it to the loaner at some point of time. I did not want to spend the loaned money. But I could not tell him that I would not take it. He was hopeless from me with respect to my inclination to perform religious duties. He was an angry and disillusioned man but I did not want to ruin my career to meet his concept of a perfect man. He did not speak frankly with me, and his voice carried a mark of turmoil within.

***

As the MA course moved towards the end, I was required to take a competitive exam, and get a job. If I had to take CSE, I would require notes on Sociology as an optional subject. Neelu Khanna, my classmate and daughter of an Indian Forest Service officer, took coaching for Sociology as an optional in CSE at Mahendra's IAS. Other four to five classmates were also taking coaching for the civil services exam. I thought of myself as an expert in Sociology needing no guidance in the subject. Yet, I thought just having a look at the notes will do me no harm. I asked Neelu whether I could have a glance at the Sociology coaching notes. While returning to Godavari hostel from the academic complex, during lunch time, she said, "Yes, why not." She gave me all her Sociology class notebooks at her hostel gate. This gesture touched me very much. She had paid for coaching guidance, spent time on travelling and attending classes, but gave me the class-notes at one word of request.

***

Now that I was here at the university for more than a year, boredom struck me. I was disenchanted with the university which was equivalent to Cambridge University to me. This institution was a dream, a place where I yearned to walk and study. I thought admission at this institution was all that made my life meaningful and successful. It was the highest thing I aspired for. But the allure which it held for me had gone, the feeling of triumph now disappeared.

I felt taking a MA degree from JNU was okay, but studying at MPhil or PhD level here lacked rigour. Pursuit of excellence at the level of the student and the faculty was missing. Admission in MPhil or PhD in a university in the USA or the UK will be more promising. I wanted to go to 'the city of dreaming spires' for higher studies. Most of the faculties at the centre of the school had taken degrees in the USA or the UK. But there was no one to guide me how to apply abroad. Then there was no internet or Youtube to guide one how to apply in those universities. I thought that if I did not go abroad, then I did nothing worthwhile in my life. I read 'Times Literary Supplement' at the Library and came across articles, advertisements, and admission schedules in the western institutions.

I heard of a few students from the University who went to Harvard and Oxford. One girl student, about whom the students spoke very highly of, had done MA, indulged in full time students' politics at the campus and then went to Oxford for PhD. One student returned to JNU from Oxford University and wrote the civil services exam and got allotted IAS in one attempt.

Another legend was that a smart young girl came to the campus and joined one of the Centres, indulged in full time student politics, became secretary general of the university's student union, took the CSE one day, and got 6th rank in the CSE. There was emphasis on the talent of the candidate, and no mention of one's hard work or the process. It was like a fairy tale.

One day after the class I approached Prof Devender Sinha who walked out of our classroom after a lecture. "Sir, I want to apply for research in a university abroad," I said. He looked at me and said, "Dear, people who are in a hurry reach nowhere." He wanted to tell me I had no status and wherewithal to take a degree from Oxford. I returned from his room in a low spirit.

I approached him one more occasion. I asked him in his office room as dozens of term-papers, thesis copies, and books lay on his table. Seeing me he said, "Right now you should do well at what you are doing." I was dismayed with his remark and did not go to him again.

I had no scope to go abroad, and I did not have much time at the university. If I left the University after an MA in Sociology, I would get no job.

I enquired from the fellow students what job I could get after passing out as MA in Sociology. They said one could aspire to become a lecturer in a college or work in a non-governmental organisation (NGO). Some government organisations also employed sociology students as researchers. One senior said a few students from sociology join newspapers and magazines. What was true of sociology was by and large true for other humanity subjects except Economics. The time was short, and I was not prepared to leave the University. I thought about my parents and poverty, and high odds.

Another option was to take admission in the university in M Phil course and prepare for the CSE. But in a batch of 60 MA students at the CSSS, only about 20 could scrape through the entrance test for M Phil. It was an entrance examination in which students from other universities also participated. I saw many MA students, who had failed in the MPhil entrance test, roaming around, looking for space in the hostel to stay in the campus. If one got admission in M Phil then one could stay at the campus for 5 years. During this long period one could definitely find a good job.

Then I went to Alok, a senior in the Centre, and asked him how to apply for a university abroad.

"For that you should have at least an MA degree from JNU."

"I would have to wait, Sir?"

"Bhai, it is a long and tedious process. You require recommendation of the Professors from the Centre," he said, sipping tea at a chair in his room.

"But it would not be easy taking recommendations from the Professors."

"Yes. Why would a Professor write well about your credential unless you have performed well at the Centre?"

"That means I have to first prove myself at the Centre."

"Exactly."

I returned to the room. I listened to FM songs on the radio placed on my study table; for me, listening to songs was one of the best things to do. Songs broadcast at night became sweeter and more philosophical.

***

My father used to say, "Student's life is a king's life." But I felt stressed and insecure all the time. Joy did not come to me. Many boys kept themselves busy studying, chasing a girl, debating political issues, watching cinema, and sitting on dhabas. I knew I could not afford to act like them. If I did not get a government job I will have to go to Zaheer's factory again. And just a thought of Zaheer's closed-hall factory, six and a half day work schedule, made me work like an animal.

The elite students spoke English with sophistication. I needed to change my style of speaking to grow and impress others. A person from a rural area and small town spoke English in a ridiculous way and distinguished himself as a novice. I tried to change my accent and speak like other students of good background. But I faced resistance from fellow students for both speaking in English and for speaking in a non-Bihari accent. They thought I adopted a form of communication which was not my own. When I spoke in the class some thought I was cheaply trying to steal the show.

But if I was not capable of standing in the face of resistance then I was nothing. One who wanted to do big in life must have courage and conviction to overcome the resistance. Ridicule of the fellows intensified my resolve and I continued. My accent became better and the people who laughed and hooted at me lost momentum after a few months. They accepted me. I remembered reading somewhere "First they ignore you. Then they laugh at you. Then they attack you. Then you win."

In the beginning, I comfortably expressed on socio-political issues in English but had difficulty speaking in conversational English. One of my friends suggested I read novels and learn conversational English. But I had no time to read novels and fiction. Gradually, I became comfortable in conversational English also.

***

End-semester exam was to commence after 20 days. Everybody became serious for studies; students collected notes and visited the library till late. Even Abbass, who remained jovial, and kept an account of who was dating whom, became serious. Now the library was to remain open till 12 midnight. Students crowded the textbook section for the relevant books.

Jasmine asked me again for my class-notes and the relevant material to read for the exam. For two days she came with me to the library after dinner and studied sitting next to me till late. After every one hour of study she went out, took a walk under the lamppost and told me to explain concepts ranging from anomie to deconstruction to super-structure. I liked her company but I did not want to spend even one moment discussing things with her during the exam time when I was already under pressure. If I spent that time on my studies I would fetched better grades in the exam. But I deluded myself telling that my power of expression would improve and revision of the notes and syllabus would be done during discussion with her.

Abhishek V broke for tea at a regular interval and went to the library canteen. He rarely carried a notebook. He got issued books, read them and returned to the textbook section of the library. I told him he should note down what he read, otherwise information and details would remain in the book. He said, "They stay in my brain. I do not believe in note making. If you do not make notes you retain in your brain what you read."

I thought he was an idiot and I did not require to talk to him any more. He was not a hard-working type and was fooling himself. Sometimes, he joined Jasmine and sat in the same row at the library. That caused me heartburn and distracted my focus.

Jasmine's commitment to political activities did not die down even during the exam time. I told her what was important from the exam point of view. She was sure of getting B plus in all papers without my help, she wanted me to assist her to raise her grade further. She said when she discussed an author or a theory with me, it became easier for her to read and grasp things from the books.

Sometimes, the faculty gave a one-day gap between papers. Then Jasmine told me to help her prepare the next paper. I felt frustrated but did not show my frustration to her. I liked her, and would have romanced her, but I did not know what feeling she had for me. When I sat with her and explained things to her, I told myself she would benefit from me, leave me and fly to another world. She would get married with somebody, with an officer, have children, and tell them that there was one fool named Hameed who studied with her at the university.

***

It was winter vacation now. Delhi witnessed cloudy sky continuously for the last 15 days, and a western wind blew through the trees and rocks. Winter seemed to destroy the spirit of the campus, its boundless beauty and unceasing activities. In a sweater and jeans, I roamed alone for hours on the campus and returned to the room dispirited.

To utilise the vacation, I went home. I had fever and the temperature did not come down despite taking medicine. My father took me to a Maulana who prescribed spiritual healing. He gave me some water and a taweez, and told me that a boy who studied in my class had cast a magic spell on me. I had no belief in Maulana and his spiritual capability, but the moment he said my classmate had cast magic on me, I became sure that the Maulana was fooling me. He prescribed me a taweez, which I wore around my neck for some days, and a bottle of rose water after reciting the Quranic verses. The taweez fell down after some time and I could not trace it. The belief goes that the evil forces removed taweez to cause further harm to the person. I told my father that I was taking water given by the Maulana. Somehow my health started improving on its own.

I met my friends in Mohalla. I felt proud to be introduced myself as a student of JNU. Friends and relatives gave me respect and thought I would achieve big success in the near future. For a few days at home I felt better. But I felt the battlefield of the university was calling me to prove my worth. I was forgetting things I had learnt. If I stayed more, my level and competence would go down.

I met Irene and Asma Zafar, who lived in my neighbourhood and whose parents shared a good relationship with my parents. They came to my house at least once a week, interacted with my mother and sisters and left after tea and gossip on the porch.

Both Irene and Asma studied in the same class as me, and they spared no chance to attack me. Irene's real name was Shabana Saleem, but everybody including her school teachers called her Irene, name of a Roman empress. She was wheatish with pink shade, and had bright auburn hair. Her lips were always deep red or ruby. When she wore golden and maroon silk cloth, she looked alluring and exceptional. Most of the boys of the Mohalla ran after her rickshaw when she went to the secondary school.

One of her followers tried to attack me with a bat on my head during a game when I said rascals stalked and harassed her while she walked on the street. Then one of my friends held his bat and saved me from a fatal blow.

Irene's brothers were young, and her father was posted out-station in a government service. So the boys could tease her and get away. She was a decent girl; she carried herself with maturity and did not fall to the tricks of smart boys around her.

Asma was a dusky girl of an average look. She read Geoffrey Chaucer, Christopher Marlowe, Fitzgerald, R K Narayan, etc. She had a great memory, and would recite several Hindi songs standing with me along the parapet wall at the roof. I saw her face when she sang the song and wished I had a memory like her. She had an affair with one or two boys in her neighbourhood. Her father was a State Bank of Patiala employee and had given her freedom to study and make a career. She studied but also indulged in affairs with boys of the locality in a subtle way. Her boyfriends brought flowers and gifts for her. Boys standing on road-corners leered when she walked in the lane to her home.

My father was hopping mad about me as usual. He prayed that I returned on the path of God rather than run after a career. He stopped talking to me after a few days of my visit to home. He said one who tried to fly in violation of God's command would finally fall. I was a friend of Nimrod and Pharaoh. My father's words and behaviour hurt me but I bore everything with patience. I had a cute new sister born, she was yet to be named.

When I returned to Delhi my condition was better. I was at half of my ability, but even that was enough to take me far. Then as the days progressed I became better. I was in a condition to work hard again.

***

Registration for the fourth semester started at the university. This was the last semester of my MA course. I had about six months to go and my next target was to take admission in the MPhil course at the university and then finally pass CSE.

I got registered on January 7, at the administrative block. In a maroon sweater, I visited different buildings for completion of the registration process. Then I went to the Centre's office to deliver registration folios. Jaswinder Pal, the head clerk, was typing on the computer a letter of invitation to Delhi based sociologist Prof André Beteille for a lecture at the Centre.

After submission of folios at the Centre's office, I passed through the office room of Prof Devender Sinha. The door was half open and Madam Sophia Kaur Deol was sitting with him discussing some academic issue. Associate Prof Sophia sported short hair, and used to wear a red blazer during winter. She spoke in a British accent and had done schooling at a school in Edinburgh. Her books were published by Oxford University Press, and she appeared on Doordarshan to speak on political issues.

***

Classes started immediately after the registration. I was among the top four students of the class with my grades. I felt other students could have scored more than me if they worked equally hard. My thrust was to change my status and that of my family through hard work and studies. Others already had what I aspired to achieve with my studies. So they had no hunger. Jasmine continued with her B plus and some A minus grade in her papers.

***

I got the idea that I should read 100 pages a day. I thought if I read so many pages daily, my life would not remain ordinary. Things will change for the better. The first book I read at this rate was Haralambos' work 'Sociology: Themes and Perspective'. This book was then 450 pages thick, now in new editions it comes in about 1000 pages. I finished it in three to four days. In an ordinary course, I would have taken a month to complete it. The book was immensely beautiful and readable, giving a wide range of concepts, theories, findings on many sociological topics. Reading it was very rewarding, and even a non-sociology student can hugely benefit from it.

Then I picked up books by Bertrand Russell, the British philosopher and logician. Faiz Mustafa was a great fan of Russell. He gave me a copy of Russell's 'Marriage and Morals'. He said though a philosopher, Russell got a Nobel Prize for literature because he wrote so well. Faiz Mustafa made me buy 'A History of Western Philosophy' with a beautiful painting of Plato and Aristotle over it by the Italian Renaissance artist Raphael. The book was a sweet mixture of biography, history, and philosophy.

The window of my room near my table opened in front of a neem tree. Sitting there, I relished reading the sections in the book dealing with St Augustine's Philosophy, Christianity during the first four centuries, St Benedict and Gregory the Great, St Thomas Aquinas, Franciscan Schoolmen, etc. as these topics were completely new to me.

***

Many times I went to the library to finish my reading quota. Sitting under the dazzling tube light, at a chair and table, I read books. Smart boys and girls sat around with books and note-pads, taking notes from 10 a.m. to midnight. Books appeared to me like a hot, spicy, pizza with cheese. I wanted to devour it. I felt better after reading in my otherwise depressed life. Many times my depression was triggered by the thought of why I was poor and when my status would change. I thought other boys like Ronnie, my neighbour at Jashanpur, did not work as hard as me. Yet his life was better, his shirts and shoes costly and branded. Reading diverted my thought, and I stayed with the thought, plot and characters of the book I read.

After the classes and day-long study in the library, I walked to the hostel with a bag on my shoulder, carrying big dreams and thinking one day my life would be great. Glistening silvery leaves hung on the eucalyptus trees on the route along the residence of the faculties to Kaveri Hostel. They smelled like black cardamom and made me feel I was walking in a dream, in place and time centuries ago. At the hostel room, I kept the bag on the table, washed my face in the washroom and rushed to the dining hall.

***

One morning at the Nilgiri Dhaba Jasmine told me to come with her to Sarojani Nagar to buy clothes. In the beginning, I resisted but when she said I would have to come, I went with her. In the afternoon in February, the blueline bus drove on the empty roads. I looked outside at the crowd, pheri-walas, buildings and bungalows. At the market I walked with her at the gallis, saw kiosks of garments strung along the streets, went to a darzi for fitting of the cloth, took a glass of ganne-ka-juice, and so on. We returned at about 7:0 p.m. I had no energy or mood for studies. That day I decided to say no to Jasmine for her request for an outing and time-pass.

In the evening during the walk after dinner, I told her I had a few months left and the MA course would be over. I have no job, no secure future. I will have to be cut off from friends and study.

"You mean you want to be cut off from me?" She stressed the word 'cut-off'.

"I mean I will have to stop going out and post-dinner walks and activities like that."

"You think I am a distraction for you in your studies. For you I did not go near anybody. And you think I am a person to be avoided?" she said.

I held her hand and said, "I am sorry, I hurt you." She returned abruptly. I walked with her to her hostel and after leaving her I walked alone for half an hour under the lamp on the road. I remembered Mirza Ghalib's line," Yahi hai aazmana to satana kis ko kahte hain?" (If this is a test, then what is the definition of tormenting?)

***

I thought about deprivations in my life, how I could contribute to society, how I could leave an impact and a legacy, what was the shape of the future, how could I inspire the generations to come. Inferiority complex battered me all the time. My concern was how to come into reckoning.

I thought this life would be useless if I was not able to be rich and famous, if I was not able to make a difference in the lives of millions. Would I be able to speak like Winston Churchill, or look like Arnold Schwarzenegger? The smart and intelligent students around me, people in the media and in power circles made me think that they were living one type of life, and I was living another type of life—bereft of song, excitement, and power. How could I get that kind of life?

The students in the campus enjoyed things like good clothes, physique, good speech, etc. not because they achieved these things with their ability and hard work, but because they inherited those things from their families. And those things set them apart from a boy like me. How could I equal them? Through hard work, perhaps. So I worked and worked to rival and surpass them.

The problems of my life and the deprivations I suffered crowded my mind. That prevented me from indulging in a pleasure trip. I thought living under stress was a normal way of life. If I laughed or indulged in gossip I thought I was committing a crime. I told myself that my life story was different, not like the lives of the other boys around me.

***

My fascination with writing and getting things published continued. I got published an article in a magazine. I loved published words and considered an author next to God in reverence. I told a few friends about the publication but they did not say a word to appreciate it. Fahad Ahsan in CSSS got published articles in Mainstream and the Economic and Political Weekly magazines. My writing did not match his level of scholarship and style but I felt happy that my words could also be published. I could use the published articles during the MPhil entrance test in my favour claiming that I was a serious student in academics. That would have enhanced my chances of selection for the admission, I thought.

Then there was one journal published by the JNU seniors. It was called some Quarterly. I got three articles published in it. The publication of articles gave me self satisfaction and confidence.

Once I went to 'The Times of India' on a blue line bus with my article. There I met one Mr Jha working at a senior rank. He asked me about my background and why I was writing. I told him I was from Bihar and I believed writing in the newspaper would open my career options. He told me to stop wasting my time and focus on the civil services exam. I thought because he did not want to publish my article, he gave me that reply. I took the bus from Bahadur Shah Zafar Marg and returned to the university.

I kept on writing under the impression that the articles would give me academic credence and repute. But, seniors at the Centre said such articles in magazines had no academic worth. Only researched articles published in journals like 'Sociological Bulletin' or 'Economic and Political Weekly' had academic value. But that did not dampen my spirit. I kept writing wherever I could get published including the JNU Magazine and felt being on cloud nine.

***

Most of the time I remained conscious of the value of time. When I talked to somebody I wanted to cut the talk and move on. Many boys appeared aimless to me, they were in no hurry to end the meeting and gathering and rather wanted these to continue. While they had no dearth of time, I felt restless and short of time. When I sat listening to or participating in gossip, a dozen of work waited for my time and attention. Why would I start discussion after dinner at 9:0 p.m. and indulge till 12 midnight. I had to read 'The Economist', go for a walk with a friend, and read 'The Iliad'. Shakespeare's line "I wasted time, and now doth time waste me" rang into my mind and I ran to the library.

In my childhood, I read a story titled "Guzhra huwa zamana" by Sir Syed Ahmed Khan where the protagonist, an old man, was alone at a dark, stormy night. He remembered his gone days and regretted how carelessly he wasted his time. When the storm stopped and the cloud scattered he saw a beautiful bride in the sky. She came close to him. The old man asked her who she was and how he could attain her. She said she was the reward for good, noble works. The old man looked at his gone days and realised he wasted his time and had no good work in his kitty. He cried, "Oh, Time! Would you come back." Later, the old man got up and realised that he was still a young boy and had a bad dream. The young boy decided to use his time on noble works all his life. This story my mother reminded me several times.

One great favour my father did to me with his threat and care was that he drove love for cricket out of my heart and mind. Otherwise, I was in love with cricket like any ordinary Indian and wasted lots of my time on this. This saved my time from unproductive activity, and I used my valuable time for studies. At the hostel at the university, I saw students watching cricket, football, and tennis matches for hours. I never felt drawn to the television screen, as I thought I had to contribute to society and country, rather than being a passive consumer.

I came across in the philosophy section of the library a book with an essay titled 'On the Shortness of Life' by a Roman philosopher Lucius Seneca. The title attracted me and I sat with the old book on the table. Seneca said we complain to God for giving us a short life. But the time given to a person in his life is long enough if it is used for achieving the goals of life. On the other hand, if we waste it in heedless luxury, even a life of a thousand year would appear short. He wrote, "It is not that we have a short time to live, but that we waste a lot of it. Life is long enough, and a sufficiently generous amount has been given to us for the highest achievements if it were all well invested."

Seneca compared time with property. He said if somebody asked us for money or estate, we would be miser; or if somebody encroached upon our property, we would leap upon his throat. But we would happily give our time, which is life itself, and which is more valuable than property. This was an insight for me. The book further helped me cut on nonsense around and focus on my goal.

***

The chill of winter and fog was gone and life became pleasant. Holi arrived at the campus while we were busy with mid-term exams and seminars.

In the morning at the hostel mess, the cook mixed some intoxicant in the milk to make our day heady. The milk looked pink and smelled like rose petals. At around 11:0 a.m., a large group of the students—boys and girls—assembled in the soft sun at the Jhelum Lawn flanked by three hostels—Jhelum, Ganga and Sutlej Hostels. The revellers used dry and water colours to welcome others to the ground. All played the colour game with decency, and gave no one a reason to complain.

After breakfast, I was reading 'A Brief History of Time' lying on the bed. Then my classmates with Sasikumar came and pulled me out of the hostel. We walked round the campus, associated more classmates and went to the houses of the faculties and greeted them. Then we poured into the Jhelum Lawn. The place was crowded.

Jasmine with a band of her hostel girls put coloured powder on the faces of the friends and acquaintances. Her face capped with colours was barely recognisable. One of her group members held a tambourine and all danced in a circle.

Jasmine now maintained a slight distance from me in order to distress me. Perhaps she wanted to tell me that she was a blessing which came near me without asking. But I did not respect her. Hundred boys ran after her and she could choose any of them. I should not act pricey. I saw her and poured colours over her.

One Shahzad, a student from Persian centre, and favourite of many, sang the kawwali "jhoom barabar jhoom sharabi...kaali ghata hai, mast fiza hai...jaam utha kar ghoom..." With face and cloth soaked in colours, he stood in one corner of the lawn with a mic and swayed everybody on his tune as if there would be no tomorrow.

***

The campus' student politics was one of the distractions. Students thought that they could shape the politics of the county and bend the policy of the government by their activism. The student leaders fired the imagination of idealism in the students. They thought of making India a rich and powerful country, lifting millions out of poverty and illiteracy. The slogan was to change the course of history. The campus was always politically charged. An event at the national and international level drew reaction from the students in the form of protest march, procession, hunger strike, public meeting, and so on. Faculties of different political persuasion addressed the students on different occasions. These activities were not secondary to studies there but defined the life at and character of the university.

One memorable occasion was the Presidential debate at Jhelum Lawn during the students' union election. Student leaders contesting elections spoke like eminent speakers. Boys and girls sat in the lawn on blue-red colour mat under a large canopy, heard and cheered the speakers on the dais. Held during March every year, the students listened to the debate till late evening. It was said that the quality of the speech and the speakers were degrading with every passing year. University's election commission, run by the students, conducted the election process. The students and political activists respected the commission's verdict on any dispute.

Jasmine would come and sit with her political group. She brought chocolates, a bottle of Coke and cheered loudly along with others at the speaker's rhetoric. I stood at the end of the crowd and listened to the selective speaker and returned after a short while. The debate was politically charged, theatrical, similar to the gladiatorial fights with the spectators watching, cheering, and hooting. There were young, beautiful faces splashed with youthful charm and idealism all around.

Sometimes a session of the General Body Meeting (GBM) was called by the students' union to discuss and debate issues which were considered of utmost importance or which threatened the students or the character of the university. One such issue was fear of the privatisation of the university and higher education. This thing scared me while I tried to make the best use of time.

All the students assembled in the GBM, debated the issue. The student leaders said university education would become extremely costly after privatisation; poor and disadvantaged would not be able to study at the university. They said fees would be hiked and students would have to pay lakhs of rupees for the courses they were currently paying almost nothing. The scenario portrayed by them was scary, and a large number of students participated in protests and demonstrations led by them. The university administration and the government were the target of their ire.

The GBM passed resolutions and submitted them to the university administration or to the higher government functionaries.

***

Every hostel celebrated Hostel Night once in a year, and the residents of a hostel invited their friends, lady friends, parents, relatives, etc. Some students had no money to contribute for the Night and had to borrow from their friends. One evening's dinner tariff was equal to the whole month's mess bill. Lots of events including debate, cultural evening, sports competition, etc. were organised.

At my Hostel Night, during the cultural evening, Saurabh Ranjan, a senior resident of the hostel, stood on the stage in spectacles, black band-gala and regaled everybody- men and women. One of his favourites was reading news headlines in a way which completely distorted the meaning of the two news headlines in sequence, creating humour. A politician from Bihar and his wife bore the maximum brunt of his creative spurt.

In between the singers took the stage and regaled everybody. Padma, a dusky girl of tall frame in striped T-shirt and jeans sang the song 'Athrah baras ki kanwaari kali thi' of Anjaam movie at the stage with huge stereo sound boxes. In a deep, rugged voice, the girl from neigbouring Godavari hostel evoked lots of amusement among the boys. Then Jamaal from Kerala, who spoke a few words of Hindi, sang the song "Aye Ajnabi Tu Bhi Kabhi Aawaaz

De Kahin Se" in the glow of the light and won everybody's admiration.

I invited our faculty Prof Harjot Singh with his family and Jasmine. The Professor accepted my invitation easily, but Jasmine required several requests for joining. My time was spent attending them. Jasmine made Prof Singh and his wife comfortable. She said Priya Jhingan's elder sister was married to an Indian origin engineer in New York, but later it came out that the groom was suffering from schizophrenia. The life of her sister was ruined.

After dinner, my Professor and his wife departed. I told Jasmine to take a walk on the empty night road of the university. I wanted to unwind and still my mind. But she said she was tired and would go to her hostel.

The discussion after our visit to Sarojani Nagar had changed her. Perhaps her point was that for friendship with me she had distanced herself from the world, rejected offers from others, but I had not accepted her as an intimate friend—a friend who was everything for me, above my career, my future, my parent's hopes and concerns. Perhaps she did not see any contradiction in my going along with her and pursuing my ambition. But I knew I could not act like everybody around, going around a girl, and missing the bigger prize which was a government job.

I requested her again and told her to come for a short walk. She again declined. Then I walked alone and came back to my room. I did not know how to handle her now. I liked to be loved and possessed by somebody. To be a hope and trophy of somebody. The only person in this world, after my mother, who liked me, was likely to withdraw herself from me.

***

Still I had not decided which line of career to choose: academics or civil services. I looked at the University and the life of the faculties. Life could not be better than those men and women in academics. Nothing was more fascinating. One was surrounded with books in a beautiful campus.

I went to Brahmaputra Hostel to ask Fahad Ahsan what to do: whether academics or civil services? He said I should take the CSE; the process of selection in this exam was objective and fair.

He said, "One could study books even when one joined the civil service. Who and what will stop you from reading, suppose once you are an IAS officer? Rather you will have more resources and facilities for reading and writing."

I told him the story of a person who was wrongly incarcerated by a king. In the prison cell, he read all the books of the world over the years. Later, the king came to know that the person he jailed was innocent, he released the prisoner. The king also tendered him an apology. Then the prisoner said there was no need to be sorry, because in the gaol he read books, which was a great pleasure. In the books, he conquered territories, romanced with beautiful women, toured the distant worlds. He discovered the secret of the universe, understood the meaning of life.

I added, "Nothing gives me more happiness than reading a book."

Fahad smiled and said, "What you are saying appears good in the story, but has a terrible denouement."

I did not contend with him.

He said, "The basic things you require for a good life, like, a house, a vehicle, you will not get with a career in academics or in any other service. Your meagre salary and huge family responsibility will disillusion you. While in civil services, you will be able to help dozens of people. Life will be more satisfying."

He said the selection process for the university lectureship was not fair. One or two vacancies came for an institution in years. Several factors came into play in selection of a candidate. If you went for an interview to 10 places and did not get selected, you would become disillusioned. And then how will you support yourself once your fellowship was over?

"But for the civil services, you will have every year 100s of seats. If you prepared well, you would be selected."

He further said, "In academics there was no end to knowledge acquisition. There will always be somebody more knowledgeable than you. Academicians most of the time do hair-splitting. Contribution at the level of thought had stopped."

Fahad Ahsan was a core academician and it was interesting to listen to his views.

I was convinced with his argument and left him after thanking. A few days later, I talked to another senior student Murad Raas. He also argued on this line.

Both counsellors were knowledgeable and had friends in academics and civil services. They had seen their classmates and friends working in different streams. Their advice ended my confusion.

***

In the evening I felt low. I realized one more day had gone from my life. I asked myself how I spent the day? Did I use it for my goal or I wasted it? Every evening the crimson light over the earth and chirping birds in the red horizon made me feel that.

I did not want the sparkling, crisp, and beautiful day to go. I wanted to hold it in my hand, lengthen its span and kiss it. But it was stubborn, and it's inevitable forward movement like an arrow was a mystery to me. My heart did not thank God that He had given me one day to work and realise my potential. I felt I did too little with the time I had been given and the day was gone forever in an unreachable past.

I saw the students around. Students with sharper brains and greater abilities extracted more from the days, achieved more with less effort; and did not suffer from inferiority complex or lack of facilities. The university was a stage for them and they played deftly on it. While others like me struggled.

***

I wrote four term papers for myself and four for my friend Abbas, each term paper in 5,000 words. Abbas Nasir offered me fresh Kashmir apples for writing his term papers. He requested me to write his term papers so many times that I could not say no to him. And somehow, I enjoyed writing. I tried to use big words and complex sentences to impress the faculty. I learnt the format of the paper and played with the words. After writing the term-papers, I felt I had authored 'Meghaduta' or 'Hind Swaraj'.

I took the Bank PO exam and qualified for the written test. I was awaiting a call for an interview. If I was finally selected, I would have to leave the university. MA was a good degree; after this I could take a job at manager level in a bank and settle in my life. I would get a decent salary, get government accomodation and the fight in my life would end.

***

Now, the end semester exam arrived and I had to take six papers. But on April 30, three days before the start of the exam, I caught fever. I exerted beyond my capacity and bowed down to high fever. I read class notes lying on the bed as I had no energy to sit on a chair. After two days, I was a bit better and walked to the exam centre in the sun heat but I was not even at fifty per cent of my energy and ability. I regretted that I was not fit to take the challenge because of my mistake but I knew it was a battle, I had to fight. This day will not come again in my life, if I did not give my best I would be a loser. I had to be fast, accurate, and prolific. A good result will bring accolades and an average will push me to obscurity.

***

On the last day of the end-semester exam, I accompanied Jasmine from the exam centre to the hostel. She said she was very stressed and will come for a walk after leaving her belongings at the hostel.

I said, "What is your plan during the summer vacation? How is your preparation for M Phil entrance test?"

She said she was not interested in doing MPhil at JNU. She had applied for a personnel management and industrial relations course at Tata Institute of Social Sciences (TISS), Mumbai.

I was shocked to hear that. Date for applying for MPhil was gone. Now she will have to vacate the hostel.

She said, "My admission is scheduled in June. It is a course equivalent to a master degree. I had taken the entrance exam for this course."

I said, "What are you saying?"

"I did lots of work for this exam. I wrote an essay, took up group discussion and an interview. It was a massive exercise. The course will give me a job. I will also get a scholarship for the course."

I wondered what nonsense she was saying. "You did not tell me while you applied for this course."

"You are always busy with yourself."

"Who advised you for this course?"

"Ritu Bhatti is also taking this course. I talked to her."

"After studying at JNU, I would have gone to a place no less than Harvard University. It is only preparation for competitive exams which keeps me tamed." I said.

"There is a difference between you and me, Hameed."

"Please do not go. I would die without you."

"You are so happy without me. Always looking for an opportunity to avoid me. I am a thorn in your pursuit of ambition."

"I cannot live without you. I have nobody on the campus."

"You have friends. Your books and your ambition."

"Is friendship with books a crime? I have to make a career. I have to study more than others. Work harder."

"Many students make a career at the campus. But one does not lose basic courtesy."

"I need to work harder to overcome odds in my life. You do not know what I am undergoing," I said.

"This is just an excuse. I am not a daughter of Ratan Tata. I also have to work hard to survive. You avoided me all the time and now you say you cannot live without me. Whom do you think you are fooling."

We reached near Godavari Hostel. She was in a bad mood. I did not want to provoke her more. She entered her hostel gate saying bye to me. I returned to my hostel. Jasmine's decision to leave the university was a bolt from blue for me. I avoided her to study but now she had decided to leave. I felt a piece of my heart was separating from me. In the room I opened the pages of Aesop's Fables. At one place Aesop said, "It is in vain to expect our prayers to be heard, if we do not strive as well as pray."

I thought not to take a meal. My room-mate asked me whether I had a fight with somebody. I said, "No." He did not probe the matter further. He went to meet Farah Mirza who was waiting for him at Godavari Dhaba. They had planned to go to watch a movie at the theatre at Plaza Cinema. They would return to the hostel at midnight when I would be trying to sleep.

***

The next day, when I got up, I felt I had no energy in my body, I had no purpose in my life, no battle to win. I left the bed after a lot of effort. Sameer was still sleeping with a bed-sheet over him. I felt somebody was sleeping next to him on the bed. I thought it must be Farah Mirza.

I felt embarrassed at being in the room with a lady. My low energy and meaninglessness became secondary to me and I ran out of the room with a T-shirt and track-pants before she got up. I stealthily moved in the room to collect my belongings and got ready within minutes. I stepped down to the mess, took a cup of tea and watched music on the television. I was still thinking about Jasmine. I felt I had no work to do. All the four semesters of the MA course were over. I was looking at an uncertain future. If Jasmine left the university, I would be alone, nobody would be around to give me strength.

***

I took a walk with Abbas at the university ring-road. He said, "It is good that Jasmine was going. You would be able to concentrate on studies. She wasted your energy."

I kept silent. I did not like what he was saying. He continued, "I can see how disturbed you are because of her."

"I will miss her badly."

"You will be fine after sometime."

"I do not want to lose her. I want both a job and Jasmine."

"I believe in destiny. Whatever happens that happens for our good. Can you imagine Jasmine going to another university, another city for a course? None of our classmates are going. If she is going, then this must be in your interest."

***

In the afternoon boys assembled in the common room to watch a cricket match between India and Pakistan. They were waiting for the match to start since morning. I tried watching the match to divert my attention but I could not think of anything other than Jasmine's abrupt decision to leave the university.

I went to Godavari hostel and told the security guard to call Jasmine. She came down after 30 minutes in white kurti and blue jeans. It seemed she was sleeping. She knew I would discuss with her about her decision to go. We walked out of the hostel towards Sabarmati Hostel and sat there near the dhaba. She was silent, I looked at the blue sky with scattered grey clouds.

"Don't go. I would not succeed in any endeavour in my life, if you leave me."

"But you thought I was some kind of obstruction to your way to success," she said looking at the kikar jungle in the distance.

A boy came to us to take order for a cup of tea.

She said TISS was closer to her home and JNU had no charm left for her any more. "I wanted to study at the top university of India and I did that. There was no point further wasting the time here," she said.

She continued, "JNU gives you academic rigour. It gives you a grasp over theory. The course at TISS would give me an opportunity to practice what I have learnt."

"Tell this bokwas to somebody else. I know every bit of you," I said.

She said, "You are a loser. You would never be happy even if you conquer the earth."

"Stay here. I will change. I will be with you all the time."

"But what will I do here? I have not filled up the form for the MPhil admission test.'

"I will arrange a room for you."

"And what about my academic session? I don't want to waste my one year."

I held her hand and said, "Dear, don't do that."

"I cannot turn the clock back."

Then Sanyukta walked to us. She could not have come at a worse time. I wanted to talk to Jasmine and convince her to stay at the university.

Sanyukta talked about the recent episode of a sexual harassment of a girl and polarisation of the student on the party line, rather than helping the girl get justice. Jasmine said the day was not far when this university would be like any other university of the country.

***

After three days, Jasmine packed her luggage and started from the hostel to board the Rajdhani Express. I along with Abbas went to see her off to the New Delhi Railway Station. The train was scheduled at 4:30 p.m. I took her luggage and sat with her on bus no. 615.

I looked at her dusky face. Her skin glowed, she looked beautiful. I felt something of my own was going from my life for always.

She said, "Had you shown me as much care as you have in the last two days, I would not have been going."

"That is atrocious. You are putting all the blame on me."

We got down from the bus and reached the platform through a rickshaw. I kept her luggage in the coach. A youngman opposite her berth sat with a walkman. The train announced one to be careful from the pickpocket and to take care of one's luggage.

She came out of the coach and stood with us at the platform. The platform smelled foul, some portion of it was dirty and wet. Abbas Nasir said when he saw so many people he felt claustrophobic. The solution to India's burgeoning problem was to check its population. I kept silent and looked at the hair of Jasmine. I thought within minutes she would be away from me and only God knew when I would meet her again. I thought I only got pain during interaction with her in the last two years. Whether I would be able to study with focus after her departure only time could tell.

"When you reach there, call me and give me your contact number at the institute."

"Okay", she said, tightening her hair lock with a clip.

After 20 minutes, the train blew a horn. I said, "Thanks so much for being nice to me in the last two years."

She said goodbye and climbed the steps of the red coloured coach of the train.

I walked back from the platform. The university campus was 15 km away. We walked to the bus stand without speaking a word. We took bus and on the way I looked at the the Ministers' bungalows in the Luteyn's Delhi. I kept thinking about Jasmine. I thought it was a dream. She came in my dream and disappeared before I could see her to my satisfaction, hold her in my hand. God had not done a fair deal to me. Had I been a God I would not have made this world like that. We reached the campus at 6:30 p.m. Abbas left me and joined the boys and girls at the dhaba. I went to the room and looked at the setting sun from the balcony.

***

It was a bad time for me. Jasmine was gone from my life. I did not realize that even if I was avoiding talking to her, or trying to distance myself from her, mere her presence around me was a source of strength to me. Even if she was in her hostel room, I felt she was there near me and could come to me any time if I called her. She was the solution to the longing for being loved, cared and possessed. Now, something vital was gone from my life. I felt I would break and my heart would choke. I could not share the pain of her absence with anybody. I felt as if God withdrew His grace from my life. I had no hope, no enthusiasm, no purpose in life. I remembered her face, her voice. I wept and felt I would die. I looked at the notepad in which she had scribbled her home address in Kerala and phone number in capital letters. I kissed those words. I asked myself what have you done? Would you be able to recover from this? Who would meet me at the canteen, library, green boulevard and come rushing to me? And I invited this separation myself.

I thought to leave the university. Everything reminded me of her. The place looked empty and frightful. The evening light lost its charm. Birds stopped singing. Hot wind seemed to scorch the earth. My body became pale. I felt a dagger was stabbed in my stomach. I did not want to touch a book.

❑

Chapter 6

Packing up Your Life

Now, after the MA end-semester exam, I was no longer a student of the university. The room I stayed in was allotted to a student named Faisal Sayed. Sameer Khan was already there. Faisal Sayed, though known to me and had sought guidance from me on academic issues, treated me as an intruder. He wanted me to leave the room immediately. But I had no place to go. He stopped talking to me. I slept on the floor in the room for some days, and in another room on other days. One day, I went to sleep in Abbas' room, but his room-mate took objection to that and I had to go to a third room. After the end-semester exam of the MA course, students generally stayed in the room allotted to them till the result of MPhil entrance exam. I was not doing anything unconventional by staying in room No. 152.

All this made me realise that I may slip to the days of the Zaheer's factory if I did not work hard to avoid that. I remembered reading an interview of Lata Mangeshkar, the legendary playback singer, where she said, she took every song as if it was her first song, and if she failed she would slip into poverty. I thought I was given an opportunity at the university to jump high, I should not fail to benefit from it at any cost.

The M Phil entrance test was scheduled on May 17, about 15 days after the end-semester exam. I had applied for three courses—one for MPhil in CSSS and two courses in the School of International Studies. The main objective was to get a hostel till I qualify the CSE.

On the day of the MPhil test, I went to a distant Kendriya Vidyalaya in north Delhi in the summer morning and attempted the questions. I knew the questions were to be answered to the point. But I wrote lots of relevant and irrelevant things under one question. Only three questions were to be attempted out of five choices. Sitting on a wooden bench in a dimly lit hall, I wrote as much as I could do. This was a make or break exam for me. If I qualified, I could live at JNU hostel for another 05 years. One had an address in Delhi at a premier educational institution of the country.

After the written test for M Phil entrance, the other frog which I was to eat was the Prelim of the Civil Services Exam scheduled on May 27. It was an objective type test and it consisted of one optional subject like Sociology and one General Studies paper. I started reading for this exam in April. I thought I was good in Sociology optional, there was no need to prepare much for this subject. I focussed on the General Studies paper, reading the books and guides available in the market, including relevant NCERT books. I had got one guide on History from Ahmad Aamir, and it was a useful book. People suggested that I read voluminous Unique's guide on General Studies. But I could not bring myself to read that unwieldy book. I bought a General Studies guide by Tata Mcgraw Hills. I studied sitting in the room during all the disturbance by my roommate and his affairs. When it became too much, I carried the books to the study hall called Dholpur House on the ground floor of the library where one could bring one's book and study. At the table, I scanned the lines of sociologist Vilfredo Pareto, "The world has always belonged to the stronger, and will belong to them for many years to come. Whoever becomes a lamb will find a wolf to eat him."

My cousin Shah Zafar used to tell me that you are born either intelligent or duffer. If you are intelligent then you need not work hard or study much. And if you are duffer then also you need not work hard, because all efforts would go down the drain and no result would accrue. Thus, hard work was a mark of being incompetent and imbecile. This argument ran in my mind many times but I knew if I believed it and stopped working hard I would lose in life.

This was my first CSE Prelim. During the preparation, I had boil in my waist and the thumb of my right hand was crushed in the hostel's room door. Because of these, the pain in my body was unbearable. Then, I realised that I was losing my eyesight. While I was taking a post-dinner walk with Surya Prakash, he saw a girl walking at a distance, while I could not see clearly who the person was. Surya told me that my eyesight was getting weak and if I did not wear specs, the eye sight would further deteriorate rapidly. Nextday, I consulted an eye specialist at the university's health centre. The doctor administered liquid drops into my eyes because of which everything appeared blurred and I was not able to study for two days. The situation was worsened by regular power-cut in the evening. At the top of it, Delhi recorded the hottest days of the century. Abbas was in my room holding the pink pages of 'The Economic Times, reading an article by Srivatsa Krishna. He looked at me and said the indications for me were not good and everything possibly was going wrong.

I thought very few things were good in my life, but I was not afraid to face the reality. If everything was great in my life, if I had a car and a farm house, and I qualified CSE, then that was not an achievement. It would be credit worthy when I achieved success despite all difficulties. My father used to recite a line of poet Mohammad Iqbal which meant: O eagle! Why are you worried about the adverse wind? It blows to help you fly even higher.

***

The next and the last exam for me this summer was the UGC JRF exam on 26th June. I was eligible to take the Junior Research Fellowship (JRF) exam conducted by the University Grants Commission (UGC) in the fourth semester of MA. Passing this exam would make one eligible for a monthly stipend of ₹ 8000, which was a good amount. I did not take this exam earlier because of my ill-health and I had gone home. My class-mate Vivek Yadav took the exam and passed it. He became the only student in our class to qualify for this test. That year the Commission raised the monthly fellowship from ₹ 2000 to ₹ 8000, and ₹ 15000 for the Senior Research Fellow. This was a huge jump and it made the fellowship much more attractive.

This test was held every six months, and all researchers of all disciplines were eligible. Each discipline had about six seats, 50 per cent of which was reserved for SC and ST students. Qualifying this exam was tough because of the limited number of seats. But the financial support it provided to the scholar during the studies made it a coveted exam. This exam was also called National Eligibility Test (NET), an eligibility test for being appointed as a lecturer to a college and university. The scheme of exam provided that those who ranked high in merit, say, 10 candidates, will be Junior Research Fellow getting monthly fellowship, and an equal number of candidates will be NET qualified, but they will not get any fellowship and will be eligible for being appointed as lecturers in colleges and universities. A candidate who had not qualified this test will not be eligible for being a faculty at an educational institution.

Many top shots of the Centre could not qualify this exam, and would take it till their last semester at the university.

I met one senior Ruzbihan Shirazi at the Centre, who had qualified for this test. He gave me tips on how to crack this exam. The kernel of his guidance was that the time for writing the answers in the exam was limited, there was no time to think and write, I should make notes on all topics and practice writing; questions asked were straight as per the topics given in the syllabus. I took his guidance seriously as passing this exam meant studying for five years without tension for money. I prepared notes on all topics and practised writing daily sitting at Dholpur House, in the sweltering June heat. I remembered my father, a fan of

Christopher Marlowe, used to quote him, "He that loves pleasure must for pleasure fall."

On the day of the exam in June, I took a bus from Godavari Dhaba bus-stand in the morning. Though it was my first attempt, I treated this exam as a do or die situation. Many seniors enrolled in MPhil and PhD were also part of the team visiting the exam centre for the test. I was taking this exam to change my destiny. I thought God didn't create me to live in poverty and deprivation. I should work and the situation would change. Everything the rich and privileged possessed I would also own.

***

Then the CSE Prelim result came in the evening of June 28, two days after the JRF exam. My roll number was printed in the list. I was one of the 5000 candidates for 500 seats for civil services. I felt happy, the summer sky looked pink even at 10 p.m. It was as if God was angry and was planning something untoward for the residents of the earth. My friends told me to take them to Ganga Dhaba for a treat.

I agreed, and a group of five friends strolled on the main road in the hot night and reached the Dhaba. Boys and beautiful girls sat around the rocks at the Dhaba with cups of tea and toasts and discussed the nuclear test at Pokhran and civil unrest in Malaysia. The dhabas were a nursery of new ideas, an arena of student leaders, a garden for romantic affairs, and other such things. The place mirrored the idea of a university, a free space, where bright minds gathered and discussed issues. The dhaba remained open till past midnight, served snacks and beverages to an assembly of star students. But I had no time to sit and discuss issues the way these students did. I had to work hard, sleep on time and get up early to take work again. I went there occasionally, and absorbed the things from the air. That night we returned to the hostel room at 2:0 a.m.

***

After the UGC test, I picked up books for the CSE Main. I had no notes or guide books, no money to purchase books. My banjara nomadic life continued. I shifted from one room to another. The room no. 152 where I stayed could accommodate only my books, and I slept one night in one room and another night in another room. Most of the nights I had no good sleep, and the students in whose room I stayed had their sleep also disturbed. The rooms were not made to accommodate three persons, and Delhi's summer made sleeping more difficult.

In the daytime, I went to the library and collected books which successful candidates suggested the civil services aspirants like me to read. All the books were not available, and those available were old. I also borrowed some books from friends in the hostel and the university. They were happy to lend the books.

***

The result of the written test for M Phil entrance came in the first week of July. Final result would come after viva-voce. Some of my close friends failed to clear the written test. Now, I worked hard for the viva voce, as everything was at stake. Abbas said if one stayed at the campus as a student one could go to America, but if one failed to get admission one had to languish at Munirka, the neighbourhood opposite to JNU. I was yet to get admission in MPhil and secure a room for stay and study. For admission in MPhil, I worked and prepared a draft proposal for research, which

I would undertake if I was given admission at the Centre. This research proposal was to be presented before the faculty, during the viva-voce, and they could question me on the proposal. If my presentation was good, they would give me good marks and I would be able to take admission.

Thus, while I should have studied for the CSE Main, I worked to secure admission at the University so that I was able to take the CSE. But I had no choice. Ruzbihan, my seniors, once told me, "Beggars are not choosers." I felt offended by his words. But he was correct. The day of viva voce came, the board of faculty for MPhil Test at JNU were kind to me. My performance during the test was good.

***

After the viva-voce, I had no target except the CSE Main. I thought if I qualified, everything would change in my life. I prepared notes on Sociology with the books in the library and also used the notes for Sociology which Neelu Khanna had given to me.

I took my notes and books in a backpack to Dholpur House at the library building and studied there from 9:30 a.m. till night. I took a break of five minutes after every 55 minutes, and returned to the seat. A pack of dogs sat at the entrance of the reading hall. The hall smelt foul. Toilet adjoining the hall was never in a good condition. Around 100 students-- girls and boys sat at the reading hall. My target of reading 100 pages helped me cover the syllabus fast.

When I read one subject I wanted to continue with that, but I had to study all subjects. It was like the law of inertia at its work. When I wrote on a topic I wanted to continue with that and did not want to read. It took some effort to take a different task. Then I fixed a time period for different subjects, and one hour of writing answers to the probable questions daily.

I read books like DD Basu's 'Introduction To The Constitution Of India', Dutt and Sundaram's 'Indian Economy', Rajiv Ahir's, 'Indian History' Bipan Chandra's 'India's Struggle for Independence', Subhash Kashyap's 'Our Constitution', etc. I read three-four books for one subject like polity, geography, history, science, and culture, etc. These books covered only General Studies paper.

Reading these books was a wrong strategy. But that I did not know then. When I took up a magazine and read which books the CSE toppers went through, they listed these books. But coaching notes and coaching guidance were keys to the success. None of them, however, talked about that. Reading these books once to take an overview of the issue was fine. But one required notes written in simple and short sentences, not the type of English language DD Basu used in his book. Anyway, I relied on these books, read and re-read them and went to the examination hall like a novice.

I copied the editorial of the newspaper,'The Times of India' and wanted to answer questions in the CSE Main in that kind of language. When I copied the editorial on a piece of paper, I was never short of words, expressions and speed. But it was a mistake. The examiner did not want difficult words and bombastic expressions, using which I fancied writing the answers. They wanted clarity of thought, specific details and an easy language to understand. But then I did not know I was committing a blunder.

Faiz Mustafa told me to read sports pages of newspapers which published articles and reports from agencies like Reuters, and Associated Press. Such pieces celebrated heroism, grandeur and physical strength. They told me about chess masters, Olympians, grand slam winners, football legends, and their achievements written with flowery words. They packed me with momentary energy and passion.

***

In the evening, I returned to the hostel thinking about Jasmine. The absence of Jasmine had started eating me. I thought how good it would have been had she been at the campus. Now this place looked desolate to me. I felt I was alone and abandoned. The uncertainty of the MPhil result and no room to stay made me more depressed. I felt I had somebody, who cared for me, whose shadow always covered me from the hardship, had left me. And my behaviour to her was responsible for her departure. I thought where she would have been and what she would have been doing. I wanted to dial her phone number and weep, but I could not weep. My cousin Shah Zafar had long back told me that men do not weep and those who look like men and weep are actually not men. Since then I believed that I would violate the code of manhood by weeping.

I felt if somebody like her was with me, I would win the whole world. I would be stronger and gallope the length of the earth like Augustus. I would feel there was somebody in the world who cared for me, I was important for somebody. Otherwise, my life was a long dreary track on which one was walking alone. Negative thoughts flagellated my mind all the time. It was difficult to walk alone for long.

***

During this time, Papa came to Delhi and gave me ₹ 1000 several times. Had he not given me money, my study would have been stalled. Rather, I would not have been able to pursue it. At the university, I took him around the campus, to the mess, and the room. He felt good seeing the brick architecture of the buildings, forest patches, greenery, students gathered at dhabas and the library. He met his acquaintances and friends in Delhi and returned to Jashanpur. I feared him, I hated him. I also loved him. When I thought of my childhood, remembered his glowing face, how my those days passed, I felt like weeping. His voice caused terror in my heart. At Jashanpur, when he came home from work or the market, my anxiety took over my happiness. I stayed subdued at home, lest I was berated by him on any issue. Sometimes, he was happy with me and he thought I was a good son. But his belief that I was reluctant to offer prayer drove him to rage.

***

I had to decide on an optional subject other than Sociology for the CSE Main. I had spent one year in the Persian language centre, and students said one could score high marks with Persian as an optional. This was a tempting option for me. But an ability to understand simple sentences, and being able to understand Sadi's Gulistan, Firdausi's Shahnama or Khayyam's Rubaaiyat was a different thing.

A few months back, I discussed pros and cons of taking Persian language and literature as an optional with seniors. They told me to start studying Persian after the CSE Prelim. They told me that I should memorise some pages and write them in the exam. I wondered how I could memorise pages of words and sentences which I did not understand. They tried to convince me that everything was easy and I would be able to do that. But I was never convinced with their argument.

Amir Subhani, a student from Bihar, topped CSE in 1987 with Persian as a paper, and made many Muslim young men think that they could also qualify the exam with this subject. I met many such candidates preparing for the exam, planning to take Persian as an optional. Students said Amir Subhani attained a high score in Persian paper as an optional in the civil services exam. Many boys like me thought Amir Subhani had unravelled the civil services exam for the Muslim students. And we could just walk in the hallowed civil services with the Persian door. But I think that was a trap, and choosing Persian as an optional ruined the careers of many ambitious students. Students, who opted Persian at JNU, where a full-fledged department existed, had no notes, nor relevant books of Persian language for barging into the civil services.

I asked for notes from friends and seniors in Persian language centre. They were non-committal. I gathered an impression that they did not have notes, though they had been preparing for civil services for years. I thought it was dangerous to rely on them.

I changed the track and scanned the CSE syllabus. I looked for familiarity with the topics given in social science subjects. I zeroed on History, Political Science and Psychology. But the syllabuses of History and Political Science were vast and of Psychology manageable. The advantage of reading History and Political Science was that they covered a large portion of the syllabus of General Studies for CSE Prelim and Main. But I settled for Psychology as it was similar to

Sociology and the syllabus was not heavy and extensive. However, I had no notes for this subject.

I talked to Shahid for Psychology notes. His friend Shruti Singh enrolled in the School of International Studies was taking coaching for Psychology paper from a well known, Delhi-based coaching guide.

Shahid talked to her for the notes. She agreed immediately and gave her class notebooks to me for getting a photocopy. Shruti Singh a native of Bihar was very committed to the cause of the poor and weak. Extremely beautiful, tall, looking mysteriously similar to the famous actress Catherine Zeta-Jones, her aim was to join civil services and work for the last man on the social margin.

This was a big favour from Shruti. Generally, a student, who took coaching class, spent time on visiting the coaching centre, paid money for the classes, and so on, did not give the class notes. Even a close friend would throw 10 excuses why he could not give the notes. Or if one gave notes, he would do it in exchange for some benefit. Shruti's notes did not cover all the topics comprehensively. Some portions of the syllabus were not covered at all. But these notes were the best thing available in the market to tackle the Psychology paper of the CSE Main. Later, I supplemented it with some material from Jawahar Books, and I was ready to take a plunge.

Raj Karan, my friend, also guided me in reading Psychology books, including one by Morgan and King. I would read the whole chapter of the book for a topic given in the CSE syllabus. But he told me to read only the topics which matched with the topic in the CSE syllabus, and not the whole chapter or the whole book, which I did. That cut lots of unnecessary reading and made things easier for me. Now, it looks idiotic why one would read the whole chapter when one is required to read only a topic in a chapter. But that was what I was doing without Raj Karan's guidance.

Studying Psychology benefitted me otherwise also. It made me know more about myself, about the concepts of attitude, intelligence, motivation, deprivation and the impact it had on the personality of the person, etc. The concepts made me understand myself, my personality, my attitude better. It also motivated me and made me work harder.

***

Many times, I felt I would change the line of fate with my work and intelligence. But then depressing thoughts took over me and made me see darkness all along. I felt I was lacking the brain power and skill required to alter the things, or achieve what I aimed for. Earlier, I believed that I would break the hard rock with my will. Work gave me lots of returns. But now I saw that success also depended on the network and contacts one had. Coming from a humble family, I had no contacts, did not know even an MLA, and hence success would not be easy for me. But after going through the Psychology syllabus, I felt I could break the code of success. It made me understand that everything was psychology. If one had determination, there was nothing one could not accomplish. Victor Hugo had rightly observed, "People do not lack strength, they lack will."

During those days, one speaker K. S. Sudarshan addressed the students packed at the SSS Auditorium—a place where the best of the minds came and spoke to us. He was deliberating on the idea that power gets you respect.

If you are weak, and sound helpless, nobody will treat you well, much less one will respect you. He narrated the fable of a baby goat who went to God and complained to Him that everybody in the forest looked for an opportunity to devour it. God then did not sympathise with it. God said, "Baby! After seeing you, my mouth is also watering."

Message was that you have to be strong. You have to work to enhance your strength. None will come to aid you. It was a relevant message. In this world, the fittest will survive. Strong will prevail. Weak will be devoured.

❑

Chapter 7

No Resting on Your Oars

I was waiting for the MPhil entrance test result. The whole day, rumour galloped around the campus about the M Phil result. One afternoon, I was having lunch at the mess at 2:15 p.m. Most of the residents had finished lunch. My senior Shrikant Verma, and two friends Chandrakant Patil, Rashid Jamshed walked to me at the dining table and said, "Congrats! You topped the entrance test." I could not believe what he said. I thanked them and finished the food in a great hurry. I looked towards the clear blue sky from the glass window pane, and said, "Thank you, God. You have been gracious to me." I knew what it was like to live in Delhi when I was not a student at the University.

After finishing the food, I walked to the Admin Block of the university in the hot sun and saw my name 'Hameed Akhtar' in the list. I might have topped the list because I got extra marks for being a native of a backward district and for coming from a backward class. For these considerations, JNU provided marks to a candidate. After seeing my name, I went to the library to study. I knew I could not stop and rest. I had to keep running to reach my destination.

***

I took admission in a two-year MPhil course at the end of July and soon the classes started. Many new students joined the course and many who were in MA had to leave the university as they could not crack the entrance exam. Leaving the old friends was depressing and adjusting to the new ones was taking time. But the university and the campus was a ground where people came, displayed their talents, earned something and left and new people arrived. This cycle was so regular and routine that no one marked it or complained against it.

Now I was busy with the class, its assignments, and activities at the Centre from 9:0 a.m. to 1:0 p.m. for at least four days in a week. While I attended MPhil classes, I knew my competitors in CSE would have been studying the material for the CSE Main. After the classes, I spent my time on preparation for the CSE Main.

The period was boring and stress filled. I worked continuously under pressure to perform without any break for a long time. A presentation at the Centre or requirement of a term paper within a short period, or the exam schedule, all caused me lots of stress. I loved reading but the kind of material I read for MPhil class and CSE did not interest me. I became tired of self-imposed restrictions and discipline.

One evening at 5:0, while studying at Dholpur House I felt depressed and lonely. I felt nothing was good in my life. I came out of the reading hall and looked at the rocks with the hanging leaves in front of the library canteen. Jasmine would sit there with me and friends and discuss term paper topics over a cup of coffee or a plate of masala dosa. I felt an urge to talk to her. Who knows if she changed her mind and returned to me at the university. I went to my room at the hostel, fetched Jasmine's phone number from a notebook, where she had written her home's address and phone number in her handwriting, memorised her phone number and went to dial the number from a PCO at Nilgiri Dhaba.

A woman took the call and spoke in Malayali. I guessed it was her mother. I said, "Aunty, I am calling from JNU in Delhi. I was Jasmine's class-mate. I want to speak to her."

She said, "My Son, she is not heret in Kerala."

"Anty, I wanted to speak to her. If you could give her contact number, please.

"I will have to look for that. I will give you. You call me in the evening."

"Thanks a lot, Aunty. Regards."

I walked to the library building through a narrow lane from the Ring Road. Kikar trees and bare rocks stood on both sides of the lane. I often walked on this stretch for five minutes after every one hour of study. That evening I dialled Jasmine's home again with shaking hands. I thought I would get her phone number but I received no response. I walked out of the PCO man. Then I told myself "Don't worry. Dependence is a sign of weakness. A weak person cannot fight the world which is constantly throwing challenges. You have everything within you to face this world."

***

After the admission, I was allotted a double seater room on the ground floor at Periyar Hostel. My life as a banjara ended, and I had a place to stay and dream.

My new room-mate Javed Younas was an intellectual prodigy. He was enrolled in MPhil at the University's prestigious Centre for Political Studies (CPS). He was sharp and had elephantine memory. He read fast, possessed tremendous comprehension power, and spoke like the US President Franklin Roosevelt. Musarrat Nazir, a milky-white, slim girl in shalwar-kamiz in Economics Centre from Baramulla district, was his friend and she visited him frequently at the room.

He will take a book like 'The Social Contract' or 'The Critique of Pure Reason' at 10 p.m. after dinner and will finish it sitting on a chair in the room by 4 a.m. He will sleep from 4 a.m. to 10 a.m. and then attend morning classes without showing signs of tiredness. What he read was printed on his mind, and he could shoot ideas, names, figures in your face at the speed of light. While others drafted an article, refined its expression, and corrected grammar, he typed an article for a newspaper at one go on his old Remington typewriter. No revision, no refinement required. His sentences were perfect. He folded the typed papers and dropped them in a red cylindrical postal box near Kamal Complex. One day, I saw his one full page article printed on Salman Rushdie's Midnight's Children in the Literary Review of 'The Hindu' with coloured cartoons and illustrations. In the first semester in MPhil he published a 10-page article in the reputed EPW magazine.

He would dictate the pamphlet for a student party without revising or refining the sentences. Political pundits and office-bearers of political parties would sit and give him the idea or the line of argument for a paragraph of the pamphlet and his fingers on the typewriter churned words and sentences. That was a miracle for me.

Many times his genius pushed me into depression. His extraordinary capability intimidated me. I prayed God to give me even half of his genius. We had a long discussion on several issues sitting in the room after lunch or dinner. Other students also joined the debate.

During discussion with him and others, I realised if one differed even with the most liberal person, who vouched every moment for freedom of expression, he considered the other an idiot. Below the skin, most of us are the same, whether one is a champion of liberal thought or an enemy of freedom.

***

This was the first semester of the MPhil course at JNU. It was also my first attempt at CSE Main. This exam started in the last week of August and stretched up to November. During this period, I had not one moment to enjoy life. I worked all the time. Enjoyment for me meant going for a walk, sleeping once in a while in the afternoon, gossiping with friends, listening to a political leader who had come to the campus, etc. These activities gave me a respite from the books of Sociology and pressure of the civil services exam. I stopped these activities for studies. I told myself if I qualified the exam, I would have lots of time to indulge in the pleasure trip.

My academic life and engagement for the MPhil course wrecked my chances of success in the CSE. However, I had no option but to attend to the academic responsibility. With JNU classes and course, I was in competition for CSE, not vice-versa. I gave time for the CSE after I gave everything at my disposal to the MPhil course. I could not tell anybody in the centre that I would be absent from the activities because I had to take the CSE.

One evening, a friend of my room-mate came and stayed in the room. The General Studies exam paper was scheduled the next day. It was an important paper, and if one performed poorly in this, one was out of the race. My room-mate and his out-station friend sat and discussed their college stories in the room till 2:00 a.m. with the tube-light switched on. I lay on my bed trying hard to sleep. But I could not. I got up at 6:30 a.m.

Sleep was an issue with me; if I had even a slight disturbance, my sleep would break. A guy or a group of guys would pass along my room singing a song or talking loudly and I would lose my sleep. My friend Surya Prakash said, "Lord Sri Krishna said 'Sona' would be very precious during the kalyug. Whether he meant sleep or gold by 'sona' was not clear." If there was a birthday party on the floor, I would not sleep till the party ended. And if I did not sleep 7 hours or more, my brain did not work. I was good for nothing.

In the morning, when I got up, I had no energy in my body. The battle seemed to be already lost. I went to a school at Jhandewalan Extension, Karol Bagh and took the exam. The paper was easy, I wrote answers at a relaxed pace. When I wrote an answer lots of points crowded my mind. I jotted down those points at the top of the page and elaborated them in the main text of the answers. My brain was exhausted after writing continuously for two hours.

If I took water served by the staff at the exam centre my stomach would react violently and if I did not take water I was dehydrated. I left questions of over 50 marks in the paper of 300 marks unattempted. During the break in the afternoon, friends from the university taking the exam assembled together, and ate chapatis and vegetables sitting on the lawn. We revised the material for the second paper.

I was not sure that this exam was going to change my life. I felt enthused as if I would drink the ocean, I told myself I was on a mission, but when it came to practically executing the work, stress gripped me. While going on a bus to take the exam, I did not feel like I was going to conquer a territory. The fear and stress of the exam poured poison in my bloodstream.

***

The exam which began last week of August ended on November 26. The last paper was that of Psychology. The optional subjects like Sociology and Psychology papers were held at Exam Halls Building in the UPSC at Shahjahan Road. The exam stretched over two months and kept me in a state of perpetual stress. This period was also dotted by responsibilities like classes, presentations, seminars, and term papers.

I spent most of my time before the exam on collection and consolidation of the notes for the two optional subjects, though I could not prepare final notes for the optional subjects. I read and added new facts, information, ideas, etc. continuously in the notes. On several topics material was available in abundance and on many topics no material was available anywhere. So one went to the exam hall with dread. And UPSC asked questions on all topics whether reading material was available in the outside world or not.

And if one left even one question or did not satisfactorily reply to the questions with good inputs, one could not hope for success or good rank.

***

CSE Main was over. Now the winter chill descended on north India. Vegetation and Aravalli rocks at the campus made the cold all the more difficult. After CSE Main, I took reading the classics in English literature, philosophy and politics . Not reading them for so long, I felt I had become intellectually bankrupt. All the thinkers and philosophers whom I had read, I had forgotten their theories and arguments.

Abbas could not qualify the MPhil entrance test, and went to Delhi University north campus to prepare for civil services. Thus, Jasmine and Abbas, my two friends, gone, there was no joy in my life. I had hardly anybody with whom I could walk, sit and share the matter of my heart. I was alone and forsaken. Days passed without talking to anybody as it was winter vacation for the whole of December and most of the students had gone home. I felt my heart would burst and emotions would choke me. I asked God why he made life so difficult for me. If we were his children, why did he make living on this earth a challenge for us? What "lamp of destiny was there to guide her little children stumbling in the dark?" I kept thinking, lying on the bed during winter night, while the clock ticked on the wall. I got no answer. There was nobody like the son of Mary who could ease the pain of mortals like us.

I wanted to go home after so much continuous drudgery but I could not do that. The total cash at my disposal was ₹ 30, with this much amount I could at most have reached only the railway station. My room-mate had gone to London to meet his father. My home at Jashanpur was not a place to relax. After a few days at home, tension built up in the relationship with the family members. When I saw poverty, deprivation and backwardness around me, I felt my work was incomplete. There was no scope for relaxation or break. So I continued plodding at the university.

I took George Bernard Shaw's book at the library. I remembered my father discussing Shaw's book 'Arms And The Man' as anti-romantic comedy. I thought about Jasmine, her shining hair and ample bangles. I felt her smell was still present near the table where we sat on the fourth floor of the library. There was nobody around me except the shelves of books, and whispering sounds of a few couples sitting in a corner. Outside from the window, it appeared the leaves of kikar and gulmohar trees covered the earth like a canopy.

Returning from the library in the evening, I felt depressed. Company of Abbas or Sasikumar would make me feel okay, but the moment I was alone in the room everything seemed to be haunting. I had nobody to sit with near a heat pillar and discuss thinkers and philosophers. At the time of the sleep, I told myself that each passing day was bringing more responsibility to me. I had to work harder. Life had given me an opportunity in the form of the university and its facilities, it was a lottery prize I had won. If I squandered it, everything would go from my hand. I remembered Faiz Mustafa quoting Winston Churchill: "You cannot afford to indulge even for the shortest period of time in resting on your oars. You must continually drive the vast machine forward at its utmost speed. To lose momentum is not merely to stop, but to fall."

***

I kept reading but not at the rate of 100 pages a day. I lost momentum. I realised reading 100 pages a day could help me qualify the exam but not place me in the top rank. CSE required reading and memorising the material. I came across the statement of one successful candidate saying "Read one book six times, than six books one time." My method of reading a lot and reading fast gave me breadth but not depth. In the exam hall one was not required to think and write. Time given to the candidate was short as compared to the words to be written for answering a question. One could answer only when one remembered the things. If one spent time thinking and recollected ideas, facts, and information, one was bound to lose the race.

The result for the first semester was declared by the end of December. I walked to the Centre and I found I secured the highest grades in the class. This time I had no bouts of fever so I could perform better. I could get this much grade despite the fact that I was studying for the CSE Main also. Then I was also taking other competitive exams. I thought had my health been good, I would have topped MA class also.

***

I also filled up exam forms for state civil services of states like Madhya Pradesh, Uttar Pradesh, Bihar, Himachal Pradesh, etc. for a gazetted post. If I missed the civil services conducted by UPSC, I had other options available. I borrowed books on the history and culture of these states, and read them. Syllabus for optional subjects for the state exams were by and large the same. I also scanned every week Times Literary Supplement seeking guidance on how to apply for universities abroad. I was scattering my energy and focus, it had advantages and disadvantages. I had towering ambition and aspiration, but very little achievement. And the only capital was my average intelligence and hard work. The odds were against me. I had no option but to succeed. It was a state of war and I could not afford to lose. The words of the American author Dale Carnegie were my guide: "Most of the important things in the world have been accomplished by people who have kept on trying when there seemed to be no hope at all."

***

The UGC declared the result for JRF in December, almost six months after I had taken the exam. I went alone on a bus to the UGC office at Delhi University's South Campus. I wanted somebody to accompany me, alone I felt diffident and insecure. But nobody was around to come with me. At the Campus, a police constable stood there with a cane stick. I went near the locked gate, and told him to enquire my roll number. He walked to a tall pillar on which the roll numbers were pasted, and looked for the number I gave to him. He came back and said, "Your number is there, Bhai Ji."

I was thrilled, but I was not sure he was correct. I told him to go and cross check my number. He obliged and said, "When I say it is there, that means it is there." I had nobody around to share my joy. I came back to the bus stop and waited for the 620 Blueline bus to arrive. I qualified this exam solely due to the guidance of the senior Ruzbihan. I thought how my life was going to change with this scholarship. A loaded bus came to the bus stop. I boarded it and returned to the campus. Now, I was going to get ₹ 8000 per month with an annual contingency fund for buying books, copies, pens, etc. for ₹ 10,000. This was a huge amount of money for me.

***

It was December 30, and the year was to end. I reflected on how the year was for me. It was a kind year, but it passed like an angry river. I wanted the time to stop, it should let me feel it and then go at a slow pace. It gave me no time to take a stock of the situation. Weeks and months galloped like horses of race and where it went I did not know. It did not return. I thought one more year had gone from my life; I had one less year to live on this earth. The more I thought about the time and its ruthlessness, the more insecure I felt. I looked at the books on the shelves and on the table and thought about the books I read that year. I spent most of the time reading and writing. But were there better things which I could do? Maybe tour the world on a motorcycle? Work for the life of a poor man in a remote village or a slum? Work in politics or at IBM? But I had no better alternatives. I had no resources. I had to build knowledge through which I could be employed or be able to serve society. I thought reading was the best way to make use of the abundant time at my disposal.

***

The winter vacation in the month of December was over, and the registration process for the second semester of M Phil started on the 6th of January. Students came fresh from their homes, and all looked full of hopes and aspirations. I felt I was stale. I did not go anywhere and remained confined in the same room and the campus for one more year.

This was my second semester for the MPhil course and there was to be regular four classes per day-- three days a week. After this semester, there will be no classes; the Centre will give me one year time to write dissertation. I would have to find a professor who would be my guide to write the dissertation and allow me to take the CSE also.

A professor who was not considerate enough to allow me to take CSE would frustrate me and would not release the JRF. The release of scholarship was linked with my performance in academics and progress in writing the dissertation.

As the session started, routine work took over my life. Before me stood the task of attending classes, writing term papers, taking term exams, and state civil services exams, etc. Apart from that I had to prepare for the interview for CSE, and Prelims. I also had to refine and upgrade my notes of the optional subjects, so that if I got the chance to write the CSE Main again, I would have better notes and score higher marks.

Now new people had arrived on the scene at the campus and new dynamics of relationship emerged. Girls in t-shirts and jeans, walking from classes to hostels, looked as if they would take over the world. Boys ran after them like butterflies flitting and sipping over lilies in a rich garden on a sparkling day. Sometimes I felt if I were physically as smart as these boys, I would have been no less than Keanu Reeves.

Abbas had come back to the campus and he stayed with me. He was most of the time free and spent time with friends on Dhaba and at the gatherings. His sense of humour was inimitable and he told stories of his village and his graduation days adding spice and wit. He was a ready reckoner on which boy was going with which girl, and whose affair had broken, and who had got secretly married and so on. Boys and girls kept him surrounded, listening to his stories and his analysis of the issues on the campus. He was wary of the political parties and maintained distance from the activists.

Abbas came in contact with a fresher Sunita John in Sociology Centre. The girl approached him for guidance to cope with the pressure of the Centre but Abbas won her heart with his smile and wit. And the bond between the two intensified within a few days. Though he was my class-mate, I addressed him as Abbas Sab and gave him high respect. My room-mate Javed Younas also valued him and the two gelled very well.

Many times Abbas came walking with Sunita John to my room in the hostel, and animated my otherwise sombre days. Sometimes Abbas brought spicy chicken preparations, sausage rolls, chutney and dined with Sunita in the thali full of rice which I brought from the mess. Sunita was an easy going girl and did not show the trappings and hesitation which the girls from the middle-class families generally displayed. She was the only daughter of her parents and had a seductive laughter. Her symmetrical teeth shone like pearl beads and added to her beauty. I liked their presence and forgot the challenges which besieged me.

Sunita loved designer clothes. She went to Sarojini Nagar and Lajpat Nagar market every week with Abbas. Always surplus with money, Abbas now borrowed money for Sunita's fancy dresses.

***

I started getting the JRF. It was one of the big things I had seen in my life—something as big as admission at JNU. A man who could not arrange ₹ 800 in a month was getting ₹ 8000 per month for four-five years! Now I had much more money at my disposal than I required. I wanted to buy a motorcycle as most of the scholars receiving the JRF rode a motor-cycle with a lady friend. Riding a cycle attracted ridicule from friends and acquaintances. Walking was more honourable than cycling. Abbas also suggested that I should go for a motorcycle. But after a few days, my desire for motor-cycle dissipated and I told myself I had responsibilities to shoulder. I could not afford to behave like other boys.

I sent ₹ 2000 to home to my parents, gave ₹ 2000 to my sister who studied at Motilal Nehru College, South Campus of Delhi University. My parents did not want her to come to Delhi and study. They dissuaded her from leaving home. But she said she would go to the capital, and got enrolled in BA (Hons) in the college at South Campus; fellow students at JNU appreciated me when they found I had facilitated the study of my sister in Delhi. She was also a victim of my father's personality. When she came to Delhi, my classmate Anju Sani accommodated her in her room for several days before I could find a room for her to stay.

I spent ₹ 2000 money on books and hostel mess fees. Now I had good, branded clothes to wear for the first time in life. Before this, I never had any clothes of my choice.

***

It was more than six months since Jasmine departed from the campus. I thought about her while reading books and felt she would walk to my room any moment. I thought she would give me a surprise and she would come back. She had played a prank leaving me alone and she would return. I remembered her shirt and pinafore dress. But every passing day dashed my hopes. I received no phone calls, no letter, nothing. I would forget her and then she would jump in my thoughts and ruin my evenings.

Sometime, it seemed to me somebody new would take Jasmine's place. Some acquaintances were pushing the thin wall of privacy to enter my world. Many students had a girlfriend and that made the guy without a girlfriend appear incomplete. The environment created a need for a female friend.

Shereen Ali, a MA student at the School of International Studies, whom I met at a hostel night party talked with a honeyed tongue and seemed to be courting me that beautiful evening. Then she met me at the book shop at Kamal Complex while she was buying 'The Chronicles of Narnia" by CS Lewis. She walked back to the hostel with me and talked with a penetrating voice. She addressed me as "Sir" as I was senior to her and said "Sir, I heard a lot about you. I will come to you for guidance." That evening I kept thinking about her.

But the love affair was still not on my mind. I knew the girls stepped in one's life like a barbie doll but soon they became overbearing and poured stress. At best I wanted friends with whom I could have discussed globalisation, Erich Fromm and Charles Baudelaire without a romantic entanglement. I told myself I would be ruined if I entered into a relationship. I had no wealth, no armour, no ship to weather a shock. I had to crack the exam and leave this campus. If I failed in the exam, I would be worthless.

***

Javed Younas churned article after article sitting on a chair in the room with his typewriter. I looked at him in disbelief. I accompanied him to drop the articles in a post box, and they came published in 'The Hindu' after a few days. Younas sometimes offered me an ice-cream from a Mother Dairy vendor as a treat. He suggested that I should read a lot. He said when we read, facts, concepts, and arguments get synthesised in our brains; then there is a burst of ideas from our soul and writing comes on its own. If we do not read, this process would not occur. So, he recommended that for being able to write a good article and paper, one must do extensive reading. But what he did not tell was that reading was one part of the writing process; one must do actual writing, however poor or pedestrian in quality. If one did not write, one would never learn writing. And we believed that an ability to write and get published was as an ability equivalent to fire a battle tank. With our power to write, we would change the course of history.

I reflected on my father's studies and writing. I read like a machine. I took a book in my hand, and finished it in a week or days, and took another. But, my father would read slowly, finish a book in a year. When I was young I asked "Papa, would these books be mine when I grow up?" "Yes Beta," he would say. I remembered one book lying on the table: "100 Great Modern Lives" by John Canning. I calculated that if I read even 40 pages per day, I would finish it in a week or ten days. And I did that. Similarly, for writing, I took up topics and wrote term papers in 5000 words. My effort was to make it difficult and verbose. Scholars like Emile Durkhiem, Karl Marks, Bergson, Dipankar Gupta, etc. were on my mind when I scribbled words on the white pages. Ideas, structure, arguments and expressions were supreme for me.

I read books thinking that it would make my life better. After all, I had nothing else to do at the university. I could either read books, write articles for a magazine or newspapers; or indulge in idle gossip and run after a girl. The second option did not appear to work for my bright future. So I read extensively, whatever I could lay my hands on. It was more rewarding, and faithful, I thought, than learning about who was going after which girl. Reading gave me exciting ideas; I felt I was witnessing the historical events; I was privy to the thoughts running in the minds of the powerful people. I could see the problems of my life were nothing in comparison to the problems of men like Abraham Lincoln, Benjamin Franklin, and Albert Einstein. With my small problems, I was perturbed much more than them.

***

Classes became boring to me. The professors talked about ethnography, Alfred Radcliffe-Brown, Edmund Leach, T N Madan and Trobriand Islands in the afternoon and I felt sleepy. But Prof Amulya Banerjee still fascinated me with his knowledge, power of expression and creative way of teaching. I thought he was a prophet. He spoke the way Kahlil Gibran wrote. His words pierced the soul. The objective of the teacher was to promote a habit of reading, shape us into a person who had a spirit of inquiry, who had courage to question things, and who respected the views of others. He quoted Paul Feyerabend, "The only principle that does not inhibit progress is: anything goes."

One of my hobbies was reading 'The Times of India', its editorial page. I loved its presentations, and its glossy newsprint. I became almost addicted to it. On Sunday morning, the menu for the mess was jalebi, puri and aaloo-sabzi. Boiled egg came at the top of it. I had breakfast while reading the 'Sunday Times of India'. Nothing seemed to be better than doing that. I loved the article by Swaminathan Anklesaria Aiyar. Other students read and emphasised the importance of 'The Hindu' newspaper, and 'Frontline' magazine. They said the level of 'The Times of India' and its editorial was falling every day. It had become a proponent of capitalism and an advocate of liberalisation. People bought it to see the photos of semi-clad women, it had no substance. But, somehow I could never bring myself to read 'The Hindu', and 'Frontline'.

***

It was the end of March. The high temperature was now heating the days and the wind became dry and strong. Dry leaves of eucalyptus, kikar, ashoka rolled on the roads. Campus had celebrated holi and now stress of exams had taken over the young minds. Presentations, seminars and term-papers had kept me busy. Now I had to think of the end semester exam, and preparation of CSE Prelims if I did not qualify for the CSE Main.

The result of the CSE Main was announced. I got the marks-sheet and learnt that I missed the call for the interview by 5 marks. Low marks in the General Studies paper was the reason. It came as a bit of a shock for me. I thought I would overcome the days of deprivation and gloom, but that was not to be. I was back to square one and had to take the CSE Prelims again. This test was the knotty part out of the three tests of the CSE.

The cycle of .events of the previous year repeated. Summer heat seemed to scorch the plains of north India. I had to take end-semester exams, one test for Uttar Pradesh (UP) civil services exam, and then the CSE Prelims --all within a period of 20 days. I went on a night train to Meerut and stayed in a hotel room to take the UP test at a women's college. I was excited to go to Meerut thinking that this was the city where the 1857 revolt started. I passed through the army cantonment area, which would have been the scene of action against the British then.

After the test I returned from Meerut and read the same books and notes for the CSE Prelims as the previous years.

It was a sort of revision. This time while I was taking the CSE Prelim, the situation did not appear that uncertain to me. I had two-three years in my hand, which meant I could take two-three more attempts at the exam. I knew I had no option but to qualify this exam, otherwise I would have to work as a waiter in a restaurant or as a road-side fruit vendor.

I took the CSE Prelims in the first week of June. I was not sure how I performed at the Test that day. The General Studies paper with 150 objective questions to be solved in 120 minutes was a challenge for one and all. Bad performance in this paper was a reason for failure of many. After CSE Prelim, in the evening I sat in a session at Sutlej Hostel with Raj Karan and others, who had taken the Test. The night was hot, and most of the residents had gone on summer vacation. Friends came with their question papers with answer ticked and discussed the possible correct answer. I concluded from the discussion that I scored high, and I was to qualify CSE Prelims.

In my room at 11: 20 p.m., the FM Radio played the song:

"Yeh jeevan hai

Is jeevan ka

Yehi hai, yehi hai, yehi hai rang roop

Thode gham hain, thodi khushiyan

Yehi hai, yehi hai, yehi hai chhanv dhoop."

I thought these lines were worth several books of philosophy. My roommate Younas was out with his friend Musarrat Nazir. I lay on the bed looking at the old ceiling fan and thinking that one day life would be good. I should start preparation for the CSE Main without wasting a moment.

But I was totally exhausted with exams. I wanted to go to a world where there was no place for tests and exams. I loved books, and sitting with friends discussing ideas from those books over a cup of tea. But putting myself in a never ending rhythm of study for CSE was nightmarish.

The university was closed for summer break, the best of mind and beautiful faces had gone to their homes to take a break. Boys like me were there to slog and sweat lonely. Summer heat made the situation horrible. Two semesters of MPhil were gone from my life. My routine was to go to the Dholpur House reading hall in the morning and to return in the evening. I did not talk to anybody for the whole day and felt I would cry. Dogs with foul smell and scabs on their skin assembled and barked at the entrance gate of the House, while the boys and girls poured their focus over the pages of the guide books like Wizard and Spectrum under tube lights. Some out-siders who were not students of the university spent more time running after the girls and impressing them than studying. From them I learnt how not to prepare for the CSE.

❑

Chapter 8

Sick and Pale with Woe

The University had opened and it was now the start of my third semester of MPhil course. Late July rain had made the rocky campus lush-green. Wind was humid and the scent of the earth after rain made one feel good.

Musarrat Nazir returned from her home in Kashmir valley to the university after the summer break. She brought a problem for my room-mate Javed Younas. Musarrat's parents in Kashmir planned to get her married to a US based business-man of Indian origin. But she did not want to get married to him. She told Javed to marry her in order to counter the efforts of her parents. Javed was not the least ready for that. He wanted to carve a career in academics and for that he had to do a PhD at least. That will take at least four more years. He tried to convince Musarrat that what she said was not possible. He would have to talk to his parents and take them in confidence; he had to make a career, and so on.

Javed Younas also did not want to lose Musarrat who in silky chocolate-colored hair, and rouge lips looked stunning. Though from a conservative family, she wore jeans and a shirt, and participated in university's Dramatics Society. She sang any hindi song in a sweet voice with an ease.

Their problem became my problem in the sense that she came to our hostel's room frequently and sat and wept with Javed. She left the room quite late, sometimes at 1:0 a.m. That affected my studies.

I required a room where there was no room-mate to disturb me for good preparation for the CSE. Mid-campus and its hostel rooms were full of activities, and stories. Apart from studies and exams, boys sitting with girls, theatre activities, political contests, etc. occupied the mind and disturbed focus. One day a girl would be teased and a session for the committee against sexual harassment would meet. There would be debate, fracas, assembly and procession. Everybody was politically charged, as if the person who would wear India's crown would be decided at the campus by the students.

Again, I did not sleep the night before the CSE Prelims because of a disturbance in the room. Nobody in the hostel went to bed before zero hour. But one was not fresh and energetic for taking the exam after a night without a good sleep. I thought if I stayed at mid-campus, my CSE Main would again be spoiled.

***

Single rooms were available to the students at Brahmaputra Hostel, located 2.5 km away from the mid-campus, in Purvanchal area of the university. I decided to go to Brahmaputra Hostel at down-campus as it was called. During the registration for the third semester in Mphil course, I opted for a room in the east end, away from the mainland of the university.

To reach Brahmaputra Hostel, one had to travel through thorny babul forest, and renounce the sight of gorgeous faces. The architecture of the hostel, unlike other buildings of the university, was unattractive. Many students did not prefer it because, in this distant land, one was cut off from the developments of the main campus life. But the lure of the single room for a researcher brought me here and I was allotted room number 210 after one year of admission in MPhil. I did not want to come here but I had no option as I wanted a disturbance free atmosphere.

Brahmaputra Hostel, like Rajya Sabha, was a house for the elders of the campus. The students doing M Phil and PhD stayed here. The elan of graduation days was gone from the spirit of these men in their mid-20s. They were busy submitting a thesis, looking for a job, and assuring their lady friends of settled life in the immediate future. The beautiful days of university life slipping like grains of sand from the fingers tormented them. Life and culture here was different from the mid-campus. A girl's hostel did not exist around; that made life simple and uncomplicated.

Every researcher at the hostel was an institution, a bundle of stories, and of dense experiences. Some had taken an interview for the civil services exam without a final success, some had suffered multiple break-ups with their girlfriend, some had their lady friend join the civil services and if they did not crack the civil services exam in the near future, the lady was to slip away from their lives.

The morning at the hostel started with a large mug of milk tea from the steel tea-can kept at the centre of the dinning hall. In the adjoining common room, the 7:40 a.m. BBC world news brought before us the images of Kosovo war, the Kargil conflict, coup d'etat by Pervez Musharraf in the neighbourhood, and of similar other incidents at the coloured television. Some viewers seemed to be sitting at the common room overnight.

Post-dinner, at 9:0 p.m., the residents again came drawn to the common room to watch news laced with the images of violence, destruction, simmering tension with Sonia Singh as anchor on NDTV. Then followed the thrillers and romances on the Star Movies. Those who wanted to study and become successful decamped, and others who were not much bothered with the challenges of life stuck in the room to watch the Hollywood stars like Salma Hayek or Nicole Kidman burn the screen or players Steffi Graf and Gabriela Sabatini run on the tennis court in short skirts. Several movies played on Star Movies channel umpteen number of times, "Golden Eye" by James Bond was one of them. Mukul Dev many times told us what the actors in the movie was going to do next before the scene actually unfolded.

***

In the third semester of my MPhil course, I had no classes to attend. I was supposed to write a dissertation sitting and researching at the library. My topic and research proposal was accepted and approved, and I was to work under Prof Harjot Singh. The time allotted for writing the dissertation was one year. I had heard from the seniors that the guides were tough with the researchers; they prescribed books to the students, went into detail of the chapters of the dissertation, and directed several changes in the draft chapters. It was believed that the quality of the chapters and dissertation reflected the scholarship of the guide also. A third rate dissertation meant the professor was actually not doing his duty.

***

Then my health broke. I had continuous fever for about 25 days and I grew weak and looked like an old horse. Lying on the bed I read Hindi novelist Premchand's Godan. Among other things, the complex web of relationships between an educated single woman, Miss Maalti and an idealist Professor of Philosophy Mehta fascinated me. Maalti was a physician and had worked in England and Mehta was a Professor with high ideals. They liked each other but did not marry. They discussed issues like man-woman relationship, meaning of life, nature of reality and so on and feared the pitfalls of marriage. They somehow represented Mahatma Gandhi's ideal of celibacy, and an ideal relationship between a man and a woman. They thought marriage imprisoned human beings, it prevented the best potential in the man and the woman from unfolding. The idea that a young educated man and a beauteous woman should give themselves to the service of the poor and disprivileged rather than fall in love, marry and waste themselves appeared very original to me. An unmarried man could be of much more use to the society than a married man who would be busy raising his children.

After this book, I read four other books of Premchand-Karambhoomi, Rangbhoomi, Nirmala, etc. This was my first introduction to a Hindi novelist, though I had read

Premchand's short stories. The constant theme of these books were leading a pure life, making sacrifices, performing selfless duty, etc.

After a brush with sickness for a long stretch, I started reading spiritual books. Earlier I was critical of religion and God. I thought religion was an instrument of the weak, a hope of the wretched soul. Rational action could get me ahead in life. There was no need to pray to God for every little thing. If I prayed only instead of studying, I would not get success. But my frequent illness made me believe that there were things more than planning, dedication and rational action. Lying helpless on the bed for almost 25 days continuously I had spiritual experiences. The books I read made me believe that suffering was a part of life; and it was pain rather than pleasure that made us great.

***

After about one-and a half-months, the result of CSE Prelims came and I had qualified for the test. This was the second round of my Prelims-Mains-Interview for CSE. Now, I had to prepare for the CSE Main.

I took up the books for the CSE, though weakness hassled me. From July to October, I could not sit and study. I had pain, cramping, heaviness and bloating in the stomach. This was accompanied by bouts of diarrhoea. I could not sit on a chair and therefore I studied standing with books on the table. When I became tired of standing I lied down on the bed and started again. My friends who saw me pitied my condition. They said I would not live another six months. But, I thought I would fight and survive.

The doctor at the medical centre of the university said I had some syndrome and there was no treatment for that. I knew if I went home, and had a change in food and environment I would be fine within days. But I could not go home because of the impending exam. My weight fell constantly and I grew weaker.

I went for a walk after lunch and dinner, and many times after breakfast for 10 minutes. I thought walking would relieve me from the problem, but it did not cure me.

***

The Centre put me under the guidance of Professor Harjot Singh for research and writing of the dissertation. For reasons unknown to me, the professor was sympathetic to me since I studied in MA. He always wore a maroon turban, and his face looked red with a rush of blood. He spiced his lecture with Urdu couplets and humour.

While he guided me for research, he knew I was preparing for the civil services exam but he did not create a hurdle for me and allowed me to prepare for the exam. A guide for the research could have wrecked the preparation of the student if he did not want the student to take the CSE.

I read several books suggested by him including Ivan Illich's 'Deschooling Society' and 'Medical Nemesis'. I took the book 'Medical Nemesis' issued from the university library to him to discuss something. I had underlined many passages of the book. He saw the book and said, "Who has done such a violence to the book?" I did not know a library book should have not been underlined. I kept quiet.

I heard the name of Austrian psychiatrist and holocaust survivor Victor Frankl and his book 'Man's Search for Meaning' for the first time from him. He was full of praise for Frankl and said what Stephen Hawking was to Physics, Victor was to Psycho-analysis. I borrowed Frankl's book from him and read every page of it. At one place Frankl said "What is to give light must endure burning." I wanted to tell Frankl that I have been burning for years, I did not want to burn anymore.

Prof Harjot loved discussing Austrian psychoanalyst Sigmund Freud—his theory of unconscious, the concepts of id, ego and superego, and the idea of repressed desires. Prof said 'id' contained basic animal and primitive impulses and it was a "seething cauldron of desire". He prescribed us to read Freud's 'Civilization and Its Discontents'.

His love for Freud would make the girls in the class blush. He extensively quoted Freud during his lectures. Two quotes made everybody in the class squirm. The first was: "Unexpressed emotions will never die. They are buried alive and will come forth later in uglier ways." Abbas would whisper, "Holy God! Save us." And the second quote was: "The virtuous man contents himself with dreaming that which the wicked man does in actual life." Boys in the hostel used to quote two lines of a ghazal expressing the same idea. It remained a mystery to me whether our Professor quoted Freud to educate us, or to sink us in the "seething cauldron of desire".

***

My neighbour at the hostel was Pradeep Mishra. He frequented my room to pass time after studies. He was also taking the CSE and attended coaching on his LML Vespa. His theory was to get enrolled at the coaching centre which would make him study and revise the syllabus rather than to study at the room. He was a jovial person and loved wearing fashionable clothes. When he passed from my room he did not forget to knock on my door, spend a few minutes, see what I was studying, pull me and disrupt the order at my room. He kept the environment on the floor relaxed, funny and friendly, bantering with everybody. My other friend Bhanu Singh, who lived outside the campus and prepared for civil services, came to me regularly to update himself with my notes and material. Bhanu had a fleet of cars and a flock of girl friends. His memory was sharp, his focus was developing communication skill to speak like a statesman, being presentable. I could ask him anything—car for driving, notes of the coaching he attended or money for dining at a restaurant—and he would happily give it to me.

***

The CSE Main was scheduled from September. When I thought my notes for Sociology were complete and ready, UPSC changed Sociology optional's syllabus. It was a big shock to me and my old notes became mostly redundant.

To prepare new notes, I visited the library regularly during illness and collected relevant points on a topic. If the topic in the syllabus was social movement, I looked for the definition of the topic, its theories, its types, its manifestation, etc. I could not have asked anybody notes on Sociology, both because I was myself a Sociology student and the guides at coaching centres were themselves grappling with the change in the syllabus. Preparation of notes was not a difficult process if the material on the topic was available in books in the library. But it was not so, and even the books with topics similar to the topics given in the syllabus had not much to offer. So whatever was available, I compiled and kept searching further.

A few students known to me were taking coaching. There was no use asking for notes from them, because they would not share these. A discussion with them showed me that they had a general and common sensical understanding of the topic. On a topic, for example, 'reasons for infant mortality or poverty', they would think of a range of commonsensical causes and write them. But I would do it differently. I would find out what the sociologists and the experts had said on the topic, what were sociological reasons for the phenomena, who were the scholars who contributed in the area, etc. That limited the number of points I would write on a topic, while a student who took coaching for three months could write lengthier answers and score marks equal to or even more than me.

I got one note-pad for each chapter of the syllabus, and noted down points for the topics. I focussed on the structure of a topic: introduction, concept, features, causes, advantages and disadvantages, conclusion, etc. It was a herculean task. The topics of the syllabus did not match with the topics and chapters given in the books. The chapters in the books, if matched with the syllabus, were long and tough. I spent many days at the library working on this. I told myself that studying in itself was not my objective, I had to cull out relevant points. Whatever I read—newspaper, magazine, journals, etc. I looked for the points given in the syllabus. If I read something on middle class, family breakdown, globalisation, I collected points and added them in the notebook under the relevant topic. But the notes I collected did not cover all the topics and chapters of the syllabus. Material in the notes were excess on some topics while nothing or sketchy on some other topics. With such preparation one could not answer a question in the examination hall.

But, I did not feel disadvantaged. Sociology, like other social sciences, had two papers: Paper I and Paper II. Paper I was connected with concepts, theories and the western society. Material was available on this as lots of western authors had written books and done studies. Paper II was connected with the Indian Society, and material on this portion was insufficient as studies on different aspects of Indian Society were not done. Many researchers and faculties at the top Indian universities contributed poorly to the academics and research. And if they wrote something, with a few exceptions, they wrote in bad English and made the subject abstract, complex and difficult to understand. They conveyed simple things in tough language.

***

At the library, Ragni Gupta was getting issued a book from the Text Book section of the library. She teased and said, "Read all the books. Leave nothing for anybody else."

I said, "I started in the morning, but this section has much beyond I can chew."

"You continue till after dinner..."

"The library is closed at night."

"Hameed, some break is also necessary. You should not be greedy."

"I was wasting my time before I came to the university. Now I want to make up for the lost time. But I am getting nowhere."

"Don't worry, soon, you will reach the top," she said and walked to the table with the books. She sat next to her boyfriend Jayant Yadav, a native of Begusarai district of Bihar. Jayant did MPhil in Political Science from the university and had joined a government college at

Ghaziabad as a lecturer. He stayed outside the university at a private accommodation and came to meet Ragni in the evening. Ragni had met him during political activities at the campus.

***

Regular fever and stomach problems broke my spirit. I could not digest what I ate. It was difficult for me to sit and study and standing for a long time caused me dizziness, and tired my legs. But I did not stop. I believed that I had more talent and energy than what this exam required. I thought about the great men who changed society, built empires, founded religion and earned billions. I thought what kind of person I was, who was not able to earn a livelihood , and crack an exam. I read the biography of Napoleon Bonaparte and realised that this captain level officer of the French army rose to become a king, and won palaces and kingdoms. What obsessed him all the time was whether he would be able to leave a legacy after his death—a legacy as big as Alexander the Great. He used to say, "The reading of history made me feel that I was capable of achieving as much as the top men who ever walked on the earth." He was restless all the time. And here was a young man at Brahmaputra hostel struggling with Sociology and General Studies notes. What a shame! I thought.

I believed I would beat the disease and achieve my target. On the notepad, I had noted from a sports magazine the words of basketball player Michael Jordan: "Obstacles don't have to stop you. If you run into a wall, don't turn around and give up. Figure out how to climb it, go through it, or work around it." Such words lifted my spirit and gave me energy to work despite weakness and gloom in my life.

***

Seeing my bad health condition, my seniors, Fahad Ahsan asked me why I looked so weak. He told me to visit one Dr Walia who ran a clinic at Munirka locality. I went to Dr Walia; he gave me medicine for amebiasis. The medicine worked like a magic bullet. After taking one tablet, I was able to sit on a chair and eat food as a normal guy. I felt good and thought everything would become normal in my life. For a month I was fine and was able to take the CSE Main.

One afternoon I went to the mess to fetch water in a bottle. I saw the Blue Star water-cooler at the mess being cleaned. The staff opened the cover of the cooler from the top, picked out a jug of mud. I was aghast and peeked into it with shock. I saw a layer of thick soft mud at the bottom of the water cooler. The dirt came with the municipal water and sat at the bottom of the water cooler. The filter attached to it soon got filled with silt and did not work. I understood drinking this water ruined my intestine and I had lay sick in bed for days, many times a month. I did not know that the cause of pain in my guts was the flourishing community of bacteria in the muddy water-cooler. Bald white-haired Dr Bansal at the health centre of the university had no medicine for me. Whenever I went to him, he gave me a look of 'Why this good-for-nothing fella has come to me again?'

***

Shahid, another scholar on my floor, had a milky white Italian lady friend named Cristiana Fontane. She was amiable and down-to-earth but intellectually average. She wore chic brown frame glasses and looked like a fascinating figure from the fairy tales.

In the hot, sweaty summer, she sat with Shahid in front of a water cooler in his room at the hostel, while he studied

Bipan Chandra for the CSE Main. How the two came into contact I did not know. I never asked him about her, lest he was offended. The only thing I knew about her was that she came from Verona city of Italy.

I showed her one article which I wrote for a newspaper. She suggested a few changes. I posted the article to Narayani Ganeshan of the 'Times of India'. It was published a few days later.

I wanted Shahid to study with me and prepare for the CSE. That would have supplemented my effort. But he had Cristiana to attend and take care, and he could not have left her alone. If he did not give her time, she could have gone to some other guy. Thus, Shahid had to propitiate two goddesses--Cristiana and UPSC at one time. But, simultaneously keeping the two goddesses happy was perhaps not possible. Shahid could not crack CSE Prelims even once. Till today, I feel, had Cristiana not come to him during those crucial days, Shahid would have cleared the CSE.

***

After relief from the stomach problem, I visited a university employee who practised homoeopathy medicine for my fever problem. His medicine worked and I felt better. But the fever returned after a few days. For a long period, my routine was staying 10 days in bed, next 10 days in recovery mode, and the last 10 days at full energy. And then again I fell sick with fever for 10 days.

I realised if my health continued like that, I would return home as a failure. I needed to work on my health and therefore I deliberated what to do. Shahid told me I should start running. That will take care of all problems. So

I started running at the university stadium. But I could not continue. Running made me sick with fever and I stopped. I felt frustrated. I could not work on the chapters for my dissertation.

***

I had set a target to study at least 10 hours a day and read at least 100 pages per day. What I did after studying this much did not matter. I avoided sleeping in the afternoon even for half an hour. I considered sleeping in the afternoon a sin. I had to tire my body and only then I deserved food. Sleeping post-lunch also made me depressed till evening. I also stopped taking curd served by the mess daily in the afternoon. I loved eating curd like ambrosia but it induced sleep, caused fever and upset my stomach. It took me a lot many days to figure out that the villain behind my fever was the curd at the mess and something which I loved the most.

Sometimes, I visited the Dholpur House in the morning, revised my notes under the whirring fan on a humid day and took a walk after every 55 minutes of studying. When I walked I visualised I had passed CSE and I was already an officer. I felt a strange sensation in my body when I made this thought run through my body. I thought about American boxer Mohd Ali's words: "It's the repetition of affirmations that leads to belief. And once that belief becomes a deep conviction, things begin to happen."

While preparing for CSE Main, I also took the civil services exam of the states. I went to take the Prelims exam of Bihar Public Service Commission for state civil services at Ganeshlal Agrawal College Palamu district. The left wing extremists had exploded the railway track and our train stopped at midnight in the forest in Palamu. I kept waiting for the train to move in the coach without a bulb-light in the dark forest. It was a strange experience. In the morning I got down from the train with my bag and somehow reached the exam centre. I took a biscuit and a cup of tea before the exam.

After this exam, I appeared for a lectureship interview by the Public Service Commission, Allahabad. One person in the three-member interview board at Allahabad was hostile. The board interviewed me with objective type questions for about 10 minutes. The questions were like who built the Taj Mahal and when India got Independence from the British. I had revised the dictionary of Sociology and answered most of the questions asked to me in the interview, but I expected them to ask me serious questions which tested the knowledge of a scholar. I returned from the city without much expectation.

***

In December, after CSE Main, I again turned to the library for general reading. Perhaps I did not know what else to do if I did not read books. I also feared that if I stopped reading I would forget all that I read, and my intellect would go down.

I parked my cycle outside the library building at 10:0 a.m. and studied till 6:00 p.m. with a break for lunch. I came across Swami Vivekanand's "The Complete Works" on a shelf in the basement. I felt if I had enough time I would read all the books of the great men. For some reasons the books of swamis, monks, spiritual men and their experiments attracted me. I thought I would get something in those books which would guide me to success; they would give me a shot-cut. With a target of reading 100 pages per day, no book posed a serious challenge to me.

I had come across the quotes of Swami Vivekanand and was familiar with him. His words gave me energy and hope. I picked up different volumes of "The Complete Works" and started reading like a hungry man. The lines like "You will be nearer to Heaven through football than through the study of the Gita," or "The earth is enjoyed by heroes— this is the unfailing truth. Be a hero. Always say, 'I have no fear' " infused energy in me, and made me feel that the challenges before me were nothing in comparison to the power God had given me. I also got his books issued at the library and read them as self-help books in my room while going to sleep. Prof Devender Sinha once told our class that if we read even 10 pages while we went to sleep at night, we would read 300 pages in a month. That stuck with me, and I read one or the other book while I went to bed.

I finished the Rajyoga portion in Swami Vivekananda's Complete Works, without skipping even one word of it. As this book suggested, I tried to make my life occupied with just two things—study and meditation. Earlier, I had read Sigmund Freud's line: "love and work, work and love… that's all there is." But now, I wanted to be on the track of study and meditation and fill my life with these two things. When I meditated at night I felt my wandering thoughts and unruly emotions become still. I fell asleep immediately.

Many times I felt being a Muslim was a disadvantage and being a Bihari was a double disadvantage. But it was a feeling which came and went, and did not stay with me for long. I could not live in a low state permanently. If I was sure that nothing good was ahead in my life then I would have killed myself. Many more times I felt that the world would be at my feet, I needed only to work and wait. Lots of my efforts went on keeping myself believing that good, happiness and great success was possible. I told myself with studies and hard work, I would overcome the challenges. Later, I read somewhere, "Almost every successful person begins with two beliefs: the future can be better than the present, and I have the power to make it so."

In that kind of state of mind, a book and a monk told me "You are made of the same constituent of which the stars and the universe are made; believe first in yourself and then in God; you can do anything, you fail only when you do not strive sufficiently to manifest infinite power," and so on. Such words and quotes like pearls were scattered over all the pages of the Swami's book. At home my father used the word "Mardood" to snub me. This word was used by God for Satan to address when he was kicked out from Paradise. Now I felt I was special, I really had worth. Success was achievable, things were under my control, I was a hero.

***

One day, though I was down with fever, I sat in the library with books. I walked in the shelves stacked with books on psychology, health, spirituality, etc. I saw a book 'Run and Discover Your Strength' by Air Marshal PV Iyer and started rummaging over its pages without a break.

This book proved to be another turning point and changed my life. Earlier when I ran in the stadium and fell sick I carried some assumptions about running and exercise acquired at my native place Jashanpur. The assumptions included one could run only in the morning preferably before sunrise, run bare footed, only on the grass, without eating anything and so on. These conditions were hard to meet as it was very difficult for me to leave bed before sunrise without completing my sleep. This book told me that I could run anytime (except upto two hours after taking meal), run with shoes, eat something light like a biscuit or a banana before running, run anywhere even on the road, take lemonade or juice after run, start with a short distance, and so on. I waited for fever to go, and then I took up running, 400 metre the first day at the stadium at 6:0 p.m. I systematically increased time and distance of running. From that day my fever and stomach problem left me, and my memory improved.

After Swami Vivekanand and PV Iyer, I came across books by Mahatma Gandhi about his experiments with health. I read Gandhi's "Key to Health" and "Indulgence vs Self Restraint" published by Navajivan Trust, Ahmedabad. The book told me about the benefits of continence. Gandhiji said one should redirect his sexual energy to positive ends. Our body uses a huge amount of energy for sex and that energy could be put to better use than satisfying one's animal lust. Sex drive should be sublimated—it should be transformed into creative energy by inhibiting its expression. Doing that would make us healthy, happy and live longer. Sex energy according to him was the source of creative energy of all geniuses.

He said his productivity and genius was attributable to continence. "I have no manner of doubt that the self-restraint is responsible for the comparative freedom from illness that I have enjoyed for long periods and for my output of energy and work both physical and mental which eye-witness have described as phenomenal...It gives a strength to body and mind such as no other process does with equal effect," he said.

I followed the advice and felt that the energy level in my body had shot up. I read the book "Indulgence vs Self Restraint" several times and underlined its pages. My body became a site of experiment. I became obsessed with the idea of self-restraint all the time. I started feeling better. I ate half of what I used to eat, my depression and constant low feeling came down. Half of my energy was consumed in keeping myself afloat, telling myself that the things were not so bad, there was hope. Continence helped me keep my mood good.

I read somewhere that Mahatma Gandhi was a prolific writer. If all the words he wrote in his lifetime were counted, it would be 500 words per day. He attributed his energy and power of writing to continence and sublimation of the sex energy. Sex energy could be converted into painting, dance, writing novels, flying to space.

***

Winter semester had started. Now I was ready to take on the world. I had wasted four months of my life, being sick and weak; that too when I had to take CSE Main. Now, I felt all the health issues were over, and I would enter into IAS in one year. January had come and this semester was the last semester of MPhil. I had to write a dissertation and produce it before Prof Harjot Singh. After that I would enter a three-year PhD course.

I was waiting for the CSE Main result, though I was not hopeful of qualifying it. I also waited for the results of a lectureship interview conducted by the Public Service Commission, Allahabad. All the time I thought of the quote: "It is important that we do not miss it because it may not come again." So I wanted to grab and make use of every opportunity to prepare for the interview.

I went to the library, wrote eight chapters of the dissertation, showed them to the guide and revised them as per his suggestion. My condition was like a mad scientist sitting in the lab, experimenting all the time. The only difference was that I was going to run for half an hour to the stadium.

After running, I felt a rush of energy in the body. I realised running was much better than medicine. My stomach problem was gone, and fever did not grip me even once in four months. I started gaining weight and muscle. I thought had I started running 04 years ago, by now I would have been two years senior in civil services. Now I did not feel melancholic. I continued practising continence and felt I was more productive.

I read a few pages of Mahatma Gandhi's book "Indulgence vs Self Restraint" regularly. Every page of the book implied that sexual energy can be transmuted by depriving oneself of sexual pleasure. The energy can then be used for achieving one's goal. A man ejaculates the energy which is spent to run 20 km during one time masturbation. That is a humongous amount of energy. Wasting so much energy for sexual pleasure was idiocy. These words helped me conserve my energy.

But I did not find any such word in modern literature, i.e. in the books I kept reading. Sometimes, I thought sexual abstinence was an obsession of the Indian mind. Great men like Julius Caesar, Voltaire and Albert Einstein never talked about adding power to oneself by conserving sexual energy. Rather men like Julius Caesar, Robert Oppenheimer, Raphael had a series of affairs. However, I kept going.

I read books on how to write a dissertation. There was no guidance from the faculty on how to write it. I noted down the format of a dissertation after seeing the dissertations of senior scholars at the library. I bought cards on which I wrote ideas about the dissertation. For the first time in my life with the JRF release, I had no shortage of money for buying stationery, yet I used slate and chalk in my room for the rough work. I felt guilty for wasting even one piece of paper. I remembered days when I had no money to buy a copy and a book.

***

Then I received a letter from my sister at Jashanpur; she said she suffered from a severe headache and I should call her to Delhi for treatment. I felt shocked. Scholarship was not sanctioned as I had not submitted the chapters on time. I had no cash and the family needed money. I had given ₹ 10,000 to a person to type the chapters of my dissertation. Anyway, I called my sister to Delhi assuring her that she would be treated at a good hospital and she would be fine soon.

A few days later Murad Shah, who convinced me to take CSE, proposed that I assist him in writing a dissertation for which he was awarded a scholarship by a media house. He said I could buy books on the topic of the project and write chapters structured by him. I said okay. I did not know the amount of labour and time it was going to take. He said he would give me some money and I would learn a lot while writing the chapters. I agreed. I took up the work and went to the library. I worked on this project like a donkey for two-months. But after taking the project I realised it was a blunder. I was divided in my effort and focus when I should have been working for CSE and dissertation. March and April were important months for CSE Prelims and CSE interview. I completed his work and got out of the obligation. The senior gave me ₹ 6000 for two months of his work. I felt I was a fool.

***

The result of CSE Main came and I was invited for an interview. Though I did not expect a great result because of my illness, it came as a trophy. This was my second attempt at CSE. But, I knew I was hanging by a thin margin as I appeared for the CSE Main exam when I was in the worst of my health. If I scored 200 marks in an interview out of the total 300, I would get a job; otherwise I would be at square one.

I took up preparation for the CSE Interview. Writing on Murad's project had wasted a large portion of my time. I was also revising CSE Prelims material. Now, I geared up to prepare for the CSE Interview, and I studied day and night. I practised speaking and told Abbas to ask me as many questions as possible in a simulated interview. I prepared a list of the 100s of questions on my social, academic, educational background and current issues. I went to two coaching centres for interview guidance; they conducted two interview sessions for ₹ 100 each and gave me no tips. I wrote whatever important information I came across on a notepad during reading for the interview.

With the call for CSE Interview, respect for me in the hostel and at the campus suddenly increased. People saw me as being in the race of becoming an officer. Amitabh, a resident of the hostel, took me on a walk and asked me how I wrote the answers that got me marks. I told him the way I had approached the questions. He was impressed by me. He was otherwise very reserved and did not think anybody else to be as smart as him.

I took up the interview headed by the Chairman Ashok Kumar at the UPSC. Neither he nor other board members were impressed by me and they asked me difficult questions. I knew the answers but I was so stressed that I could not collect myself and answer them. During the Interview, I saw the opportunity which had come to me slipping from my hand and I was not able to do anything.

After 15 days of the CSE Interview, the result came. My name was not in the list. I was devastated. I thought I missed it because my health did not support me during the CSE Main. I thought of my disadvantages, the reasons why I would not be able to qualify the exam even if I tried the exam a hundred times. And if I was not able to qualify the exam after giving all my time and resources, I was good for nothing. My whole family was dependent on me. If I did not get a job even after one year, how would my family members survive?

After the result, some of my friends were selected for IAS and IPS. I considered a few of them to be less intelligent and qualified than me. I knew these men inside and out; they could not match me in their comprehension ability, writing skill, and memory power.

CSE Prelim was again on my mind after 10 days. I could not afford to be low and down. All men had to pass through such difficulty. Roman emperor Marcus Aurelius said : "Do not think that what is hard for you to master is humanly impossible; and if it is humanly possible, consider it to be within your reach." The success of my friends rattled me but it also made me confident. Now, I believed that IAS was within my reach because a man who was less capable, a man with flesh and blood like me, had qualified. So I would also definitely qualify. Till now, the candidates whom I had observed from a distance had qualified, but now I saw men, whom I knew like the back of my hand had succeeded.

Day for the CSE Prelim had arrived. On Sunday morning in June, I went to the Kendriya Vidyalaya, near Karkardooma Court in east Delhi for the exam. The road was relatively empty, but the destination was quite far. I tried to give my best for the exam. I was at the peak of my health and energy.

After 10 days of the CSE Prelims, I took a train to Patna to appear at the Bihar Public Service Commission Main exam. I stayed there for 15 days in a hotel and attempted 05 subjects. My exam was good and I hoped for a good result. Exams and more exams had tired me out, but I had no option.

I loved the ambience of Patna. As I stepped at the railway station, I felt it was my land, a place I was bound with. The roads, the river Ganga, bazar, traffic, music, the voices of women—everything made me feel at home. I told Patna that I would come back to her after getting a sarkari job, and I would spend my whole life looking at the waves forming and dissolving in the Ganga. No evening was more enchanting than the evening here, the unruly youths at the exam centre appeared normal and I felt hustle and bustle around as music to my ear. I returned to Delhi on Magadh Express with a heavy heart.

While on the way back to Delhi on the train, I thought I had to submit chapters for my MPhil dissertation. My monthly JRF was spent with my mess bills, family members, and my sister's education. I had no reserve of money to meet contingency expenditure. My one sister was ill; I had brought her to Delhi for treatment.

***

I reached the hostel at the university in Delhi after the exam at Patna. Sudhir Pathak, passing through my room, knocked on my door and entered the room. He gossiped about the girlfriend of a resident of the hostel, who had fallen down from the first floor. The rumour was that the girl was sitting on the window and the boy was kissing her. During the act, she slipped and fell down with a shriek on the grass. While eliciting from me some details of the incident, he took my hand and said the lines on my palm were not in my favour. He then told me about my past, exact years when I faced a particular difficulty. He told me about my grandfather, his profession, and the age at which he died. He said my grandfather was only one son of his father and he was connected with the army profession. He said my grandfather served in the eastern part of India. In reality my grandfather served in the British army in Rangoon. The more he said the more flabbergasted I became.

I thought what kind of thing was palmistry, one could even know about the relatives of a person and their profession, age, disease, etc.

Then he came to my life and career. He said I had no bright prospects in my life. The possibility of me qualifying a competitive exam was nearly zero. If I ever cracked any competitive exam that would be because of my hard work and not because of luck. In the end he said, hard work could change negative into positive and failure into success. He said if I wanted to crack civil services I would have to slog a lot because success was not going to come to me because of luck.

The words of Pathak broke me. I kept thinking about his words for hours after he left. I came out of the hostel building, took a fresh whiff of air. I wondered what Jasmine would have been doing now. How she would have been looking in maroon dupatta. Had she been with me I would have been scaling Mount Everest. Then, I went to the mess, had dinner of rice and aloo-gobhi. At night I meditated for 20 minutes. I remembered the words of Kerala born Vedic scholar Adi Shankara, "I meditate in my heart on the truth of the radiant inner Self." I felt a little better and after some time slipped into deep sleep.

I felt meditation calmed my sexual urge. I told myself this was perhaps because my sexual energy was channelled from the lower part of the body to the upper part to energise my muscle. The words of Swami Vivekanand ran in my mind that by meditation we are able to reach the house of creative energy.

Good thing about me was that I remained under stress for about two hours after listening to such apocryphal predictions. Thereafter, I was full of ambition and belief that I would make it to the top. I thought I was also made of the same mettle as Julius Caesar, Pulakeshin and Attila the Hun. The next day was another day. Morning was bright and promising. The sun told me the earth was for you to run and conquer.

***

Next day in the morning I went to the library and worked on the dissertation. I had forgotten all the nonsense Pathak had filled in my brain. I told myself, God had sent me in this world's battle to be a hero.

At the library, in a corner, I surrounded myself with the books, old dissertations, blank-sheets under the soft tubelight. I wrote sections of the chapters thinking how students at Oxford University would have been writing their dissertations and theses. Then my three classmates—Anju Sani, Alka Jamwal, and Nirupama Menon, busy with their MPhil dissertation, saw me and came to me for time pass.

Anju said, "It would be good if you get into IPS. Imagine a young angry man full of anger and idealism joining IPS. You would thrust all the scoundrels in jail".

"If I get into IPS, I would issue an arrest warrant against three university fairies and ask them why they tortured a poor soul in the university library".

Nirupama said, "We will come to you with Jasmine. She will also sit in the interrogation room".

"Jasmine will also go to jail," I said.

"You are so angry with her," said Alka.

Anju said, "There is a reason for that. She has gone, leaving *bechara* alone."

I smiled. Jasmine's name evoked in me the memories of gone days. I folded my hand and said "Madam, we have a few days left to submit our dissertation. Let us work on that." They smiled and went to their seats.

I returned to the hostel at around 5:0 p.m. and changed into a sports dress to go to the stadium for running. I read somewhere that the important thing was to gain a passion for running; to love the bright morning, to love the trail, to love the pace on the track. Then everything was going to be great in one's life. So, I was now going to hit the track in the stadium to fill myself with freshness and energy.

In front of the hostel sat Asad Rahman, Apurva Vishwanath, Chandrakant Patil, Raghav and others on the paver benches amidst thick foliage on the dhaba shaded with broad, leafy trees. Sun was going down behind fern-like leaves of gulmohar trees. They discussed the works of Rainer Maria Rilke and Pablo Neruda. They were charismatic characters of the hostel. I wished I had the memory power like them and could speak as they did.

In their discussions, governments rose and fell; civilisations and cultures clashed; monarchs and prime ministers came and went; centuries and millennia passed; Karl Marx, Thomas Macaulay, EH Carr and Edward Gibbon dropped in and intervened.

Many times their discussion continued till 2.0 a.m. over a plate of aaloo-parantha, boiled egg, omelette, egg-bhujiya on the tables strewn with yellow petals of amaltas flowers. A chance visit of a lady student in finery to the hostel distracted the students for a moment, but then they sprung back to the topic.

Asad Rahman, Apurva Vishwanath and Chandrakant Patil argued like orators and statesmen with command over language and facts. But seniors like Raghav Pandey did not like high flying ideas and arguments, and used crude words to silence others.

Asad Rahman would say, "There was a myth that if a girl liked a useless fellow but was shy of expressing her love for him, and if that fellow smoked, then the girl would reprimand him. She would extract a promise from him that he would never smoke again. Thinking this, I smoked bundles of cigarettes and burnt my lungs. I wished somebody would come and snatch my cigarette. But nobody came to me."

My departure from the hostel for running in the stadium provoked adverse comments from many fellow students and friends sitting at the dhaba. These comments did not dampen me a bit. I told myself any fool and idiot could complain, criticise, condemn; I should not bother. I returned after half an hour of running on the ground. It took twenty minutes to make it to and fro.

***

I completed chapters for my dissertation in June and got it bound. The university was again closed for three months for summer vacation from May to the second last week of July. I dedicated the work to my mother, who always supported me, whether I was right or wrong. She stood with me when my father bullied me, and made my life bearable. She gave me unconditional love and told me not to worry. She blessed me and guarded me always from assaults and streams of invectives of my father.

❑

Chapter 9

Out of Darkness, a Ray of Hope

It was May afternoon. I walked into my hostel room after lunch. The FM Radio played the song "kahan tak yeh man ko andhere chhalenge". I stood at the window and absorbed the intense melody of the song. One line of the song said: "Those who departed in the journey would come across you again." I thought it was a lie. I was not going to meet Jasmine again. Films and songs created a feeling of void in our life. Or it intensified the void existing in life. If I thought about her, saw her photo, or read her writings, the tempest of emotions would wreck me. I would not be able to study. I had to prevent her from infiltrating into my thoughts.

From the window of the room, I looked at the grey sky. The lone gulmohar tree faced the hot sun. Rain was few and far between. I wanted rain pouring from the sky night and day in Delhi and cooling the thirst of my soul. But that did not happen.

***

CSE Prelim result came and my roll number was in the list. I thought I was hanging by the cliff, I had to secure my position and climb the mountain top. I saw it as another life chance and opportunity to come out of misery. I picked up all the notes of Sociology and Psychology from the shelf of the room and started revising and upgrading them. On the top of a notebook I had written from somewhere a quote of the American chess player, Bobby Fischer, "A strong memory, concentration, imagination, and a strong will..."

I did not want to read even a word of these notes; I had read them several times and they had grown boring for me. But I told myself I would get a job, a position and status by reading these books. Reading 'One Hundred Years of Solitude' by Garcia Marquez will get me nowhere. Those notes were my bread and butter and I should focus on them. I had read them in the drowsy summer afternoons, sweating evenings and lonely nights like they were a passport to my success.

When I was not reading books or revising notes, I used mnemonic techniques, and recalled the names, theories, studies, and points. Sometimes I recalled the names and concepts starting with one letter, say, 'T' and they triggered a chain reaction of words, names and concepts, e.g. Tocqueville, T H Marshal, citizenship, Anderson, and so on.

***

In the newspapers, I read that floods caused extensive damage in Bihar. My mother told me on phone that at Jashanpur it rained as if a cataclysm was to devour the earth; as if everything would sink in darkness. I yearned for that kind of rain in Delhi.

I remembered, at Jashanpur one afternoon in July at 4:00 p.m., the weather suddenly changed. Black, dense clouds hovered in the sky while rain loaded cold wind blew after a sultry day. I rushed to the rooftop of the three-story building which was like a large playground to enjoy the evening. The sky appeared closer and the strong wind seemed to blow us off from the brick-roofed floor.

Asma Zafar, my neighbour, also came to the rooftop to see the magic of nature. She would usually drop in at our house to interact with my sisters, Mom or with me, when she was bored of studies.

Children of the families living in the different flats of the building also came up to the top. I played with them 'Chhuaa-chhuyee' game in which one child tried to chase and touch one of the several children around. After the game, I stood with Asma at the railing while her dupatta fluttered in the wind. She dressed her thick hair everytime the wind dishevelled it. Lightning flashes appeared in the dark sky like blood arteries and veins on the heart. Asma said she would go to Patna to take an Assistant Grade exam. I told her she should practise the test papers, that would give her speed and accuracy.

Then Zulekha aunty came on the roof shouting at the top of her voice, "O! Chhora! You go out of control when you see a girl?"

I had done nothing to receive such a remark from her.

As aunty uttered these words, a thunderbolt from the dark sky descended and passed over us. It struck the adjoining house at a distance of 30 metres. We were stunned and our revelry stopped. The passing charge scattered us all over the roof and we fainted! I got up, saw all around, it was dark and everything smelled like charred flesh. Our hair and skin were burnt. I noticed some children fallen and some trying to stand up. Asma was holding the hands of two children and rushing them towards the staircase. I picked up aunty and tried to make her stand. I felt somebody had lobbed a grenade over us. Then, I did not know lightning killed lots of people every year in Bihar. It was a narrow escape for about 15 of us.

***

In between, I wrote a synopsis for the PhD thesis in the library. I had two years to write my PhD thesis. I thought I should complete this before I left the university. Also, if I did not submit synopsis and chapters for the thesis, scholarship under JRF would not come.

For the thesis, I wanted to work on the model of development which would suit India. We had a capitalist, socialist and mixed-economy model for making India a developed country. I wanted to know which of the existing models was good, or should India follow an entirely new model of development. I studied theories of developments, different models of development and their interplay with the society and community, international institutions pressurising a country to follow a particular model and so on. It was mainly a field of economics, but sociologists also studied society and economy.

I prepared a synopsis and showed it to my guide Prof Harjot. He wanted me to work on some other topic. I stuck with my area of interest. I had to do quality work in that area. Finally, my guide agreed. He suggested changes and I worked on them sitting at the library.

That evening at about 5:00 p.m., my three classmates—Anju Saini, Alka Jamwal, and Nirupama Menon came to the library and stood near the desk I was sitting on. They started ragging me.

Anju said, "With this much labour, you would top the exam."

Alka said, "It seems you have fallen in love. Only love makes one work so hard."

Nirupama said, "Who is inspiring you to work from morning till evening, may I know?"

I laughed. I could not outwit them. I said, "I may be spared, if I committed any mistake."

They smiled and walked towards the textbook section.

I worked on the synopsis for hours for a month and finalised it. Next, I made a presentation to a board of faculty members who approved it. The synopsis contained an outline of the research and chapters. After this, I had to write the chapters.

***

Many of my classmates had left the university. Two had gone to Harvard University and others to Australia and England. Girish Appu, a senior and masters in History, was going to a university in the USA for further studies. He also came from my native place Jashanpur. I thought those working in academics were showing some progress, joining a university as lecturer, going abroad or getting published a paper. But I was not going anywhere after doing MA. Life for me was sickening and boring.

My classmates at the university were now like senior citizens of the campus. Exuberance and enthusiasm in them were gone. They were scared of the future. Four years back, the future looked promising to them. They were to rule the stage of the world. Now, they thought if they got even a small job, that would be worthwhile.

I had moved forward from the aim of going abroad for studies. I was fighting a battle for the civil service. I did not now request anybody to guide or help me get admission in a foreign university.

I filled up a form for Prelim of Uttar Pradesh Public Service Commission (UPPSC), as many students from the hostel had done it. Now the date for the exam had come. Though it was a diversionary task, I took up the exam in June at Jagdish Sharan Kanya Inter College, Begampul, Meerut, travelling from Delhi in the early morning. Exam was good and I expected I would pass.

Then, CSE Main started. I took General Studies CSE Main at a school at Geeta Colony, and the rest of the papers at UPSC building. This time I was better prepared. At the exam hall I wrote answers at a relaxed pace. For the essay paper I wrote on a topic related to the status of women and argued for their freedom and empowerment. I mentioned the studies and theories of Sociology.

For the current affairs portion of General Studies I studied Spectrum guide book. It was a thick book with lots of points. One reading was not sufficient to make one able to answer the questions in the exam. I revised it thrice but it was voluminous and difficult to master.

The CSE Main concluded at the end of November and it exhausted me completely. Mere thought that I had to take an exam caused me stress, it seemed to gush unlimited adrenalin in my blood. And an exam on which depended my future caused me much more stress and ruined my present. I was supposed to use every moment available before the exam to prepare for it, and not waste time gossiping, sitting idle, or watching television. All the time I had to work. But I wanted a bit of leisure time, the time when I could have sat on a rock and seen colours ripening on the slopes of a hill, an antelope passing through the bushes, a flying peacock sitting on the wing of a babul, autumn leaves rolling aimlessly on the metalled road.

***

I came back to my routine of reading in December. I also started writing chapters of the thesis. Using the free time for academics would keep me free in the coming semester when I may have to take CSE Interview and CSE Prelim.

Three classmates working on their thesis again saw me at the library and surrounded me.

"Why are you blushing so much?" said Alka.

Nirupama said,"Jasmine was asking me about you."

Anju said, "I have not seen a man who turns away a beautiful girl like her."

I was looking for a book in the catalogue. They spoke in soft voices and pulled me, while students sat and studied books.

I said,"Yes, Jasmine called me last evening."

"Haan? She called you?" said Alka.

"What did she say?" said Anju.

"She told me 'I love you'," I said.

They felt embarrassed. Alka smiled and pulled the other two to go. I thought I would have to invent this kind of reply to counter them.

I came to the desk with the book 'General Theory' by English economist John Keynes and made notes for using them in my thesis chapter. The book was the magnum opus of Keynes and a senior suggested that I go through it at least once while writing anything on development models. Everyone who came across me suggested a book to read, such was the environment at Brahmaputra Hostel.

Then, at 6:0 p.m., Abbas came to me at the library and told me to go with him for a cup of tea at the canteen. He had taken the JRF exam conducted by the University Grants Commission and looked tired. It was the month of Ramazan, and he had gone to the exam centre while fasting.

He said his mind went blank during the exam. Things looked dark, and he felt giddiness.

I said, "You should not fast while taking the exam. In fact, till you are a student you should not fast. One has no energy left in the body when one is fasting."

He said, "God's help will come. Fasting is farz, mandatory. Even a rickshaw puller fasts."

I said, "Religion is pulling us down. We should eat and be strong and not starve our body. When you are supposed to sprint, you are depriving your body of energy."

He said, "I believe in God. He gives success or failure. Books and hardwork are pretexts. Behind the scene the will of God is at work. Energy comes from God, not from food."

I said "God wants you to act, work, strive and struggle. Not to sit idle and wait for the loaves of bread to come. It is our work which gives us success or strength, not prayer or fasting. When Atilla the Hun slaughtered the Christian monks in 450 AD, God did not come to rescue them. Frustrated St Jerome asked God 'O Lord if their sword will kill me why did I embrace Thine exalted cross.'"

We finished tea and returned to the hostel. Sun had set long back, and the chill numbed my body. The vegetation around was invisible in the fog. My head and fingers were frozen, and I shivered in a brown sweater and jeans.

In the room after dinner, Abbas talked about the French philosopher René Descartes. I loved Abbas's talk on philosophers and philosophy as he simplified the philosophy and told the matter in a story form. He said, "Descartes was the founder of modern philosophy. He was a rationalist and contributed to the rise of the Age of Reason. Philosophers like Spinoza and Leibniz belonged to his camp. He loved travelling and mixing with people and one time he even joined the Dutch army. It is said that he read a little and did not work hard. Though he never married, he had a daughter with a servant girl Helena in Amsterdam. He was always well dressed. His famous line is 'I think, therefore I am'. What Prof Amulya Banerjee calls 'arrogance of science' is rooted in Descartes' thought."

I listen to Abbas as if he was telling me a fairy tale. I thought Descartes, as one of the greatest modern philosophers, must be a scholar with woolly hair sitting with books at a library.

Then my room-mate Javed Younas came to the room and said the environment at the university was deteriorating day by day. I said, "Javed Bhai don't think so much about the environment. Let us go for dinner." We walked to the dinning hall as the students savoured rice with mutton and mutter-paneer under the milky light.

***

On the evening of December 31, I was strolling in the mid-campus near my old hostel Periyar. Moideen Kutty, a senior in the Economics Centre and a native of Kerala, parked his motorcycle near the hostel gate. He saw me and told me to come for a walk with him if I was free. It was 11 p.m. but I agreed to walk on the wet and lonely roads towards the administrative complex.

I had shared my questions about the existence, the meaning of life and the whims of the creator with Moideen Kutty earlier. Though, I made several conclusions about spiritual and religious issues, but those questions inveighed me repeatedly. Moideen Kutty was well read and worked with a library of the USA in Delhi. He said he would give me time when he was free and would clarify my doubts.

Now, he broached upon the topic. On the road covered with fog, a boy walked with a girl in a ponytail, his arms draped around her. I politely raised questions disturbing me and underlined contradictions in religious scriptures. Walking along with the tall, silent trees he listened to my queries for a few minutes, but soon he got annoyed.

He asked, "Why do you love people and why do you want to serve them?"

"Because so many people live in abject poverty, they do not have food and shelter."

He thundered, "But Why?"

"Because I feel their pain and I love those living at the margins."

He was frustrated with my answer. He had come for a walk to help me find God and clear my confusion.

He said, "You have never done deep thinking on the issues of life, death, ultimate goal, God, etc."

I said, "The questions relating to these issues disturb me all the time."

"But your answer to my questions show you never underwent any trauma thinking about these issues. You are only deceiving myself and others."

I kept silent. We walked further on the desolate road. He asked "Have you read the Koran?"

"Yes."

"What did you gather?"

"Reading the Koran, I found all the verses there could be categorised into four: one telling humans to remember God all the time. These verses are repeated all over the text."

The word 'repeated' infuriated him.

He changed from being a guide to a hostile person. Before start of the talk he was nice and affectionate like an elder brother. But now he said I was an imposter and I wasted his time.

When I finished Rajya Yoga, I realised the questions which inveighed me disturbed also Swami Vivekananda.

Swami reached the conclusion that we ought to love and make sacrifices because we are unit parts of the same total soul. But I did not understand this answer, nor was it my conclusion.

Moideen Kutty was puritanical but was well read and influenced by the Hindu religious thinkers.

He said, "Social science and its theories or the writings of the thinkers are no use to understand the basic questions of life and society. Our knowledge from books cannot help us understand the spirit and ultimate questions. They dealt with the surface reality. You read Swami Vivekananda again."

His conclusion about social science shook me. Emile Durkhein, Karl Marx, Jonanthan Turner, Clifford Geertz, Jurgen Habermas and men like them were our gods. They were final words on society and economy. Were these brilliant minds misguided, fake?

He said, "I thought you were in a real spiritual quest and wanted answers to important questions of life. But you are faking distress and an insincere person."

After these words, nothing more was left to discuss. I never did make someone change his opinion about me so quickly. I said, "Okay, Moideen Bhai." We walked back to our hostel which was about 2 km away. It was 12: 30 a.m. and fog enveloped everything. I kept thinking his remarks about me being fake and imposter, but I could not understand what made him conclude this about me.

***

Registration at the university had begun from January 5, after the end of the winter semester. Life and activities had returned to the campus after the start of the new session.

I took up further writing of the thesis chapters. My guide made several alterations in the chapters. He said, "The sentences should be tight. Every extra word should be removed. Paragraphs should be coherent." He edited the chapters, told me to read monographs, critiques of the existing development theorists, and so on. He directed me to make so many changes that the labour I put in writing these two chapters seemed to be a waste.

At the mess table Sunder Singh, a senior, said we should aim to convert the thesis into a book. One Adam Aloysius of the university published a book out of his thesis from Oxford University Press.

I said, "Sir, I am not able to write chapters which could measure upto the expectation of my guide, and you are telling me to write for publication."

"Why? You write well. But chapters for the thesis must be of a higher quality than that of dissertation. Writing a thesis is training for writing a book. It should be original and a work of scholarship."

"Yes, sir. I was trying my best to do that."

After dinner we watched the news in the common room. A large number of Indian paramilitary troops were killed by Bangladesh forces on the eastern border. The newsman showed the gory picture of the dead soldiers.

***

I had no penny in my hand. My two sisters were in Delhi and I had to give them money for room rent and food. My one sister gave tuition to the daughter of the landlady. I went to their room and guided them at least two times a week. I hoped if they studied they would become my support and the condition of the family would improve.

I would get the fellowship released when my guide approved at least one chapter of the thesis. I went to my guide Prof Harjot Singh with a lot of courage, and stood near his table. He was writing a chapter with an ink pen under a big table lamp with yellow light for an edited volume on citizenship.

Wearing a tight brown turban, he smiled and said, "Yes, Hameed?"

"Sir, I had no money to pay even for my mess bill," I said, as my voice choked.

Prof Harjot Singh became emotional and told me to bring papers, he would give approval. The sound of ceiling fan filled the room, and white blank papers fluttered on the table. Books on shelves, table, cabinet, etc. gave the room a clumsy look. "The Men Who Ruled India" by Philip Mason with a yellow cover page lay in the corner of the table. I thought while some men ruled India and I was struggling to meet two ends meet. It was such a big shame.

After a month, I resubmitted two chapters, making the desired changes. My guide kept them at his table and said he would call me after going through them.

***

I received a letter from UPSC in April informing me that I had passed the CSE Main and I should be ready for an interview. The letter with a form to be filled up asked for several information including the names of two referees to whom I was known. I gave the names of Prof Harjot Singh, my guide and Prof Raj Kishore. I got the filled-up form attested by the Administrative officer of the School Bhanwar Lal, a bearded, nice man. Date of interview was by the end of April.

Now I had to prepare for the interview. I had around 20 days to go. I made notes and prepared for the expected questions on my educational qualifications, places I lived and educational institutions I studied. I had nothing to show for my extra curricular activities, leadership qualities, achievement in sports and talent in school or college. Nor could I sing the song of my poverty and deprivation. I had no answer to the question why I wanted to join civil services, except that I wanted a job.

The chief of the board was George Matthew. He was a nice and kind man. He asked me questions about corruption, climate change, why I wanted to join civil services, etc. I could answer most of them. The interview was neither good nor bad. On the basis of my performance in the CSE Main and Interview, I hoped I would be through.

In the evening when I returned to the room at the hostel, dozens of students asked me what questions the interview board asked. I repeated the questions three--four times. But more and more students asked me about the questions, then I wrote the questions on a piece of paper and showed the paper to the students who asked me. But this offended them, and they thought that I was being arrogant.

***

Now, I felt a great life was waiting for me after a month, when the interview result would be announced. It was difficult for me on some nights to get sleep. My room on the top floor was heated and was not conducive for the night's sleep. The chain of thought about the exam, interview, and Jasmine ran uncontrolled and did not let me sleep. I would get up from the bed, meditate for some time and then try to sleep again. But these days even meditation seemed to fail to contain chaos in my mind and the rush of thoughts. In the daytime, somebody would ask about the result, and interview, and that would make adrenaline rush in my blood and disturb my peace.

On May 15, at 3:0 p.m. Persanna came to the hostel from mid-campus on a bike and said the result of CSE had come. It was time to go to an internet cafe and see the result. I walked to Shahid's room to take him along to see the result. But the room was bolted from inside. I knocked on the door but he did not respond. I thought he might be sleeping, but 5:0 p.m. was time to wake up. Then I heard the sound of moaning and heavy breathing which made me think he might be spending time with Cristiana.

I came to my room, kept the water bottle on the table and took a glass of water. I looked at the room and wondered whether it was time to leave this destination or to continue living in drudgery. I thought if I continued there like this, then when would I see the country and the world, its mountains and rivers, snow and sand dunes. The leaves of the trees standing outside the window ruffled in the wind. The gulmohar tree smiled and told me to go and check the result.

I did not want to go alone. I came to Shahid's door again. I knocked as the room was still closed. This time Cristiana in a navy-blue T-shirt and black trousers opened the door. Shahid was at the study desk busy with a biography of Indira Gandhi by Katherine Frank. Cristiana was sweating profusely though the fan was running at its maximum. Her face was red. She welcomed me and told me to take a chair along the wall. I saw Shahid's hair completely dishevelled. I told them the civil services result was out.

"Did you see your result?" said Shahid.

"No, I would have to go to a cyber cafe. Please accompany me."

Shahid was in no mood to come along with me when Cristiana was with him. Soon Anurag, Shekhar, Chandrakant and others also came to the room. Shekhar said, "This year's result from JNU was poor. Mugdha, Chibber, Anupam, etc. could not get into IAS." Chandrakant asked me whether I saw my result.

"I am going to check it."

Finally, Shahid, Anurag and myself went to see the result walking on the lane from Brahmaputra Hostel. The chai-dhaba was as usual crowded with the men in shorts and T-shirts discussing democracy, Indian Constitution and strands of Marxism.

My steps were frozen, abundant kaner, and gulmohar trees and peeping boulders along the track did not tell me what was in the womb of the future. We reached the cafe and I opened the website while others waited outside, and gossiped.

The UPSC website loaded very slowly. I was holding my breath while my hand shook on the key-board. My heart was pounding, and I could feel its thrust within my chest. The website finally opened and I looked for my name on the pages. When I could not find my name even after 10 pages, I pressed 'Ctr F' and typed my name: Hameed Akhtar. I was at the bottom at serial number 400 in the list of 430 successful candidates.

I was happy and satisfied. My objective was to get a government job and take care of my family, get my sisters married. I thought I would be able to achieve this target with any job which I got through the civil services exam.

I came out of the cafe and informed my friends. They said, "Better than nothing," and congratulated me. I dialled my mother and informed her.

After an hour, somebody pasted the result on a wall in the hostel. When the result of CSE came, I had a strange feeling. In my mohalla Gulab Ganj, gangs fought turf war and killed members of the opposite gangs firing and tossing a sutli bomb. Within seconds, the scene of normalcy of the place, movement of the people, dissolved, and blood, and torn pieces of body lay scattered all around. When a student came running in the hostel and announced that the CSE result was declared and so and so qualified the exam, I had that scene replayed. The result made and finished many lives. The entrée of an ordinary student into IAS or IPS was nothing short of a shock.

I felt the hard work had paid me. Had I been healthy, I would have cracked the exam two years ago. Had I performed well in the interview, I would have ranked higher. I thanked God I was now on the shore. The result did not bring much happiness to me as it was too little and too late. I was expecting much more.

The next day, 'The Hindu' newspaper carried the names and the roll numbers of the selected candidates. My father at Jashanpur bought the newspaper with pride and showed it to the family members. He was happy that I had qualified for the exam.

***

Students at campus greeted me but the moment they came to know about the rank, they frowned upon me.

They gave an expression as if I was going to be a clerk in a mufassil town.

When I studied in class 10th, my aspiration was to become a bank clerk. I saw Nabeel Ibrahim, a bank clerk in my neighbour-hood. His father-in-law had only daughters, so he lived at his in-law's spacious house. His wife was gorgeous and graceful. He had twin sons, whom I tutored for some time. They were a Sayed family, sophisticated in their manners and up-bringing. Nabeel went to the bank in the morning and returned with fruits and sweets in the evening on a Vespa scooter. I thought life could not be better than that. So cracking the CSE was a big thing for me from that perspective. Yet I was going to get Group B service in the central government, which was not an ideal achievement after so much of the effort.

I had to take the CSE again to improve my rank and get better service. Most of the candidates, including the one who got selected for IPS, prepared for the next CSE to enter into IAS. As I ranked at the bottom of the list, I had to take the exam again.

But UPSC had made the next CSE a challenge for me. It changed the syllabus for the Psychology paper. The topics were new, and I had no notes on them. If I went to the exam hall to attempt the Main exam, I would be blank in the Psychology Paper.

***

Now the CSE Prelim stared at me. This was my fourth attempt. This was the last year of my fellowship. If I did not qualify now, I would have no money and time to take more attempts at CSE.

I took the CSE Prelim at Senior Sec Boys School at Andrews Ganj in mid-May. I had mainly revised my notes which I had been using since my first attempt for the CSE Prelim. Some books and notes had become my lucky charm and I read only them. I bought current affairs magazines and made myself familiar with the developments. I gave one month for the preparation of this exam. I felt bored reading the same stuff and I thought I was going nowhere despite reading the material so many times and investing so much energy.

On the evening of the test, five guys including me sat in the room of Prem Kumar at Jhelum Hostel after dinner to compare the answers we had ticked. That would give us a fair idea how many answers were correct, and whether we were through or sunk. During the sitting, four guys were on one page and I differed from them. Their answers matched. By the end of the session, I was convinced that I was out of the race and was not going to qualify for the CSE Prelim. I walked from the mid campus to Brahmaputra hostel at 11:30 p.m. I was not very much convinced that their answers were correct but I believed I was in a risk zone. My success in the CSE Prelim was not certain. That evening I slept at around 3:30 a.m. I wondered how much time this exam was going to take. I have been working on it for years. I did nothing except work to qualify for this exam. I wanted to do other things after getting the job. All those things were waiting.

***

After the CSE Prelim, I wanted to go home for a week. The routine and the place had tired me. I was closed in the campus for more than a year. I came across the term 'fascism of sameness'. I met the same people daily, ate the same food, saw the same things around. The beautiful campus and its surroundings were now taking life out of me.

I took a blue bag and rode a bus to the New Delhi railway station. Whenever I went to the railway station, I stood at the overbridge, looked at the surroundings and thought one day I would be returning to Jashanpur with my mission accomplished. I visualised this while taking the train. Now, I was happy that I had achieved success. But I did not know where I was going to work and live the rest of my life.

At home, my parents and friends were happy to see me. They were nice and kind to me as usual except for my father whose condition for giving love to anyone was dependent on compliance with the precepts of the religion. Religion was the centre of life for him; and job, children and other things lay in the periphery. I wanted to tell my Dad that life was not made for religion and endless religious practices; they were made for human life and for making it beautiful or ugly or whatever way one took it. Delhi born sufi poet Mir Dard had rightly said:

"Dard-E-Dil Ke Wasty Paida Kiya Insaan Ko Verna taa-at ke liye kuch Kam Na they karr-o-bayan"

(God created humans for bearing pain. Otherwise, for worshipping alone, He had countless angles.)

One evening, one of my neighbours, Irene, walked to my house. She was going to get engaged with a lecturer in a college in naxalite affected district of Moosabad. She graduated in Psychology from Sanjay Gandhi Mahila College in the town. Years back, one of the boys with a crush on her came to attack me with a bat when he saw me standing with her on my roof one cloudy evening. I did not want to take risks for a girl and said sorry to him. Now, I did not know the status of that guy.

I was standing with her at the railing on the first floor of the flat. She said, "Now your life would be different. There would be people running at your command." I did not tell I had got a petty job and that counted for nothing. The world thought I had reached Elderado but I was still rowing a boat in search of a shore. I thought how beautiful God had made her. She would be a prize of the person who would marry her.

Then a light blue Jeep with rifles hanging on their shoulders stopped at the road near the house. The policemen carried a paper with my photograph, and asked about me and my address as they entered the mohalla.

Entry of police in the mohalla generated lots of interest among people. Everybody stopped their work and saw whose head police were looking for. Visit of the policemen to my mohalla was very common given the number of the desperadoes adorned the streets and indulged in a regular gangwar, felling a few bodies at least once a week.

I was also seeing what these policemen were doing but had no inkling that they were enquiring about me. Four-to-five tall police constables stood in khaki with .303 rifles on the arterial road. One fellow carrying a revolver on his waist was their senior and was making an enquiry.

When I learnt that they were enquiring about me, I was shocked. Irene looked at me and asked, "You really passed the job exam or there is some issue." She meant whether I committed some crime.

I was shocked at her question. Seeing the police, she was in doubt that I cleared the exam for the job conducted by the commission. I thought I would convince and impress her later; first I should deal with the calamity at hand.

I came down without wearing slippers, and told the policemen there: "I am so and so." My legs were shaking and my mouth was parched.

I saw they carried my photograph. They asked me a few questions. Then my mother sent tea cups and snacks, and my uncle Mr Rasheed gave them bakshish. Things became a bit pleasant.

At the university I had heard that the policemen came to the house of the candidates who qualified the exam for an enquiry about their address and background; and I had conveyed the same to my mother. My compatriots assembled there and tried to listen to what the police asked. After five minutes, policemen jumped into the Jeep and turned back the vehicle.

When the policemen left, men who gathered there to see the tamasha asked me what was the matter. I said they had come to make some enquiries about me. But these men were not convinced with my answer. They said, "Why they were there? They do not inquire about a person of good repute."

I thought to tell them, "Get lost. I do not owe you an explanation."

My mind was preoccupied with what Irene might be thinking and how I would convince her. I will tell her my name and roll number which was published in the newspaper.

But between all these, she disappeared from the railing and walked away from my house. She was scared of the police. She did not want the Police to ask her an uncomfortable question like what she was doing there at my home.

My cousin issued a statement that the police were searching me all over with my photo; I made them return by paying some bribe. They were suspicious that I had committed some serious crime and I was hiding at home.

***

I decided to return to Delhi after seven days. I could not bask in fake glory. But Shahrayar Parcha who helped my father financially and also gave me money sometimes proposed my marriage with his daughter. Shahrayar was sure that I was going to get a good job and he should not let the opportunity slip. I said he should give me some time to think over the proposal. I said I was taking one more attempt to get a better service. But he pressed a lot and asked for engagement. He thought if I got a better service my bargaining power would increase and I would escape his tentacles.

The girl was beautiful, boys of the mohalla talked about her grace and sophistication. She had studied at the convent school of the city Sacred Hearts Academy and was academically good. I had seen her in my childhood when she went to school in an ambassador car and after seeing her I got an idea how the rich people like her lived. Then, I roamed aimlessly in the locality and sometimes passed her house. I was not a fool to nurse an illusion that one day his father would come to my family with a proposal for her marriage with me. But, after that I had not seen her for years.

Proposal from that family was an honour, but I could not have agreed. I said please give me some time. But, Shahrayar Parcha wanted the engagement when I was there.

My parents did not impose their will on me on this issue. They wanted me to marry a girl of my choice. When I saw Shahrayar was not ready to relent, and pressed my parents hard, I told him to make preparations for engagement. That night I could not sleep. In the morning I woke up and left home with sports shoes for running at Gandhi Maidan. But, I did not go to the ground. I boarded a train at Jashanpur Junction to Mughal Sarai and from there to New Delhi. I called my mother on the telephone from Aligarh and told her that I was on the way to the university.

❑

Chapter 10

A Letter from UPSC

It was July and I returned from home after enjoying accolades. I again got busy with work. I had to write my PhD thesis and take the coming CSE Main in two-three months. I had qualified for the CSE and if I cracked CSE Prelim again, I would be at the top of the list of successful candidates in the CSE. I was fresh from home and worked from morning to evening. I had tasted the fruit of labour, I thought the harder I worked, the better my life would be. I would have a house, bouquet of roses, a friend, books of Kahlil Gibran and the aroma of incense.

Running and continence gave me wings to fly. I had energy to work on my ambition. Mahatma Gandhi's book on continence said semen retention gives man a tremendous amount of energy. One should redirect one's sexual desire for women to ultimate goals of life. I kept working on this piece of advice and felt I could drink the ocean. But then everything went into a meltdown.

One afternoon a few days before the CSE Main, I checked my letter box at the hostel gate to see if I received any post. That was a routine act. I had got a letter in my box from UPSC. I thought it was a letter informing me about the service allocation and an invitation to join the job.

I walked out of the mess building to take a walk on the open lane with gulmohar trees standing along. I opened the sealed letter and read it. The letter informed me that though I had qualified for the exam and ranked 400 in the total 430 candidates, but I was not allotted any service.

As the implication of what I read entered my mind, the world around me tumbled. I thought how could this be true? I had never heard that one could not get a job after qualifying the competitive exam. The letter written by a Desk Officer of UPSC said candidates who were included in the general merit list of the UPSC and claimed the benefit of reservation as OBC candidates were allocated to services as OBC candidates. Though I was selected as an OBC candidate, there were no seats in the OBC category. All the seats were grabbed by the OBC candidates who ranked higher than me in merit. I did not understand anything in the letter except that I was not going to get a job. I felt like vomiting. I returned to the room when I realised I could not walk any more.

With the letter in my hand, I walked into the room of Pradeep Mishra at the hostel and told him about the content. He snatched the letter from my hand, read it and looked at me with disbelief. He said, "If there was one person in the world who could be told unlucky it was you." He said he had not heard anything like that before. Within a few minutes others on the floor also came to know about the letter and looked at me with sympathy.

***

For a few days, everything looked dark to me. I did not know what to do and where to go. Everything seemed to have slipped out of my hands. Energy and enthusiasm had gone from my body. I asked God what I did to meet such a fate. A friend, Kumar Rangarajan who also got such a letter from UPSC, came to me and proposed to go to court against UPSC. He talked to a lawyer who asked for ₹ 50,000 as fee. I told Rangarajan I had neither money nor energy to fight this battle.

Then, slowly, I reconciled with reality. I realised that the time which was available to me was an opportunity to reverse fate. If I did let the time go, feeling depressed all the time, I would be a loser. Faiz Mustafa left a piece of paper on my table with the words, "I am not concerned that you have fallen; I am concerned that you arise," in his beautiful writing. I pasted the paper on the wall in front of my reading table.

I started preparation for the CSE Main. I had about two months to go for the exam; it would start in the last week of August. I shuttled between the library and the room for study. I stopped being my normal self, and cut myself from the outside world. I studied and studied. The world outside the campus was terrible, it would crush me if I went out without a job. Revision of the notes was the primary task, but as the syllabus of Psychology optional was changed, I had to prepare notes for that also. The university had no department of Psychology, and therefore the library had no book on the subject. I went to the Delhi University library in the North Campus about 20 km away for two weeks. The exercise was not useful as the material on the topics given in the books were not available; research studies to quote in the answer were outdated; and the books were old. I was tired after making it to and fro in the evening; smoke on the roads caused headache and summer heat drained all energy from me.

***

One afternoon, Bhanu came to my room at the hostel in shorts and Adidas shoes. He told me, "You scored 320 marks in Sociology. It is a shameful score for a student of this university. Students who studied for three months at a second rate coaching fetched more marks."

I said, "In social sciences you cannot score more than 320 or 330 marks."

He picked 'India Today' magazine from my reading table, and said, "You are mistaken. I know one IAS officer, whom I call Bhaiyya, scoring 400 marks out of 600 in the Sociology paper."

I was shocked to hear this. It was something unimaginable.

"Why did you stop at 320 marks?" He chided me.

I thought the highest one could score in Sociology was 330 marks, and my ambition was to touch 330. Scoring 400 marks was like trying to beat the speed of light. After all, Sociology was not Mathematics or Physics where one could score so many marks.

Bhanu said, "After studying Sociology in JNU, if you cannot score 400 marks then you are a moron. Who knew Sociology in India more than students and faculties of JNU? Bhaiyya scored 400 marks taking Sociology as second optional and studying it only for three months."

In the CSE if one scored 60 per cent marks, he/she topped the exam. The prevalent belief was that one could score a maximum of 330 marks in a humanities subject.

I remembered reading Todd Skinner, a mountain climber, "If you are not afraid, you have probably chosen too easy a mountain. To be worth the expedition, it had better be intimidating."

But Bhanu's talk made me feel ashamed. It was like a eureka moment for me. I told myself, "Scoring 400 marks is possible. And you have to score this." Now I studied the subject with this thought.

***

Then Shahrayar came to Delhi and took me to Karim's restaurant at Hzt Nizamuddin locality for dinner. I had no time to go out for dinner but I thought to bear with this headache momentarily. During the dinner, he said what I did at Jashanpur was an insult to him; it caused them embarrassment in the social circle. I said, "I did not know what to do when you pressed me. I am preoccupied with this exam. If I get engaged or married, my exam and years of labour would go to waste."

My mother had advised me to convey to him my view frankly, and we should not come under his pressure. I said okay to my mother but I did not say any hard word to him. There was no fire in my belly. Entering into a fight was not my nature. I had learnt that if you gave your piece of mind to a person, you would make an enemy out of him. I said, "Let me finish the work. I was not going to go away anywhere. I will come back to you." He relented and returned to Jashanpur.

***

CSE Main started on August 20, I took up the 4th attempt at CSE Main thinking it was a do or die situation. I knew it was my last chance. If I sank, my life would be a 'tale told by an idiot'. Running in the stadium daily in the evening kept me sane. It stilled the cacophony and the train of negative thoughts in my mind. I looked at the wall of my room pasted with the words: "It is war, you cannot afford to lose."

This time my exam centre was at Upras Vidyalaya at Delhi's Vasant Vihar locality. I wrote General Studies answer paper like a mad person. I wrote answers with much more content and speed than I did at earlier exams. I told myself I was sprinting and more speed and more content at the answer-sheets would take me ahead of others. I used pens of different colours, and left proper space between the paragraphs. I kept the sentences and paragraphs small; used simple day to day words. I wrote one point in one para and moved to another para for the next point.

In the evening, at my hostel room, I thought I had made a blunder in writing the answer of the General Studies paper. The technique taught to me was to attempt the questions whose answer one knew best. So I attempted question number (c) of 1, and then question (b) of 7, then question (a) of 8, next question (b) of 1, and so on. At home I thought over it and thought this would sufficiently ruin the mood of the examiner and he would think that I was an idiot. That dampened my spirit.

Exams for optional subjects were held at Exam Halls Building, UPSC building. I went to the exam hall thinking I would score 401 marks in Sociology optional. I answered questions in more than 700 words per question. Earlier I finished at 600 words. I also wrote 15-20 points for each answer against my earlier attempt to reply giving 10-12 points. I wrote as fast and as much as I could. I thought the more I exerted the better my performance would be.

I wrote about the political elite in the answer criticising them as a class existing for themselves, and not working for the poor and disprivileged. I was scared how the examiner would take my answer. This answer was to reveal my line of thought and political orientation. I thought if the examiner belonged to a conflicting political and ideological orientation, he would run me down. To answer the short-notes in the question paper, I defined the concepts, gave reasons and explanations, mentioned the theorists, and wrote conclusions. After the exam, I prayed to God and asked for 400 marks.

As a consequence of a target of 401 marks, I scored 360 marks in Sociology. I had never crossed the mark of 320, while writing the CSE Main three times.

One day, after the exam, I went to the residence of a Member of Parliament opposite the UPSC. The son of the MP was a student leader at the university. The boy knew me but I had a formal relationship with him. I went with my friends who were his classmates.

From outside, the flat appeared to be a modest accommodation, but from inside it was a spacious place with an ambience of a bar—loud English music, larger than large pictures of 'gori' girls all over the wall, countless bottles of wine, high tools, boys and girls with small clothes. After a few minutes we retreated from the residence as we wanted to revise books and notes in the time gap between the two papers. But that ambience shocked me and made me think what kind of life the privileged of the country were living.

The last paper, Psychology, was to be held by the end of November. But as UPSC had changed the syllabus, the time available with me was used in collection of material on the topics in the syllabus, visiting different libraries in Delhi. Pradeep Mishra at the hostel had coaching notes on the changed syllabus, but I did not ask notes from him for the obvious reason that he may refuse to share it with me.

Then the day for the Psychology paper came. I took the exam paper at the examination hall at UPSC. I answered the questions of the first paper reasonably well but my hand started shaking when I saw the questions of the second paper. I knew the answers of only two questions and very little about the other three questions. In total I had to attempt five questions, each in at least 700 words. One cannot think of success in this exam if even one paper was answered badly. I wrote whatever I could write as an answer to those three questions.

When I came out of the exam hall I was low. I believed this bad performance could fail me in the exam. I had done creative writing for answering Psychology question papers. I did not write anything from the Psychology textbook or notes. My answers were as good as a student of Physics attempting the question of Philosophy. This was my fourth and last attempt. This was also the fourth and the last year of my Junior Research Fellowship. If I did not qualify, I had no money to survive or continue my studies.

***

CSE Main was now over and it was December. After the exam I tumbled into depression. Extremely busy with exams, I was suddenly out of work. The speed train of my life had suddenly stopped. University was closed for winter vacation, only a few students stayed at the campus. The garden of roses, kikar and peacocks was deserted. My feeling of loneliness was intense and agonising. Sometimes I felt I had no energy in the body to strive; I was defeated. Bad performance in the Psychology paper of CSE had taken everything out of me: all my hope and energy. It seemed all my efforts since the last five years had gone to waste. God had not made any connection between work and result. I thought I would have to leave the university and vacate the hostel very soon. When people asked me how I attempted the paper, I said 'It was fine', but my heart shuddered with the thought of the result. Then I remembered lines of a Sufi poet: "If you find snakes and scorpions everywhere, Don't worry—God will keep you in His care."

For a few days I did not know what to do. Firoz Alam, a senior, came to my room and told me to taste liquor, I would feel better. He said, "It is the season for wine, roses and drunken friends, my dear," and laughed loudly.

Firoz was doing PhD at the Centre of Political Studies. His memory was phenomenal. He took CSE and appeared for CSE Interview twice, though never studied systematically nor prepared even one page note for the exam. He kept a plant of cannabis at his room window and consumed its leaves. He spoke English only when he was high with a peg of Bacardi. I believe he would have gone to the CSE interview board at UPSC after loading himself with a few pegs of rum in order to speak English with confidence. That would have annoyed the interviewers and they would have downgraded him.

I said, "I do not need it, life gave me so much bitterness to taste that I needed no more bitter wine."

He thought I did not drink because of religious reasons. He said, "Religion was a lie. The Westerners tell their children that as trees take birth, grow and die, similarly human beings grow young, old and die. You see the concept of hell. People in Arabia consider hell to be a furnace of fire, but among the Tibetan the hell is unbearably cold, a frozen place.

"When you dig the question, the religious people would say I don't know. God knows better. It is God's maslehat. They refer the issue to the third party – to God."

"Fear of death leads to religiosity. How religious a person is depends on how much he fears death. Fear is a personality trait. Sociologist TB Bottomore discussed one more stage after the scientific stage. Man again becomes religious after the scientific stage."

I said, "My one target is to see God as I am seeing you. And the second target is to find out Jasmine wherever she is."

He said, "You will never succeed in the first endeavour. As for the second, Jasmine herself will come to you."

He guffawed like a monster. I felt good when somebody challenged my intelligence, quoted authors, poetry, their theories. I came out of the room with him and went to the room of Faiz Mustafa. He was underlining the lines in the book of the 11th century Persian philosopher and polymath Omar Khayyam:

"When you are so full of sorrow
that you can't walk, can't cry anymore,
think about the green foliage that sparkles after the rain.
When the daylight exhausts you,
when you hope a final night will cover the world,
think about the awakening of a young child."

***

After a few days, the year was to end and to become history. But this time I was not thinking that one year had gone. I was thinking about my whole life. About the future which I did not know. About the difficulties which might come across. My heart was choked with emotions, I could not bare it to anybody and share my incapacity and bewilderment.

Friends repeatedly asked me when I was going to join the service. I tried to forget that I was not going to get any job, but repeated questions by my friend made me shudder. I told them I would join the service in March-April. I thought about the sacrifices I made, the hard work I did in the hope of a better tomorrow. I avoided listening to music, watching films, indulging in gossip, going out with a woman, and so on, all in the hope that better time would come. Today when the result of CSE came before me I was clueless as to what to do. My life turned out to be a joke. All my sweat and labour could not get me a job. My mother, my sisters lived in poverty and deprivation. Their life was to become better after my good result. But things were dark as far as I could see.

My situation was worse than the time I stepped in Delhi seven years back. Rather, at that time, I was full of hope and energy. Then I thought all the happiness and success of this world would be at my feet. I would bend my fate. But now, where was the goal which I wanted to achieve by hard work and determination? What would Jasmine think, whom I neglected for studies. This time UPSC advertised 300 posts, less than the previous CSE. Possibility of getting selected for a job now was lesser. My fellowship was to last for the next six months.

I thought I should look for a private job now, maybe to go to Zaheer again at Okhla. Looking for a job after six months when I would have no JRF money would not be the right time. I applied for a driver's licence and went to a Honda showroom to see a motorcycle.

***

I did not go home during the winter vacation from the first week of December. I continued running for 30 minutes which kept me free from health problems. I utilised the time writing articles for the newspapers. I wrote five articles for the newspapers and dropped them at their office at Bahadur Shah Zafar Marg. I got three of them published. The publication boosted my mood and brought appreciation from the students around.

I was not getting any fellowship from JRF because of a delay in sanction of fellowship by the guide. I had no money to pay for the mess bill, and get fresh registration done at the University next month. Most of the time the fellowship was sanctioned once in six months when the guide was satisfied that the scholar had made progress in writing the thesis. I had submitted two chapters for my

PhD, while I was supposed to submit three more. During the winter vacation, I worked on one more chapter. Writing two chapters would complete my thesis.

Studying for more chapters for the thesis in the library under the high ceiling, I felt the place was no longer exciting. Now it was time to go from there. This was the same library where I thought by reading books I would change my fate and this world. I looked at the places where I sat and talked with Jasmine.

I remembered the fourth floor where Jasmine sat with me. The lift, magazine section, the table, the water cooler, everything reminded me of her. I felt I had become mad. Her images, her voice, the smell of her body did not stop running in my imagination. When I closed my eyes, the picture of her face became more vivid.

***

Some winter evenings post-dinner, I spent sitting near the heater with Faiz Mustafa. He was always bubbling with infectious energy. The way he said something made the message more powerful. Though a student of Persian language, he prepared for the civil services with Political Science as an optional and was familiar with all the philosophers and thinkers of repute. His family background was good but his brothers in the cloth business did not give him expenses. Always dressed well, he knew that I kept low thinking about Jasmine. He quoted Friedrich Nietzsche and said, "Resist all sentimental weakness. You are a man. You are born for a greater purpose. You do not want to be known as a lover of a woman. You have to leave an imprint on the earth." I could even climb Mount Everest if he told me, but I could not get Jasmine out of my mind. Yet, I felt good and hopeful listening to him.

The university opened after the winter break of one month, and smart, young faces returned to the campus. The semester started with the registration process. Fog enveloped the hostel. Nothing was visible ahead of a metre. Flights stopped for days in Delhi.

I went to the library feeling as if I was an old guy, my prime was over. I sat on a chair and continued writing the chapters of my PhD thesis. My plan was to write the thesis in the next six months and benefit from the opportunities in academics. Many students taught in a college in Delhi or outside as visiting faculties and earned some salary. A PhD degree would make me eligible for that at least.

I went cycling to the library, parked the cycle in front of the building and worked till evening. I felt low all day, and did not interact with anybody. It was the autumn of my life and career. I had no energy left to write the chapters but I continued. Jasmine and the letter which I received from the UPSC haunted me all the time. I believed with hard work I would reshape my world and the world of my family members, but the CSE result broke me completely. I compared myself with the rich, powerful and famous boys around me and cursed myself seeing one life they were living and one life I was living. If God wanted me to live in penury and difficulty, why did he give me wishes and dreams? He could have made me dumb and deaf.

I read books to utilise my free time as I thought it was the best use of time and this work will give me maximum return. Though now my faith in getting output from reading books was shaken, I continued reading nonetheless as a matter of habit. One afternoon at the library I finished reading a book 'Unto This Last' by British philosopher John Ruskin. I found mention of this book many times in Mahatma Gandhi's writings. This book had helped him build his concept of 'Antyodaya' and formulate the Talisman which we found written in NCERT books. 'Good of the individual is contained in the good of the all,' he had concluded. I felt compelled to finish the book with old, pale pages. In the beginning I found it difficult to progress this 100 pages thick book but by the end I felt it was worth reading. The book was a critique of the existing political economy. At one place Ruskin said the art of becoming rich is not an art of accumulating money for ourselves, but of contriving to make our neighbours to have less wealth. In other words, it is the art of establishing inequality in our own favour.

***

I took chapters to my guide Professor Harjot Singh at his office. He was a figure in contrast to me. While I was always depressed and low, he was high and jovial. He was filling a form on his academic career and trying to recollect what he did during which year. He said he was not a very serious student and failed to make the best use of many opportunities in his life. But I wondered if he was a Professor at a top university, what more one could ask for. Then he dialled his wife and talked to her in Punjabi in a way a newly married couple would talk. He addressed her as "Meri Hukumraan." He was then 60. He recited one Urdu couplet: Ek saal gaya, ek saal naya hai aane ko, par waqt ka ab bhi hosh nahee diwane ko." (One year had passed, and a new year was to come; yet the lovelorn was not aware about the time).

While he talked, I saw a book 'Essentials of Rumi' on his table with a quote by the 13th century Persian mystic poet, Rumi:

From love bitterness became sweet,
From love copper became gold,
From love the dregs became pure,
From love all the pains will become medicine.
From love dead become alive,
From love the king is made a slave...
Sweeter than this poison I did not see any drink,
Lovelier than this illness I did not see any health."

The quote sent me thinking about love and which kind of love Rumi was talking about. Then Prof Shaili Raman in short hair and sari came there and they started talking about the difficulty in confirming a train ticket. I realised this was time for me to leave. I kept the chapters on the table of the professor and walked back to the library.

In the evening, I returned exhausted to the room after the whole day's work. Evening was the most difficult time for me because depression tortured me the most. Running at that time countered gloom and I felt better. Had I not been running I would have been nowhere.

I walked into Faiz Mustafa Bhai's room. He was reading Lebanese author Kahlil Gibran's book 'The Prophet' under a table lamp in his room. I pulled him out of the room for a walk on the road.

***

Now I waited for the BPSC exam result. If I qualified for this exam, I could serve as Sub Divisional Magistrate or Deputy Superintendent of Police in Bihar. I would be protected from the rough and tumble of the private sector. I could also try for a lectureship job but I needed some money for a year at least to finance my attempt.

Then a friend Rahul Singh, studying at a university in Delhi, approached me and told me to assist him in writing his dissertation. He offered me some money and help in learning to drive a motorcycle. I was tired of such work but I agreed as I had no money for regular expenditure or to pay the mess bill. I helped him in writing a 180-page dissertation for about a month. I worked with him for about 8 hours daily at the library. He paid money at the rate of ₹ 5 per hour for internet surfing for research. His work made me familiar with the internet and computer. This assignment exhausted me completely.

Next, I worked to write a guide for NET for Sociology for a publisher, who said he would publish the book. The publisher promised to pay me an amount of ₹ 50,000. The notes on NET with me could make a good guide for the candidates taking this exam. I sat at Dholpur house, worked for a week. But I got bored and could not move after writing two chapters.

Hundreds of ideas raced my mind all the time on how to ride over the coming cataclysm. Friends suggested repeatedly that I should go to court against the government for not providing me with a job. But the litigation cost was so prohibitive that there was no question of taking this step. My third sister had also come to Delhi for studies, and lived in the room where two other sisters were living. I hoped I would get her enrolled in a good institution.

***

I made preparation to fill up forms for the Ford Foundation fellowship. This fellowship was given to scholars from the weaker sections from Asia, Africa, Latin America, Russia, and the Middle East countries for graduate or postgraduate degree programmes in the Western universities. I thought with my academic records, I stood a good chance of getting this scholarship. If I was awarded the fellowship, I would get money for studying abroad. With a degree from a western university I would be placed better in the job market, and my life would be good.

But filling up the form was a challenging task. It required writing essays on a topic of research, clarity on the issue I was going to research, recommendation by the reputed faculties on my academic credential, and so on. Things were to be done on computer and internet. I had just picked up typing on the computer keyboard. These facilities had newly arrived at the university, and one had to wait for his slot at the computer centre to use the internet; or one could go outside the university at an internet cafe.

Yet I filled up the form, making a lot of effort and spending time on it. I sent the format to Prof Harjot and Prof Raj Kishore to write about my academic credentials. They wrote in glowing terms about my knowledge and hard work and returned the sealed envelope to me to send it to the scholarship officials.

***

I caught a new and unlikely hobby of weightlifting in the gym at the hostel. A few days ago I surfed through Nelson Mandela's autobiography, and I came across many inspiring words. He wrote: "I found the rigorous exercise to be an excellent outlet for tension and stress. After a strenuous workout, I felt both mentally and physically lighter... I attended the gym for one and a half hours each evening from Monday to Thursday...We did an hour of exercise, some combination of roadwork, skipping rope, callisthenics or shadow boxing, followed by fifteen minutes of body work, some weight lifting and then sparring." That a political leader with abundant moral authority and a role model for many also indulged in rigorous physical exercise, and weight lifting made me think for hours and I fiddled with dumbbells and barbells.

I also participated in a weightlifting competition at the hostel. It was a long journey for a man who was thinning because of health problems. What amazed me more was that I won prizes in the competition. At my early age, I thought those who built bodies, exercised in a gym, were non-serious boys, not interested in studies. And those who studied and were career conscious did not visit a gym. But experiences, and reading made me cast off my misconception.

Now with exercise and running, I was not tired though I worked from morning to evening. I felt my body was tough like a rock. I thought I was benefitting from Mahatma Gandhi's book "Indulgence vs Self Restraint".

At the gym I interacted with a fellow hostel resident Mahesh, who had a sculpted body. Unlike me, he was a heavy weight lifter, and practised at punching a bag. He was a student of the School of Languages and studied Hindi literature. Always wearing a smile, he worked hard for the civil services exam and his only engagement in the day was to study and work-out at the gym. He interacted a little with the fellow students.

Some time his girlfriend Madhulika Verma came to the hostel in a T-shirt and jeans on her metallic blue scooty and brought a spicy chicken burger for him. When Mahesh was not present in the room, she came to the gym looking for him. She also drove him to the mid-campus and dropped him back to the hostel. While Mahesh aspired to become a civil servant, Madhulika was active in student politics and stood at the forefront of all the protests and rallies. Mahesh accompanied her when she went on moon trekking in the rocky forest of the campus with a team of trekkers on a full-moon night. I saw them parting ways. Mahesh did not qualify the CSE in four attempts. Madhulika had high idealism and ambition. She could not go much further with him.

***

It was April and the advertisement for the CSE had come in the 'Employment News' again but I did not fill up the form for the exam and planned not to take the CSE any more. I had no time, energy or money to sustain this show.

Bhanu came riding on a Bullet motorcycle in the evening. He was surrounded by so many girls but showed no sign of distress. I did not know how he managed them. He told me that he enquired about the result and I would be through for sure. I felt good listening to him but I believed he had no first hand information on the issue; that was his wishful thinking.

That night I had a nightmare. I dreamt that I had lost the battle. I immediately woke up and sat down on the bed in the darkness. The fan was whirring. I thanked God when I realised that it was a bad dream. The result was yet to come. It was 2:30 a.m. and the dawn was away.

Then the CSE Main result came and I got a letter from UPSC for an interview. I bought a white shirt of Arrow brand and a new navy blue trouser. Abbas asked me for the shirt; he wanted to wear it while going to meet a top politician of the country. I told him no but he insisted. He said, "This is your last attempt at the examination. If you succeed in the interview, you will not need this shirt. You will have a truck load of shirts. If you fail, your status will be that of a dog and then also you need not wear this shirt."

Though what he said was demeaning, I saw logic in his statement. I gave him the shirt to wear. He travelled on a blueline bus and after meeting the politician he returned my shirt mauled with stains and spots.

On the day of the interview, I reported at the UPSC at 10:0 a.m. This was my D-Day, if I won this day, life was going to be less difficult and if not, life would be a punishment. My turn for the interview came in the afternoon at about 3:00 p.m. By that time I was bored, low at energy and hungry. I ate some biscuits but that was not adequate to beat my hunger. Unless I ate rice and daal, I was not going to feel normal. When I was hungry, I could hardly speak. However, there was not much that I could do.

I entered the interview board and greeted ladies and gentlemen. Anamika Mukherjee was the chairperson of the board. I took a seat and after an introductory exchange, tough questions ranging from global warming, to corruption to why you want to join civil services, etc. were darted at me. Madam Mukherjee was harsh and ruthless. She asked me about my selection last year by the UPSC. "Why didn't I get an appointment?"

I told her the reason.

"How did you fill up the priorities of the service in the Main form?"

I had given IPS as the second and IFS as the third priority. She being an ex-IFS officer, my choice and preferences infuriated her.

I said, "Ma'am the suggestions of the senior, discussion with other candidates and my family background influenced the choice."

"Oh! Public opinion rather than the information we provide to you in the Government of India gazette influences you."

One time she shouted and said she wanted me to think and apply my brain. She gave me 149 marks out of 300 marks. In the last interview I secured 173 marks. Many years later when I learnt Anamika Mukherjee passed away, my eyes became moist and I told my friends that the lady because of whom I was in the service was no more. My earnest wish was to meet Mukherjee at least once. But that did not happen and I did not try to locate her. That pain will always remain in my heart.

I took a blueline bus from Shahjahan Road in the evening after the interview to the hostel. I saw the crowd and pollution on the road. I thought if I did not qualify the exam I would mill around like the men on the road. At the hostel, a group of students surrounded me and asked me what questions they asked me and how was my interview. I said Anamika Mukherjee was the board's chairperson and she was tough. I told the students the questions the board put to me.

Next day, in the room, I removed the books from my study table. All the books and notes were connected with the CSE Interview. Now I had to work for my PhD and finish my course in six months. While removing the books, I felt I would weep. Shifting of the books and notes marked the end of one phase and the start of another phase of my life and career. I thought: "God! How many times would I be doing this? When will success smile at me? Some men rule this earth, change the course of the earth, build empires and conquer territories. But I am not able to crack one simple exam. What type of man am I?"

***

It was May. After the CSE interview, I again sat in a corner of the library and worked on the PhD chapters under a ceiling fan. Weather was terribly hot, the day's temperature hovered near 46 degrees. Reading the material for the thesis bored me. I wanted to read something else like Karen Armstrong, V S Naipaul or Samuel Huntington, but that was a luxury. I read Economic Survey, Amiya Kumar Bagchi, Gunnar Myrdal and Amartya Sen.

The three fairies met me at the library, and asked me how my interview was. They were also submitting the last chapters of their PhD.

"Today you are looking very smart," said Anju.

"Yes, do you see, his shirt is Arrow brand?" said Alka.

"Yes. Dekho, his face is like Shah Rukh," said Nirupma.

Today I had no answer to counter them. I thought they must have planned in advance who would say what.

Then I blurted, "Yes, Nandita Das has gifted this shirt to me." The film actor had come two days back to the campus to speak on women's issues.

"Oh! She must have been impressed by you."

"Yes, she is looking for an actor for her next film," I said. They realised today I was combative. They thought they had pulled me enough, smiled and walked to another table for their work.

I appeared at the Ford Foundation fellowship interview at Qutub Institutional enclave. The board asked me what I was doing at the university and on what topic I intended to do research. These were not simple questions. They were looking for a focussed researcher with good academic credentials. My grade was above 90 per cent and the topic of the research was relevant. I hoped I would get the fellowship and study abroad.

***

Several students had left the hostel and were working as senior officers in the state bureaucracy. One of Faiz Mustafa's close friends Mohd Ghazali, with whom he started preparation for CSE exam, my neighbour Pradeep Mishra, another student from the floor Sushanta Talukdar and many more from the hostel had joined IAS. We did not know those who did not get job as faculty of a university or civil servant in government. What kind of difficulties they were facing. Faiz Mustafa told us the story of "The Old Man and the Sea", a thin book by the American author Ernest Hemingway. The story was about an old man fishing in the sea but was not able to net any fish. One day he caught a huge fish, so big that he was not able to pull the net. Faiz meant to say that we should have patience, keep trying, we will qualify the CSE. I tried to read this book several times but could not progress more than 10 pages. I was more adept to read non-fiction books—books on philosophy, politics, psychology, religion, sociology, etc. than a novel. But Fahad Ahsan used to say that if I wanted to learn the art of writing I should read Hemingway. He was a Nobel laureate whose writing style should be emulated. I remembered Hemingway's words, "There is no friend as loyal as a book."

***

One week later on the dinner table at the mess, Saurabh, a resident of the hostel, told me that the CSE result would come on 15th May. The same night, Udai Pratap, a fellow civil services aspirant, came to my room at 9:0 p.m. and said the result was expected to be out the next day in the evening. Pratap's father was Chief Secretary in West Bengal. Listening to him I felt I had to fight a war at Panipat the next morning.

Next day, I went to the library at 9:30 a.m. and read Bernard Cohn's 'An Anthropologist Among the Historians'. I was thinking all the time about the exam result while I was flipping through the pages of the book. Feeling bored, I went to the Centre and collected books on sociology of development. Junior students surfed the internet and bantered. For them a PhD student who had not left the university with a job was a dead-wood. In the computer room, I accessed the UPSC website to see whether the CSE result was out. The website said the result would come on 15th May at 5:0 p.m. I felt shaken, I was not able to surf anything and came back to the hostel. I had lunch and went to the library again. This time I picked a book by French sociologist Jean Baudrillard on cultural studies. Of late, cultural studies, postmodernism, simulacra, etc. became the buzzwords at the university. At 6:30 p.m., I returned to the hostel riding the cycle.

At the hostel room, because of the stress, I did not want to face the silence of my room. I went to Shahid's room to gossip and lessen my stress. I told myself this evening looked gloomy. Had you cleared the exam Bhanu would have come to know by now and come rushing to me. The result would have been bad. I should get ready to pack and leave this artificial world, and go out of the walls of this campus.

At Shahid's room I sat in his study chair while Shahid sat with Cristiana on the bed and solved a crossword in the Telegraph newspaper. Then Dinesh, a neighbour of Shahid, knocked the door and said the CSE result was out, one could check it on the UPSC website. I thanked him and looked at Shahid. I thought either I was on the ship to Eldorado or I was sunk in the deep Burmuda Triangle. My breaths became light and short. I told Shahid that I would leave for the internet-cafe to check the result. Shahid wore sneakers to accompany me and came out of the room.

We came on the ground floor and walked towards the gate. Delhi was extremely hot, but the evening looked pleasant. The blowing wind carried the fragrance of amaltas flowers on the road. Two students stood with the newspaper stand reading Economic Times and Jansatta. I saw Tanib running towards me. He stopped and congratulated me. I thought my name was at least there in the list of successful candidates. It was not a wash-out. Then he said I was ranked 80 in the list. My joy knew no bounds. I thanked him and reached the gate. Students at the hostel gate surrounded me and congratulated me. They said, "Now you have become an IAS officer." Amitabh Garg held my hand in utter disbelief. I thanked God for what he bestowed upon me. Firoz Alam, Pramod Tiwari joined me and we went to the cafe and opened the UPSC website.

I walked in jeans, T-shirt and slippers. I was thinking about the life which this success was to bring to me. I was also thinking about the night of gloom my failure in this exam would have spawned. At the cafe, I typed the UPSC Civil Services Exam in the Google window, and the result jumped on the screen. Then I searched for my name, it was in the capital letters at serial no. 80. I saw my name with disbelief. The movement of time stopped. My breath became faster. I looked at the website, the title of the result and my name again. I was not sure what I was seeing was true. I asked myself if it was real or a dream. Then, I called my friends to see the result. They saw the screen and lifted me up.

I dialled Mom from a nearby PCO. My sister took the phone. I told her to give the receiver to the mother. Then my other sister came on the line. I told her I got into IAS. She started screaming. Then Mom came on the line. I said, "Mummy, I have passed the exam. This time the rank is better. I will get an IAS job."

"Thanks to Allah, Babu. Offer prayer and thank Him. It is good."

She asked why I was not calling her for so long. She said she was very worried. Abraham Lincoln's words flashed in my mind: "I remember my mother's prayers and they have always followed me. They have clung to me all my life."

Then, I paid ₹ 10 to the Cyber Café incharge and offered Coke to the friends at the cafe. We walked to the hostel. The world for me had changed now. The purpose for which I had come to Delhi years ago was fulfilled. The status of my parents and family members was to change. This world was to treat me a bit kindly and allow me to carry my self-respect. Now my future was not uncertain, and the world outside was not scary.

I along with the group reached the hostel gate. A big crowd stood there. The place was already abuzz with who qualified and who did not. They congratulated me. Dozens of hands moved together to wish me and shake hands with me. Then, I made calls to my sisters, friends, and my

Professors. About 35 students appeared for the interview from the university, and 20 had been through.

I came back to the hostel and sat at Shahid's room. Now, Cristiana looked at me as if I was a different person. She offered me a glass of water from her bottle. "Why do you look so stressed? Now you should be relaxed."

"I am not stressed. I was thinking about the difficulties I escaped through this exam.

"You think a lot."

"Yes." I laughed. I thought only whose life was on the line of fire could understand what I was through.

Shahid and I brought food from the Mess. Shruti had also come to the hostel room on her scooty. We all four sat for dinner in two thalis in the room. My mouth was dry, I was not able to eat much. I sipped water and ate some chapati with yellow daal.

I thought if there was one miracle in my life, it was my score in Psychology paper. After my bad performance in the second paper of Psychology, I believed I had lost the battle in the CSE. I thought I would barely scrape through. But in the end, I was in the top 100. I could attribute this to nothing other than God's blessing.

After the dinner I went to meet my Professor Harjot Singh. He was very happy. He said it was a result of my hard work and sincerity. Then Sasikumar came to meet me from the mid campus. He said, "Chalo. Let us go to mid campus." I wore sports shoes and rode the blue line bus. We reached Sasikumar's room at Sutlej Hostel. More friends and class-mates joined me. We kept talking about the result and ate payasam, a kind of sweet from Tamil Nadu.

Then at around zero hour I went to meet my sister at her lodge. While returning I met Javed Younas. Finally, I reached the hostel at 2:0 a.m. I watched TV to soothe my mind and divert my thoughts. I slept at 4:30 a.m.

Next morning my Papa came to meet me while I read 'Romeo and Juliet' by Shakespeare. Romeo at one place said, "Love is heavy and light, bright and dark, hot and cold, sick and healthy, asleep and aware—its everything except what it is!" Papa looked happy and he congratulated me. He said we should be thankful to God for this favour. I said, "Yes."

After the launch I was taking a walk with Faiz Mustafa. We reached near the bus stand. I saw a girl who looked like Jasmine. I thought it was an illusion. Since Jasmine left JNU, every other girl looked like Jasmine to me at first glance. Then I looked the other side at the gulmohar trees.

The girl stopped and said, "Hello, Hameed! How do you do?"

I looked at her. She was Jasmine. I was shocked beyond imagination.

I said good-bye to Faiz Bhai and took her to my room. She sat on the chair and her face beamed. I looked at her in anger asking her where she was and why did she go away?

She said, "Congratulations to you for your well deserved success."

"I sat near the window and said you dumped and left me alone. I will not forgive you."

I offered her a glass of water and laddoo. She said she did not go to TISS. She was enrolled at the Delhi School of Economics. She was now teaching as a contract faculty at a college in Delhi University. She said she left the university as she felt she was disturbing me. She came to the university once for a work but could not meet me. She did not want to distract me. Yesterday, she came to know about my selection, so she came to congratulate me. Her face glowed and looked innocent.